GAMERS

ALSO BY E.A. PADILLA

Rule One Twenty

Michaso

Tunnels

Sentinel Event

E. A. PADILLA

* * * * *

GAMERS

EAP Publishing

Gamers

E.A. Padilla

EAP Publishing

Eappublishing.com

Copyright 2020 E.A. Padilla

ISBN 978-1-7361460-0-2 (paperback)

First Edition 2020

PUBLISHER'S NOTE

Edited by Susan Severson-Roncone

Dedication

I want to extend a shout out of gratitude to my friends, loyal readers and family.

Thanks to those who volunteered the use of their names for the newly introduced characters: My friends, Dennis Allwardt, Burt Barnow, Susan Betts Williams, Brian Buehler, Janet Carmickle, Joe Erbes, Wes Fleming, Icarus, Jon Moore, Brian Owens, Bessie Sinor-Gebien and Jeanne Woodstrup. Also, to my brother-in-law Richard Blair and sister Lisa Padilla Blair.

Also, a special thanks to my life-long friend Patrick Gleason and his son Riley. This idea originated from a text I received from Patrick. Riley thought I could make a good story around the idea of computer gaming tournaments. From text to reality. Thanks Patrick and Riley.

1

Colonel Fangqi yawned. His eyelids crinkled as he stretched his facial muscles. He looked out from his top floor apartment window. The view was majestic. On clear days, he could see every variation along the mountain ridge, up across the grassy valley until the view disappeared on the horizon. His eyes backtracked and followed the meandering river and streams just inside the Chinese border. The river and streams flowed into Lake Balkhash. His new assignment was to run a special project inside the western most frontier Xinjiang Province.

Colonel Fangqi was promised that this assignment would help him rise through the military ranks. His commander, General Lee, emphasized that the lake was one of the biggest in Asia; the 15th largest in the world.

Lake Balkhash was unique. The west side held fresh water, while the eastern side was saline (salt). The General went into great detail about how a Russian early warning missile radar station, one specializing in Low Earth Orbit (LEO) satellites surveillance, was of big concern for China. The General even explained that the U.S. gave this location its own, not so secret, nicknames; "Hen House" and "Penchora".

Recalling General Lee's comments, Fangqi's face contorted almost into a snarl. It wasn't until arriving weeks after that he had discovered firsthand the truth. The information was technically accurate. There were two Russian stations located within two miles of each other. With excitement, Fangqi had inspected the area. After seeing the area through his field binoculars, his excitement was short lived. The bases were decommissioned in 1994. The neighboring country of Kazakhstan was retained to finalize the demolition. However, only after a limited attempt, they abandoned the base allowing them to decay. In 2004, they burned it down.

A tea kettle on the modern stove came to a boil. The pot's whistle snapped the Colonel out of his trance. Turning away from the large living room window, Fangqi returned to the kitchen and turned off the flame. He dropped a tea bag into a ceramic cup and poured boiling water inside. Seeing the water reminded him about the lake. With a quick turn of his head, he stared back out the window toward Lake Balkhash. Speaking to an otherwise empty room, Fangqi whispered in disgust.

"The lake's only nineteen feet deep. There isn't even a naval fleet there."

With a twisted face, Fangqi tensed his shoulders slamming his palms down on the kitchen counter. The vibrations created ripples across the tea's surface.

"I'm not an environmentalist!"

Fangqi's words echoed through his empty apartment. With a deep sigh, he regained his composure focusing on all the luxuries this assignment included; an oversized living space furnished with all modern conveniences. As a high ranking officer, he was encouraged to attend Xinjiang University, the highest institution of learning in the province.

China was changing. It adopted a new perspective toward other countries. Unlike the days of isolationism, China dabbled with Western ideas while adhering to their most famous Chinese General Sun Tzu, the author of The Art of War, who coined the phrase "to know your enemy you must become your enemy." While attending the university, Fangqi mostly intermingled with the younger Chinese generation and some foreigners. Half of them were foreign exchange students from abroad.

The phone rang. Fangqi checked the wall clock and knew it was General Lee. It was the routine; same time, same day of the week. Without thinking, Fangqi straightened his shirt and re-tucked his pants. Before reaching for the phone, he winched up his belt while reaching for a note pad and pen. He had an idea written down and wanted to share it with the General. During a walk through the University, while reading an advertisement, it came to him. He never knew that such competitions existed. It was a computer game tournament. This particular tournament seemed to be attracting active military personnel. With his free hand, Fangqi snatched the wall mounted phone of the hook.

"General Lee, I have an idea."

After a brief pause, the General replied. "It's about time. And it better get us closer to infiltrating the American's nuclear launch codes," grunted the General.

*   *   *   *   *

Standing behind the bar drying glasses, Susan glanced about. It was a charade. They were already dry. It gave her something to do. So, she didn't appear out of place staring out across the bar casually studying everyone. She'd worked for the Agency for ten years and had evolved into a natural part of the surroundings. Most of the clients were Westerners visiting this part of China or attending Xinjiang University. It was a perfect cover. Westerners naturally gravitated to such places hoping to lift their spirits and reduce their loneliness. Being around people that shared similar experiences and spoke the same language helped. It was a place that reminded them of home.

Susan glanced at her Agency issued cell phone. She was waiting for the time to reach seven. Just then, the front doors swung open. It was a visiting professor. He was beyond predictable. He visited Susan's bar every Wednesday arriving at the same time each week.

"The usual?" asked Susan.

With raised eyebrows and his head tilted toward the back table, Burt smiled. "Yes please."

"I'll bring it to you," Susan replied.

Just as she finished pouring Burt his drink, one of her agents, Janet, entered the bar followed by a group of women. This was Janet's first foreign assignment. She'd graduated from Southern Oregon University with a BA in Psychology and Business. The Agency provided the specialized training in wireless communications. Susan specialized in breaking in new agents and was Janet's first handler. Janet specialized in human intelligence gathering.

While Susan carried Burt's bourbon and coke on the rocks, balancing the glass on a tray, she peered over toward Janet. Susan noticed Janet's two new companions. She would later learn they were foreign exchange students; one from S. Korea and the other from Los Angeles. Later, Susan would confirm they were legitimate students with no affiliations. As part of Janet's training, Susan instructed her to hack into their phones and laptops. After a few months of snooping, Janet would also clear them as "just students".

Susan evaluated Janet interacting with her friends. She appeared natural without any hint of desperation or need for reinforcement and guidance. Susan flashed an inward smile at her new milestone. In the world of clandestine covert espionage, success relied on a lot of small victories.

Susan watched the ladies maneuver toward a table. From habit, Susan pretended wiping glasses while scanning the bar. It was going to be a busy night. The University was hosting a computer military gaming tournament. These events attracted a lot of out-of-towners and active military personnel. She'd come to expect more opportunities to identify some of the Chinese Ministry of State Agents. The less experienced agents couldn't help themselves. With such a rich target area, they tended to push too hard, eager to make an impression in pursuit of assignments. Being a successful spy required years of on the job training. The best ones had a knack of staying alive, another form of survival of the fittest.

Right on cue, a group of short haired young Chinese men wearing green military fatigues entered the bar. As they stepped through the heavy wooden framed plate glass doors, Susan was happy to see several men press their hands against the glass. She was confident that the Agency computer was busy scanning and saving the prints, followed by cross referencing them with known records. Any new military personnel would be catalogued, and a new file opened. Inside the bar, sixteen hidden cameras recorded non-stop. The regional Agency Headquarters in S. Korea had an entire unit designated to review and categorize countless potential leads throughout the Far East. If they found anything interesting, she would be contacted.

Just as Susan approached the group of Chinese military men, a high ranking officer from Xinjiang Base, Colonel Fangqi, stepped inside. Although this was his first visit to her bar, Susan knew everything about the man. She sensed that tonight was unusual. Behind her plastic smile, she approached the men.

"Can I help you gentlemen?" asked Susan, spoken in perfect Mandarin. Hearing her speak, the men all smiled, surprised to hear an obvious American speaking their native tongue.

*   *   *   *   *

X.O. (military executive officer) Newland was the senior officer inside the Agency located inside Camp Bonifas, because Director Valdez was in Germany finishing up a mop up assignment. Newland was grateful things were quiet. The only pressing issue was getting the newest computer monitoring system L.I.S.A. (Launch Intelligence Sensory Application) up and running. With the increased threat of rogue terrorist groups, L.I.S.A. was designed to monitor global communications and activities that, when considered in their totality, provided a way of identifying potential nuclear threats. By tracking and monitoring Internet search access points, telephone interactions (land, cell and faxes), and while cross-referencing all known associates to the users and end-users, L.I.S.A. would be able to make associations that would otherwise go undetected. Once these individuals and groups were identified, more traditional surveillance techniques would be employed; satellite, physical surveillance and in-depth background checks could be performed. This same form of intelligence was used by Israel to locate and eliminate Iranian nuclear scientists.

"So how is everything coming?" asked X.O. Newland.

"Right on schedule boss," replied the computer software specialist Erbes. "I'm guessing by the end of the week it will be fully operational."

"Outstanding!" replied the X.O.

*   *   *   *   *

Colonel Fangqi was in a much better state of mind. Until he stumbled upon the computer military gaming tournament being held at Xinjian University, he had no idea how he could solve his problem. The entire idea was still formulating in his mind. But having an organized and concentrated group of military personnel had potential. At first, when General Lee informed him that his principal assignment was to develop a way to hack into the U.S. nuclear codes, it seemed impossible. Until now, he felt this task was similar to solving the mystery of how the Egyptians built the pyramids.

His meeting with his computer specialists explained that hacking the launch codes was beyond a difficult task. To have any chance, they needed to narrow down the variables. They needed the system manufacturer, and a reasonable means of narrowing down the number of digits and type of data that was being used for the code. Having this information, they could design a computer algorithm. Just knowing these parameters made it mathematically possible. However, in the real world, even with this information, time became a major part of the equation. Their computers would need to run these computations and obtain the code without being detected by the U.S. Given the U.S.'s advanced technologies, with so many variables and limitations, it initially seemed like only a theoretical possibility. Having the precise number of digits in the launch code was the key.

Fangqi's computer specialists elected to go with tethered computer systems in conjunction with large mainframe computers. They were designed specifically for this task and were not encumbered with other unnecessary duties and sub-routines. Colonel Fangqi wanted to help his team reduce the variables. His intuition told him that using these military computer game tournaments might be an answer.

Unlike the free world, China didn't need to hide their efforts. The Communist Socialist government controlled everything. Xinjiang University already dedicated laboratories and computer rooms allocated to dozens of military programs. It was no secret. The secret was knowing exactly what each group was researching. Only loyal Chinese Military personnel participated in these programs. The rooms were meticulously protected and used the newest and best security systems. The Chinese assumed that the U.S. and other Western countries would try to infiltrate their research.

*   *   *   *   *

General Blair passed the tall Douglas fir as he walked across Kaneda AFB. The base was located on the island of Okinawa. The tree was transplanted during the Cuban missile crisis. Being planted close to the Pacific Ocean, only four miles away, helped the tree to flourish, growing over three hundred feet tall. In the right environment, these trees can live as long as 1,000 years.

As General Blair waited for the traffic to clear, the missile silo Launch Officer, Brian Owens was passing by. Owens paused and flashed an ear to ear grin at the General while pointing toward the top of the tree and yelled out the open window.

"I'd pay big money to see you climb that tree, General."

Keeping a stoic unflinching expression, General Blair stared through his pitch black sunglasses trying his best to suppress a grin. Without missing a beat, the General replied, "piece of cake." After checking the traffic in both directions, Blair ignored Owens staring out the car window. As the car continued forward, the General added, "Easy peazy. It's not even on fire."

Hearing the General's reply, Brian laughed. "I'll see you tomorrow, boss."

General Blair gave an expressionless nod. Once Owens' car had turned down the street, he broke into a big smile. Glancing over his shoulder, he stared back up at the tree. Back in the day, when he was working as a Hot Shot for the U.S. Forestry Service, he could have easily climbed to the top. Before entering the military, he was a Squad Boss who led groups of men into the hottest part of the fire. Part of his responsibility was to coordinate their ground efforts with Air tankers dumping 8,000 gallons of retardant and setting back fires and creating barriers with bulldozer crews. Seeing those air tankers motivated him to enter the military. Being one of the top students in his flight school class, as wells as the needs of the Air Force at the time, Blair selected bombers. He had no interest in F-15 Eagles or F-16 Falcons. He opted for the "heavy" track T-1 bombers.

During the prior Christmas party, and after everyone had a few cocktails, General Blair shared several Hot Shot stories. As the night wore on, he promised Launch Officer Owens, if necessary, he'd climb the Douglas-fir tree to signal him inside the silo complex using a flashlight and Morse code to communicate. As General Blair continued walking across the street, he thought he might have exaggerated. His Morse code was a little rusty.

*   *   *   *   *

Jeanne relaxed sitting on the rock outcropping staring out across the Pacific Ocean. The engineers designed this section of the submarine dock with oversized boulders strategically placed along the shoreline to strengthen the beach head. Turning away from the vast Pacific Ocean that extended beyond the horizon, she glanced back at the newest Virginia Class submarine, SSN-805 the USS Michelle J Howard named after the first female four-star General. It was fitting given Jeanne was one of the first female submariners in 2011. A boomer was the preferred nickname for a submarine. Jeanne's boat was permanently assigned to Okinawa's fleet. Its proximity to S. Korea, the Philippines, as well as China and Russia, made Japan and Kadena vital to the U.S.

Jeanne adapted to the life onboard submarines. Unlike other Navy assignments, submarines would deploy, remaining submerged for months at a time. Unless the boat was assigned as a defensive escort to a battle group, the boat could literally be anywhere around the globe.

Each sub was stocked with 90 days of fresh food. Given most Virginia Class subs are nuclear, the only resource that needed to be replenished was food. The subs distilled their own water for drinking, cooking and bathing. A "submarine shower" entails a brief dosing to get wet. The water is then turned off, where the sailor soaps up. After a brief scrubbing, the water is turned back on to rinse off the suds. Aside from food, these subs could remain submerged for 25 years never needing to refuel. But that is only a theory. Most certainly, the crew would go mad long before that.

Enjoying the sun, Jeanne tilted her head back and squinted her eyes. Most submariners were doing the same thing; soaking up as much sun as possible before their next deployment. These sailors found any excuse to be outdoors knowing that the next rotation would find them between 60 to 80 days at sea. She'd grown accustomed to this lifestyle and was one of the two Launch Key Officers assigned to the boat. Part of her responsibility was to verify the launch code and obtain the verbal order by the Captain or X.O. (Executive Officer). After all these years, and the countless training runs she'd participated in, simulating a nuclear launch never got old or tedious. Not once had it escaped her that one of these modern submarines possessed more fire power than all the missiles used during the entire World War II combined.

The gentle sea breeze drifted by as the bells from Okinawa's World Mission Church rang out. She watched a sailor carrying a King James bible as he strolled along the crosswalk heading in that direction. Jeanne always wondered if there was any significance that the U.S. Navy scheduled a total of 66 Virginia Class boomers and that there were 66 books in the bible. She'd come to appreciate the superstition and symbolism inside the military. Jeanne turned away from the church bells and glanced out over the waves rolling across the vastness of the Pacific Ocean. She forced her mind to relax and stop overthinking the constant connection between the military and God. She closed her eyes and took another deep breath of the ocean air.

*   *   *   *   *

Colonel Fangqi waited for his appointment to arrive. He had an idea and needed to do some research of his own. Until he had more information, he wanted to keep the idea close to his vest. The last thing he wanted was for word to get back to General Lee before he could formalize a detailed proposal. He had a lot riding on the outcome of this assignment and was determined to succeed. If he could pull this off, General Lee had to make good on his promise to promote him back to Beijing.

Fangqi propped his office door open and tapped his finger on his desk waiting for the soldier to arrive. He glanced at the wall mounted clock before studying his list of other soldiers he planned on interviewing. This first meeting would set the stage, give him valuable insight to see if this idea had any merit. Hearing the distinct sound of boots climbing the outer stairway next to his office caught his attention. Fangqi craned his head trying to get a glimpse of the soldier. A youthful face appeared. Unaware that the Colonel was watching, the soldier glanced around the lobby before settling down on the wooden bench to wait. Unable to hold his excitement, Fangqi stepped out of his office. His secretary was surprised as he was supposed to check the soldier in and then bring him inside to introduce him to the Colonel.

"Soldier are you here for the 1:00 o'clock appointment?" asked Fangqi.

Startled, the young soldier snapped to attention, saluted and replied, "Yes, sir!"

Unable to hide his enthusiasm, Fangqi flashed a big smile and waved the soldier inside.

"Bring us both some tea," Fangqi barked at his male secretary. Without waiting for a reply, Fangqi shut the door and hurried back behind his desk. Leaning forward on the edge of his chair, Fangqi tilted his head toward one of the chairs in front of his desk. The soldier glanced around the Colonel's office and was confused as to why he'd been summoned. As a tank driver, he rarely interacted with anyone outside his direct chain of command. Like most soldiers, he assumed he'd done something wrong and was anxious to find out what this was all about.

"Soldier, it's come to my attention that you and some other tank drivers are participating in a computer simulated military gaming tournament at the University."

The soldier listened to every word. He couldn't help but feel the need to be apologetic and fearful. "Colonel, I was told by my Lieutenant that it was okay. I received written approval to participate, sir," replied the soldier in a pleading manner.

Seeing the soldier's reaction, Fangqi realized that there was a misunderstanding. He wanted to set the young tank-driver at ease. Fangqi needed as much information as he could get.

"No. You misunderstand. I have no issue about your participation," Fangqi replied in a soft pleasant manner. He even tried to flash a warm smile.

Right on cue, the door opened. His secretary struggled through the doorway carrying a tray with two cups and a tea pot. Glancing up at Colonel Fangqi, the secretary was taken aback. Something looked peculiar and out of place. He'd never seen the Colonel with such an expression. The secretary actually flinched and almost dropped the tray.

Ignoring the secretary, Fangqi stood and took the tray. After setting it down on the desk, he continued flashing an unnatural forced smile and dismissed the secretary. As the secretary closed the door behind him, he recoiled in disbelief as he watched the Colonel trying to serve the tank-driver.

"So, soldier, tell me what motivated you to participate in the computer tournament? I want to know everything."

*   *   *   *   *

Buehler waved to the sentry guard as he presented his ID. For the first six months being stationed on Okinawa, Buehler rode his custom Harley Davidson EVO 107 motorcycle everywhere. He'd shipped it in from the States. Technically, the sentry was supposed to stop him each time, but every posted sentry knew him by sight. With his fatigues covering his torso and the unique custom colored gas tank, he was easy to remember.

Buehler gunned the throttle and lurched forward bounding toward the far back section of the base. He parked his bike in the farthest parking space before making his way to what looked like a small 20 by 20 foot stand-alone building. He glanced around wondering if he'd come to the correct location. He paused in front of a non-descript double doorway hoping one of his buddies would show up. After a few awkward moments, Buehler took a deep breath as he grabbed and rotated the handle and pushed the heavy door open.

As he entered, the interior wasn't what he'd expected. No old wooden desk with tall metal filing cabinets. What he found was a modern full body scanner with four formidable sentries standing post. They were all business. Two guards were armed with loaded M-16 machine guns each standing on one side of the floor to ceiling scanner. The other two sat behind a receptionist counter with thick ten-inch thick bullet proof glass.

Buehler glanced about. Countless cameras hung from the ceiling, the walls and mounted on the countertop. His image was displayed from multiple different angles on several of the monitors mounted behind the countertop. Normally, Buehler would break the tension with a smart wisecrack comment. Based on the stern unflinching expressions on their faces, this was not the time or place for such foolhardiness.

"Could you please step up to the white line and hold up your ID and dog tags?" instructed one of the seated guards.

Buehler glanced down and saw the white painted footprints placed behind a solid white line. After glancing around at the four men, he stepped forward and did as he was told. Within seconds, the other seated guard, looked up from his computer monitor and addressed the two guards surrounding the scanner.

"He checks out. Get his blood sample and handprint scanned, then you can let him inside."

"Yes sir," barked the guards in unison.

The entire time Buehler was processed through, not one of the four sentries cracked the slightest hint of a smile. Their faces were stern and beyond serious. Buehler was so distracted by their demeanor that he didn't realize that his index finger was poked to secure his blood sample.

With one of the armed guards in front, Buehler was led around a wall and directed down a steep stairway. All three men marched in step as they descended into the silo corridor underground missile complex. At the bottom of the stairwell, it opened up into a large oversized waiting room with multiple hallways leading to other underground missile silo groups. On one side there were lounging sofas and chairs. Buehler assumed it was the general meeting area. There was no television, wall decorations nor any attempt to beautify the area. It resembled a do it yourself survival bunker.

On the opposite side, there were three oversized hallways that descended further underground. Buehler glanced around unsure what to do next.

"Wait here," instructed the lead sentry guard. "The others will join you here." Before leaving, the other sentry guard pointed at the ceiling cameras.

"Don't' do anything stupid. You're being watched and taped."

Buehler hadn't noticed the cameras and nodded. As the sentry guards walked up the stairway, Buehler sat on the edge of one of the sofas. Staring down the hallway, he was curious about how much he'd get to see.

It was his first introduction to his new assignment. One of the missiles was set to be decommissioned. He was part of that team. His prior assignment was as a mobile missile launch team. The rockets were similar. The biggest difference between the mobile launchers and the Okinawa rockets was the payload. As part of a cross-training programs, he was one of the few mobile rocket launch teams that would participate in decommissioning outdated systems. This was his first TOP SECRET assignment. He would now be subject to annual polygraph exams and increased random drug testing and financial background checks. They couldn't afford to have any one in his position susceptible to manipulation by others. It wasn't just the Russians to worry about. The bad guy list seemed to keep growing.

Initially, Buehler felt privileged and honored to be selected. But finding out the extra security required to handle nukes, he questioned the wisdom of accepting the assignment. At first, he thought it was unusual that the Air Force gave him an option as opposed to just informing him of this new assignment. But he'd eventually learn all the "real" reason things were done. The military decided long ago that when it came to nukes, transparency was the best deterrent. These soldiers needed to appreciate the extremes another country might risk and do to infiltrate this branch of the U.S. defense system.

While Buehler waited, a short distance from where he sat, tucked around the bend in the center descending hallway sat eight underground ICBM (Intercontinental Ballistic Missile) silos. Buehler had no way of knowing that inside tube four, sat the oldest ICBM in the U.S. nuclear arsenal. It was scheduled for decommission before the end of the year. But because of the actions of a few, that would never happen. In six months, silo four would be the first U.S. ICBM launched against another nation. He was oblivious to what was to come. How could anyone know that from this very room World War III would start?

2

"General Lee, this idea will work. I can almost guarantee it," urged Colonel Fangqi.

"Guarantee? Why so much confidence?" questioned General Lee. "We're talking about infiltrating the most sophisticated military that ever existed. How can you be so certain?"

"Our goal is to just crack their nuclear codes. The directive wasn't to initiate any direct confrontation. I'm talking about accessing that information to prove we can do it. And with this idea, we could achieve that goal. And better yet, without the U.S. being any the wiser," replied Fangqi.

While Lee read the report for the third time, Fangqi waited in the wooden chair with his arms crossed.

"I still don't understand how creating this computer tournament helps," replied General Lee.

Because of the secret nature of this project, the meetings were isolated to just General Lee and Colonel Fangqi. Once the mission became official, others would become part of the conversation. Fangqi wished his programming expert could be in attendance. He could do a much better job explaining how accurate input of unknowns surrounding the digital code and pattern, the character types and total number of digits was the issue. From the beginning of the process, having this information greatly increased their odds of success. Not having to initiate several different computational sub-routines to hack the code meant less time required to achieve the mission.

Reducing time was essential. Also, Fangqi appreciated the time limitations to remain connected to the U.S. network before being detected. Staying on-line made them potentially visible and vulnerable to detection.

"General, my team tells me that knowing the accurate number of digits in the launch code decreases spending valuable computing time. My experts estimate that eliminating each digit could drop our search criteria from some ridiculous number to a realistic number," added Fangqi.

"What do you mean ridiculous?" General Lee asked.

"It sounds fantastic. At first, I didn't even believe my team. I went so far as to research the word," replied Fangqi.

General Lee leaned forward. With his eyebrows raised, waiting for Fangqi to continue.

"They said it drops from 19 sextillion to 3 sextillion possibilities."

With blank expressions, General Lee and Colonel Fangqi stared at each other. For an awkward moment, General Lee tried to comprehend these terms.

"You're confident those are real terms? Sextillion...it isn't a made up word your computer geeks made up to mock us? I mean sextillion, it sounds fake. Like a westernized slang word," replied General Lee.

Nodding, Fangqi replied. "Initially, that's exactly what I thought. But it's real."

After a brief pause, General Lee began nodding. Confident this wasn't some game, he pressed on.

"But it doesn't seem like much of a reduction. Hacking 3 versus 19 sextillions," asked Lee.

"My team explained it like this. The earth is about 1 sextillion cubic meters. So instead of 19 earths of data, we only need 3."

After another pause, General Lee replied, "I see." With pursed lips, General Lee nodded. "I'd like a report outlining this point. I'm certain I'll be expected to explain this to others before we can proceed with a computer tournament that you're suggesting."

Sensing the meeting was over, Fangqi stood. Before leaving, he reached inside his briefcase and slid a two page memo onto General Lee's desk. The memo went into detail about the plan and included the math and numbers comparing the differences.

"I've continued with my plans and here are my final recommendations awaiting your approval before going further," said Fangqi as he saluted and exited General Lee's office. Without looking up, General Lee squinted his eyes. With a wrinkled brow, he read the memo.

*   *   *   *   *

Janet was curious what all the fuss was. Several Chinese students stood around an oversized poster tacked onto the University message board near the administration building. She'd gone there to check on her financial aid check and was distracted by the crowd gathered around the board.

"Wow!" remarked one of the students. "An international tournament."

The group of students exchanged excited looks. The poster was colorful and included modern jets, ICBM rockets, submarines and mobile rocket launchers. In bold caps, it declared the inaugural Computer Military Gaming Tournament. There were different categories; ICBM's, Bombers, submarines and mobile missile launchers. There would be elimination tournaments followed by the final competition held in Beijing with all expenses paid. It was designed similar to the NCAA basketball tournament with 68 regions being represented. The winners from each category would receive $250,000.

"I've never heard of the sponsor," asked another student reading the poster.

"It's not Alibaba?" shouted another younger student with thick rimmed glasses.

"Who is Dragon Digital Dynamics (DDD)?" asked another.

In unison, everyone standing in front of the poster pulled out their cell phones and began searching the sponsor. The website had been under construction and went live hours before the oversized posters were displayed around the globe. Fangqi and his team selected Universities near U.S. military bases around the world. There was an on-line enrollment that was being monitored 24/7. The platform was designed to isolate and track the enrollees. Those that entered the competition, were directed to a long-winded detailed explanation about every aspect of the tournament. It included the regional locations and their corresponding winners' brackets.

As part of the introduction, sample weapons setup options were available. The program forced each participant to choose a category; presumably the one in which they were most familiar. The idea was to isolate and track the active U.S. military personnel. The hypothesis was that given the size of the prize money, these active military members would default to the types of systems they've trained in and are proficient in. The theory was this experience gave them a competitive advantage and increased their odds of winning. They were hoping to cast a large net so they could monitor active military personnel that were working in some capacity inside the U.S. nuclear defense program.

DDD posted the tournament information on all the gaming sites, Twitter, Facebook and Instagram. They even blanketed YouTube and Yahoo and other search engine sites purchasing advertisement banners that redirected those interested to the enrollment website. As each participant completed the enrollment form, a non-descript electronic authorization question that supposedly granted DDD the ability to use the participants' names and images in future advertisements. In reality, by accepting the terms, a hidden sub-routine program was uploaded into the contestant's computer, cellphone, laptop, tablet or desktop. It gave DDD complete access to their system. Fangqi had hundreds of computer specialists tapping into the users' photos, profiles and all social media sites hunting for what appeared to be active military personnel.

A large building on Xingjian University campus was converted into a makeshift computer lab. Fangqi sat behind one of his computer specialists. Each specialist represented a separate team of three additional programmers and specialists. Their plan was simple math. The more enrolled participants, the more likely they were to tap into an active U.S. military personnel.

"How many do we have so far?" asked Fangqi.

The specialist glanced toward the tracking totals. "Twenty-one," he replied.

"Where are they located?"

The specialist projected his monitor screen onto the oversized wall monitor. As the image appeared, he pointed at the table. Each U.S. active military participant's live image was projected as a screen shot. Under each image, the person's name and location displayed. Just as they'd predicted, several of the computer ISP locations were located near U.S. military bases. In two instances, the participants were on-line from a military computer.

"Perfect," smiled Fangqi. "It's going just as planned."

*   *   *   *   *

X.O. Newland surveyed the L.I.S.A. (Launch Intelligence Sensory Application) command center. There were eight groups of dedicated computer technicians, assigned to

28

each region of the globe. The concept was to funnel all electronic communications searching for unusual spikes of activity that could somehow be linked to some potential nuclear threat. The idea was to monitor, track and compare current global activities against prior known catastrophic events (i.e. 911, ISIS attacks, and other terrorist activities). The Agency learned through recent terrorist attacks that the Play Station 4 gaming system was being used to orchestrate attacks in Paris, France.

Since L.I.S.A. came online, nothing unusual was being flagged. No sudden spikes in any form of communications. They had no way of knowing that it was the calm before the storm.

Like everything, there is always a first. L.I.S.A.'s first event startled everyone, including X.O. Newland. Unexpectedly, the Far East Region began flashing. Similar to the satellite subterranean program on the other side of the S. Korea's Camp Bonifas Agency location, the L.I.S.A. project area had a red light mounted on the ceiling. It began flashing accompanied with a repetitive electronic chirp tone that resonated off the walls.

In unison, everyone looked up at the flashing light and then back at X.O. Newland.

"What do we have here?" asked X.O. Newland doing his best to appear calm and in control.

"Event level 5, sir," replied the Senior Technician Joe Erbes.

"It's centralized where?" Newland asked.

"Beijing, China. Sir."

The other technicians listened to the conversation. It was everyone's first go through with a live event. The months of training and preparation was never quite the same.

"Why only Level 5? What's China doing?" replied Newland.

"Actually sir, based on the data, it's inbound spike activity globally to one server."

"From where?" pushed Newland.

After a few keystrokes, Erbes was able to backtrack the activity to a computer software company.

"Sir, the ISP location leads us to Dragon Digital Dynamics, Corporation."

Erbes and Newland stared at the screen wondering exactly what that was. Wasting no time, Newland started barking out orders.

"Let's get support on that company ASAP. I want to know what just got so interesting at Dragon D."

"Yes, sir!"

"Keep me posted. Oh, and go ahead and deactivate the alarm. As the electronic tone stopped, the other seven technicians returned their attention to their areas wondering if anyone else's region would start to light up.

*   *   *   *   *

The Kadena's Officers' Club was a buzz. Everyone was talking about some new software company, Dragon Digital Dynamics that was sponsoring a competitive computerized military game tournament.

"Hey Dicky," whispered Launch Officer Owens as he leaned into the General's good ear.

"What's up Bry?"

"A lot of the guys are talking about some new Chinese computer company holding an international tournament. The winners get a quarter mil each," said Owen with raised eyebrows.

"Really?" replied General Dicky Blair as he chewed on his steak.

Owens tried to wait to hear what the General had to say. Watching the General chewing his food, with no apparent hurry in replying, Owens spoke up.

"So, you see any conflict with some of my guys participating?"

"Why shouldn't they?"

"It's a competitive war simulation with nuclear capabilities, subs, bombers and even ICBM's. I know we don't openly acknowledge our silos in Japan. It seems a little close to home. I just want to make sure it's okay with the boss before I give them the okay," said Owens.

"Let me think about it. But at first blush, I see it as just some computer game," After a brief pause, the General continued. "What are the Russians doing? Do you know?"

"I thought you'd ask that. I called my buddy and they're letting them play," confirmed Owens.

"Hum...who knows? Maybe this will be our military Olympics," smiled the General. "If any of your men sign up, they better win!"

"I'll let 'em know, boss. There's gonna be some happy soldiers tonight. Thanks, boss," replied Owens as he stepped away heading to the USO Kadena to share the good news.

General Blair smiled as he watched Launch Officer Owens quick step it out of the O-Club. *"What could happen from a little friendly competition?"* thought Dicky.

*   *   *   *   *

Professor Barrow's class just ended. Carrying his briefcase, he was heading to meet his handler Susan, when he noticed a group of young students gathered around an oversized poster talking about a new military computer game tournament being sponsored by an unknown company Dragon Digital Dynamics. It was apparently the buzz on campus. In fact, one of the regional events would be held on campus. As Barnow was about to cross the street, he saw a red Dragon Digital Dynamics flyer taped to a pole. As he waited for the light to change, he read the flyer. The light changed before he could finish so he removed the flyer from the pole, stuffed it in his pocket and continued across the street.

As Barnow pushed open the heavy double glass door, the blast of air conditioning brought a smile to his face. It was a pleasant change from the sticky humidity outside. With his eyes still closed, Barnow paced inside still flashing an ear to ear grin and walked to his favorite back table.

"Miss Betts," announced Barnow.

"Mr. Barnow," replied Susan. "What can I get you today? You're usual?"

"Yes, perfect. Have you heard all the fuss?"

"No. What's up?"

"A new software company is sponsoring an international computer military gaming tournament. Winners get $250,000 each."

"Wow. No wonder the geeks rule the world," replied Susan. "They're now getting rich for playing games," joked Susan. "If they start having an Asteroids or Pac-man tournament, let me know. I might stand a chance of winning that one."

"What's Pac-man?" asked Burt.

"Are you serious?"

Seeing his reaction, she realized he wasn't joking. Susan just smiled. "I'll bring you your drink at your favorite table."

Burt smiled back and sauntered back to his table. After getting his drink, she approached his table. Because of the dark lighting, she hadn't noticed that he wasn't there. Holding his drink, she glanced around before she noticed a tattered red flyer sitting under the crystal ashtray.

Susan surveyed the room. He was nowhere to be seen. Without thinking, she picked it up and returned to the bar sipping his drink while reading the flyer. She wasn't about to let it go to waste.

Across the room, Agent Janet Carmickle, posing as a foreign exchange student, continued nursing her drink. She wondered why Professor Barnow left without finishing his drink. Maybe he forgot about another engagement. Neither Janet nor Burt knew the other was an Agent.

*   *   *   *   *

The 2ndL Lieutenant glanced around the cockpit. He loved his job. Flying the newest and most advanced bomber B-2 Spirit was a dream come true. His wife and two kids loved living near Kansas City. With aerial re-fueling, these planes could reach any target in the world. Through technology, the Air Force maintained the entire 19 B-2 Stealth Bomber fleet at one location- Whiteman AFB in Missouri. A single test plane was housed at the Edward AFB in California.

The pilot was ecstatic. There was no need to move his family around. His kids could start making long-term friends and finish school with the same group of friends. A luxury in the Air Force. Most tours lasted 20 months. He was expected to spend at least one tour overseas.

The pilot glanced over at his co-pilot. Under his aviation mask and helmet, the pilot's smile was hidden from view. He felt blessed to have this particular assignment.

*   *   *   *   *

From across the table, Fangqi stared at General Lee. Fangqi was grateful that his special project received the authorization to proceed. Meaning, some of his most senior computer technicians and analysts could attend meetings. In this meeting, Colonel Fangqi was much more relaxed knowing that he didn't have to know all the answers. With his group of experts by his side, he was confident that he could answer any of their questions.

35

"So, Colonel Fangqi," asked one of the advisors. "I'm very uneasy with the notion that we will be coercing active personnel inside the U.S. B-2 and B-52 squadrons. This infiltration seems too reckless."

Fangqi held his plastic frozen expression in an unnatural position trying his best to convey a non-threatening cooperative smile. While inside his mind, he felt like screaming, *"For the third time, you ignorant bureaucrat, we will only initiate this portion of the plan in the event we proceed trying to remote launch one of the U.S. missiles!!"*

"Sir, just to be clear," Fangqi replied as he glanced around the table making certain his movements were slow and controlled. "As you may recall comrades, we would only pursue such actions in the event that our intent was to clandestinely launch one of their ICBM's."

Fangqi softened his grin and leaned forward with a slight bow of respect before he continued speaking. "As a reminder, my assignment is to provide a thorough and detailed plan from beginning to end. We are still verifying the veracity of our preliminary hypothesis."

General Lee glanced around at his advisors. With a subtle nod, he interjected, "True. We need to formulate a full set of options and details. If the plan proceeds, we need to have a clear understanding of what step comes next."

"Exactly," replied Fangqi.

"So, how exactly would we initiate contact with active U.S. military personnel?" asked another advisor. His tone made it clear that he was doubtful that such a feat could be accomplished.

Fangqi expected this line of questioning. Waiting outside of the conference room was one of his contacts.

"General, I have a non-military comrade waiting outside. He works within our government and specializes in these types of matters. Should I bring him inside to explain?"

Everyone there perked up. Only on rare occasions had any of them interacted with one of their own MSS (Ministry of State Security) agents.

"That would be helpful Colonel," replied General Lee.

As Fangqi escorted his contact into the room, the advisors began sizing him up, eager to hear what he had to say.

"Comrades, this is my contact to the outside world," continued Fangqi with a wave of his hand. "Beyond our great walls, his job is to establish relationships around the globe. The kind of relationships that not only provide us with vital information, but also a means to exact our power without having to set boots on foreign soil. Comrades, let me introduce Ying."

Upon hearing his name, the advisors' eyes squinted as if intensifying their evaluation. In Chinese, "Ying" means hawk or eagle. A bird of prey. No one for a moment believed it was his actual name. They correctly assumed it was his alias or code name.

Ying remained calm, sitting rigid while scanning the room. He waited until he was certain that he'd made eye-contact with each advisor. Only then, did he break the silence.

"Comrades," replied Ying in a scratchy smoker's voice. "I understand you have some questions. Let's hear them."

The advisors glanced about taken aback. They assumed that he would be speaking, elaborating on what Colonel Fangqi meant. His approach came across as arrogant, overly confident with no sense of subordination. It was as if he were the highest ranking member as opposed to the low level operative that answered to them. Obviously, Ying hadn't got that memo. He'd spent so much time abroad, constantly risking his life and the lives of his team members, that he'd become callous refusing to bow down to these bureaucrats and their silly protocols. Etiquette had no place within his work. Covert clandestine missions have no egos to stroke. His autonomy abroad eroded his filter, no longer able to feign respect for the Party's hierarchy. Those years of indoctrination engrained into his psyche since his youth had gone by the wayside.

38

With his hands crossed, he stared at the center of the table and waited for their reply.

"Whahum..." interjected the most senior advisor as if clearing his throat preparing to speak. "Ying, how exactly do you plan to coerce the B-2 and B-52 bomb loaders to cooperate?"

Ying glanced around the table before replying. As he evaluated the room of bureaucrats, he relaxed realizing that none of them had ever left China, let alone understood how things worked outside the protected walls. Seeing their faces, Ying was reminded that the Chinese culture is passive by nature. Ying glanced through the large plate glass window at the "Great Wall" that meandered the countryside. It was a constant reminder how much effort his ancestors invested to build it as a means of keeping invaders out. Foreigners who understand this subtle point acquired a deep seated understanding, a prerequisite if there was any hope at developing a true appreciation for the Chinese people and the way they think.

Ying's stoic demeanor began melting away. These men were truly his comrades in arms. There was no disguised motivation. They genuinely wanted to understand and approve their plan. However, as their culture dictates, understanding a logical path was step one. Like a good kindergarten teacher instructing children, Ying spoke.

"Comrades, unlike China, most of the Western World is motivated by recognition and greed. When these two goals are mixed in great quantities, Westerners' feel a sense of great power. It's this pursuit of power that becomes their currency. The West calls it prestige. It's this perceived recognition that especially motivates Americans. To them, it is a prerequisite, a required piece of their puzzle to become somebody of importance, of value."

The advisors and General Lee nodded. Everyone understood the feeling of being recognized as something that could motivate some people. It was, however, a difficult leap to understand how such a frivolous selfish goal could motivate others enough to betray their country.

"But how will this understanding help us?" asked General Lee.

"Have you heard about the Russian gangs working in the U.S.?" asked Ying.

*   *   *   *   *

It was a long night. He tried to keep his eyes open. His dwindling stack of blackjack chips no longer covered the green felt casino table. Since his assignment to Whiteman AFB, his life started to unravel.

This new assignment had started out with so much prospect. His wife and family just moved outside Kansas City. Whiteman AFB was only 70 miles away. Kansas City was a bigger city with plenty of entertainment; the Chiefs in the NFL and the Royals in the MLB. Since moving there, he learned it was known as the "City of Fountains" and the "Paris of the Plains." Only later did he learn about the river boat casinos. Six casinos in the area alone. In hindsight, he wished he'd stayed away from the gambling. Until moving there, he'd never stepped inside a casino, ever.

As the dealer swept away another set of his chips, he shook his head trying to stay awake. He glanced around the mostly empty chairs with bored card dealers standing behind vacant tables waiting for their late-night shifts to end.

He glanced down at his watch, a gift from his father for being accepted into the Air Force Academy. Unfortunately, he never graduated. For the hundredth time, he promised never to pawn it. No matter what. He kept telling himself that things would never get that bad. He wouldn't let it. He turned his attention back to the green felt blackjack table. With blurred vision, he was able to make out the time. It was almost 4:00am. He'd already planned ahead lying to his wife that there was a late night flight scheduled requiring his team's attention. She always wondered why bomb loaders needed to come in at all hours of the night.

He let the chips fall back and forth cascading down creating the distinct sound that all card players know. It didn't take him long to master that skill. It's amazing how quick something can be learned, especially when one practices the same thing over and over ten-hours a day over eight months.

He only had $100 dollars in chips left. He was about to stop so he could save some money for following night. It was too soon to hit up his co-workers for another loan. He'd just paid one of them off last month. As he was about to slide his chips off the felt top and cash out, he saw a woman walking toward the table.

Her boss Alexi told her to go sit next to the loser at the blackjack table. She'd seen him around the casino over the last several months. His late night appearances made him somewhat a regular. She glanced at his face as she sat down. He appeared too young to have developed a gambling habit. His short cropped hair was a giveaway that he probably worked at Whiteman AFB.

She placed four hundred dollar bills next to his small stack of chips. As the dealer exchanged the cash for varying chip colors, he glanced over unable to avoid the opportunity to ogle. Her low cut tight fitting mid-thigh skirt and her heavy make-up worked its charm. He couldn't help himself as he glanced at her left hand happy at not seeing a ring. Although he was happily married, and had never cheated on his wife, he found himself excited about her presence.

"May I sit here?" she asked.

Her English was good but had a thick Russian accent. He glanced up and smiled while nodding his head. Distracted by her arrival, and his senses dulled from another marathon gamble session, he seemed influenced by her presence and pushed all of his chips in. He didn't want to appear as shorthanded for funds as he really was. Before his senses could react to his poor judgment, the dealer dealt the cards. For a split second, before all the cards were dealt, he debated stopping the dealer to admit his error in judgment. Not that it would have worked even though he was probably considered a regular who knows the dealers and pit bosses all by name.

For some reason, he didn't want to appear weak in front of the pretty Russian lady. He glanced up and waited for the dealer to show his up card.

"Six for the house," said the dealer.

He and the Russian both held the cards dealt to them. The dealer turned over a queen, for a total of sixteen. The dealer took a mandatory hit and drew a face card and busted. He and the Russian both won. As the dealer paid out the winnings, he tried to act relaxed. But inside, he was very happy. *"Maybe the Russian brought me good luck,"* he thought. He quickly pocketed the winnings and bet the remainder on his next hand. He felt like a high roller betting $100 a hand. Besides, for some reason, his luck seemed to change. He received two aces and eagerly split the bet. No longer thinking about the next day, he retrieved his last chips from his pocket. Trying his best to appear confident, he fidgeted with his wristwatch waiting for the dealer to deal the next cards.

To his relief, he was dealt two face cards.

"Pair of blackjacks," announced the dealer as he slid $150 in chips on both sets of cards. He now had his original $200 in chips, plus $300. Wasting no time, he stood and grabbed all his chips and started walking to the cage to cash out.

"Have a good morning, everyone. I'll see you tomorrow."

Alexi, the Russian girl's boss, watched the man walk to the cashier. Staying out of view, he waited for the man to cash his chips while pretending to play a nearby slot machine. Alexi followed the man out the front door and into the parking lot. He texted himself the vehicle license plate information and included the make and model. Unaware he was being watched the soldier drove his truck out of the parking lot. As he turned onto the boulevard heading back to Whiteman AFB, Alexi spotted the military decal. He was certain that this man worked on base. Alexi cracked a smile. Speaking to an otherwise empty parking lot, he said, "Privyet" (hello in Russian) and watched the man drive away.

*   *   *   *   *

Buehler nodded at the sentry posted at the secret missile silo gate. He adopted the far back parking spot as his own. As a joke, he contemplated installing a sign with his name. As the newest guy on the team, a temporary at that, he thought it best to avoid making any waves. Assigned to decommission a secret ICBM hidden inside Kadena AFB, made him feel privileged to get this opportunity. From what he was learning, "Old Bessie" was the last old-school missile in the U.S. nuclear arsenal.

Later that year, the missile was scheduled for decommission. The military chain of command was going through a necessary evil; making sure the missile was in top-notch shape before being decommissioned. This seemed like a waste of time, but it's the way the U.S. military does things. An evaluation on the readiness will be conducted. Even though it will be obvious that it recently underwent a rigorous upgrade, the fact is that the decommission report is based on its readiness at the time of the inspection. Regardless, no one in the U.S. military wanted to let any system be scrutinized without first making sure it was in top working condition. That's just how things are done.

The increased threat of rogue terrorist cells acquiring nuclear weapons escalated the need for decommission specialists around the globe. The goal was to have multiple units around the world ready at a moment's notice to break these complicated weapons down safely and quietly.

As Buehler descended the silo hallway, he met a group of engineers huddled around missile four "Old Bessie's" access panel. Peering around the metal plate, Buehler leaned over the crouched technician to peek at the missile's inner workings.

With a gapped mouth, Buehler's eyes darted around examining the interior components. The other technicians glanced up and smiled expecting this reaction. There is something awe inspiring to be standing next to a force that creates a four and a half mile fireball explosion and generating 750 mph winds and had the explosive force of 600 million tons of dynamite. The light generated at detonation would be a thousand times brighter than the sun. The unimaginable destructive power of a modern nuclear bomb is mind-numbing.

Buehler tilted his head and stared up into the silo. Without turning away from the silo opening, he asked, "How tall is it?"

"71 feet, six inches," replied the highest ranking officer there. "...and it is seven feet seven inches in diameter," he added.

Still staring at the missile, Buehler asked, "How far can it travel?"

"Over 7,500 nautical miles. Not bad at $70 million each," added another technician.

Finally, turning away from the missile Buehler asked, "How accurate are they?"

"To within 131 feet," the same technician replied.

For a moment, all the men sat motionless lost in their thoughts not saying a word. The silo chamber area was deathly quiet. Only during the maintenance inspections was the access panel ever opened. This particular ICBM was supposed to be decommissioned years prior. Due to political reasons, its existence remained under wraps. It was the last of its kind, the LGM-118A Peacekeeper. All others were reportedly decommissioned on September 19, 2005 located in F.E. Warren AFB in Wyoming. At that time, the powers that be had no plans of abandoning Okinawa's secret missiles. The Air Force planned to swap it out when Okinawa expanded to eight total silos.

But the Air Force soon learned that adding the bombs was much easier than removing them. Over the years, because the missiles were less sophisticated, it was susceptible to a cyber-attack. With ever increasing cyber-technologies and expertise by other nations, the decision to decommission could no longer be delayed. In anticipation, Kaneda's General Blair understood that its systems would be checked and evaluated potentially scrutinizing the management responsible for maintaining its readiness. Part of his responsibility was to assure that all nuclear protocols were maintained. On General Blair's orders, "Old Bessie" was getting its last full maintenance tune up and upgrading any obsolete systems. They wanted everything to check out as it was being taken down.

Just like that, it was a perfect storm. Buehler took a final peek at "Old Bessie's" internal workings before the access panel was closed. No one there could have imagined that in a few months, the last active LGM-118A would be flying out from this very silo in route to Moscow. If it weren't for the tune-up and standard operating procedures, everything could have been avoided. Very soon, "Old Bessie" would be in perfect working condition – especially the remote triggering mechanism.

3

Fangqi stared out across the vast room. Long folding tables were set up end to end. With twenty tables per row and ten rows deep, it looked more like NASA's launch control center than an isolated building inside Xinjiang University's makeshift computer lab. For the next few months, it was going to double as Fangqi's headquarters. With three computers and monitors per table, Fangqi had 600 desk top computers pinging out across the Internet searching for a way into any U.S. military base or location that was even remotely affiliated to their nuclear weapon systems.

He had the brightest Chinese computer scientists not already gobbled up by the free-world on his team. It wasn't something new. For many of them, they'd been used with financial and informational hack jobs. Some had experience from SONY and South Korean missions. For these comrades, it was a badge of honor to have hit two enemies; Japan and S. Korea. Until now, the Chinese avoided direct attacks on the U.S. leaving that to the Russians and Indians.

Now, things were different. Times had changed. To attack the U.S., with their top level and most sophisticated software programmers created by some of the most educated people in the world was a challenge. Taking on the Americans was the biggest game of them all.

"Colonel," said one of the senior computer scientists and programmers.

"Yes?" Fangqi replied as he redirected his gaze into the mousy scientist's eyes peering through thick prescription glasses.

"All our computers have been searching for any backdoor access through known locations. We're bombarding all variations through multiple ISP address hubs." After a deep exhale, he continued. "Unfortunately, we haven't had any success," he explained in an exacerbated manner.

"What seems to be the issue? What's in the way?"

"The access points are rock solid. There are multiple layers of password protocols, combined with very restrictive time constraints to get through. If I redirect more computers, we might be able to get through. But we don't' even know if these entry points will get us to where we want. Accessing the U.S. personnel emails is one thing. But getting into the other higher classified areas is altogether different."

After a pause, Fangqi replied, "I see. Given so many security breaches, it's no surprise that they've tightened up these areas."

The computer scientist rubbed his chin and glanced out at the rows of computers. The constant hum of the computer fans and distinct clicking sounds from the programmers typing away sounding like a swift running stream of constant noise.

"If only," continued the computer scientist before stopping mid-sentence lost in thought.

"What?" asked Fangqi. "What do you mean by saying that?" he said asking for clarification.

"If they had an older less protected system. A system that isn't necessarily tied into their main hub. We'd stand a better chance."

Fangqi thought he had an idea. "Let me look into something. I'll get back with you on that. Keep me posted on any progress."

*   *   *   *   *

Launch Officer Owens glanced down the stairwell leading to the silo launch rooms. The guidance technicians were still busy working on missile four "Old Bessie". It was being retrofitted and brought up to modern standards only to be dismantled later in a few months. He'd heard the rumor that one of their ICBM birds belonged to the grand-daddy models that had been previously retired. Until then, he thought everything he heard was exaggerated. Unable to hide this issue from the others, like everybody else, he wanted to see, up close and personal, missile four as it was upgraded and retrofitted. Even the exterior looked somewhat obsolete. The color was dull from being hidden away not subject to this type of visual scrutiny.

"Excuse me, sir," said one of the guidance techs as he side-stepped Lt. Owens descending the stairs.

"Sorry about that," Owens said as he smiled back. By his expression, the technician detected the Lieutenant's sense of awe.

"These missiles are amazing aren't they sir?"

"Absolutely."

"Hard to believe they made them like this back in the 50's," the technician added.

"I thought all these old ones were swapped out decades ago." Lt. Owens replied.

"Well, after the Cuban Missile Crises, it was tough to access this area without the world watching."

Lt. Owens nodded as he contemplated how isolated this underground missile silo was from the rest of the base. It was miles away from anything.

"True. Our little one room shack kind of stands out all by itself."

"With the Air Force denying the presence of any nukes on Japan, and back in the day with the Russians flying more and more surveillance satellites to get a peek at what we're doing here, Washington figured it was better just to leave it alone. Now, after all this time, it's been practically forgotten. Outside of Kaneda AFB, only a few old timers even know of its existence."

*   *   *   *   *

For today, Burt finished his final class. As he crossed the Xinjiang University campus, he saw a small group of students huddled around a large computer monitor. He was about to turn the corner when something caught his attention. He had to double take to be certain what he was seeing.

Burt cut through the student union and found a window from inside the bookstore that gave him a direct view over their shoulders. It had to be a mistake. Were they actually looking at an U.S. nuclear launch code panel? "It couldn't be," he thought.

Burt glanced about making certain no one was around. To get a better look, he leaned up against the glass. He noticed that the console was an older version, similar to the ones used-on the old LGM-118A Peacekeepers. Unlike the new modern LGM-30 Minutemen that used twelve digit passcodes. But still, Burt thought, *"What the hell are these kids doing having access to this classified information while playing some computer game, in China of all places?"*

Burt watched the men toggle through several options. It looked like the game they were playing was allowing them to select the type of launch command center and type of system to use. He recognized only one of the consoles. From his memory, it looked identical to the ones he'd seen during the peak of the Cold War.

When they finally set down the controller and left, Burt noticed the game reset allowing the next player to select their platform choice; ICBM's, Bombers (B-2 Stealth or B-52), submarines or mobile launch systems. The shop was getting ready to close. The crowd cleared leaving the system area vacant.

Burt exited the adjacent bookstore and made his way to the computer gaming system. Above the oversized monitor, he read the large banner that announced the inaugural International Military Computer Gaming tournament sponsored by DDD. The prize was $250,000 award for each winner.

"Excuse me," announced Burt. "What is this tournament all about?" he asked the clerk.

"Oh, you mean the DDD tournament," replied the clerk as he pointed to the banner. Burt nodded. The clerk grabbed a multi-page flyer and handed it to Burt. "Let me explain."

*   *   *   *   *

Jeanne was prepared to leave the USS Michelle J Howard submarine launch room. She'd just completed her ten-hour stint and was heading to dinner in the galley before a quick shower then off to sleep. As she held her tray, she was reminded that eating was one of the benefits as a submariner. Maybe it was a reward for their perceived suffering working submerged under water for weeks at a time. Or adjusting to the red running interior lighting and lack of natural light. Whatever the reason, the U.S. Navy made sure boomer cooks fed the crew well. It was normal to be fed corned beef, ginger pot roast and even gourmet fried chicken, followed by pies and pudding for dessert.

As she gazed at her entry choices, she over-heard some of the sonar guys talking. Their conversation caught her attention.

"I'm telling you guys," one of the crew said as pieces of fried chicken crumbs fell out of his mouth. "This tournament is so cool. You get to choose what platform to compete in."

"Which one are you going for?" asked another crew member.

"What else? Subs," he replied.

The other crew members continued eating while listening nodding as they stuffed their faces.

"After grub, I'm gonna practice on the simulator I downloaded from the DDD website."

"When's your first tournament again?" asked another crew member.

"Next month. We should be back from our 60 by then."

"Did you okay it with COB (Chief of the Boat)?" asked another.

"Yup. The Captain even ran it up the pole. General Blair gave his okay too. There's only one stipulation though."

The table fell silent. The crewman paused and glanced around with a serious expression before continuing. "If I win, I gotta buy everyone a drink."

The entire table erupted in laughter. Jeanne listened to everything and was curious. She paused with her full tray next to their table. When they saw her, they stopped eating and stood and saluted. In unison, the men spoke, "Ma'am."

56

"As you were sailors. But what's that you were talking about. What's up with this tournament?"

"It's a military computer gaming tournament," he replied.

"Did I hear you right that you downloaded a program onto your laptop? A simulator program?"

"That's right ma'am."

"Huh? I'm interested in taking a look. Can you show me after dinner?"

"Yes ma'am."

Jeanne nodded as she walked back to the officers' area. The crew settled back down to finish their meal. Lt. Jeanne Woodstrup was a WEP's (Weapons Officer). She'd graduated from the Naval Academy and was part of this boat's ballistic missile launch room command team. She carried some heavy weight and everyone on board the sub paid her great respect.

*   *   *   *   *

"X.O.?"

James Newland's head snapped up. It was the tone of the technician's voice.

"What you got?" Newland asked as he walked over to the computer tech's workstation.

"We've been getting a steady flow of robo-calls knocking on all our nuclear bases located inside the continental U.S. L.I.S.A. picked up on it about an hour ago."

X.O. Newland listened and nodded.

"We started digging deeper to back track and isolate the origin. No surprise that we're getting multiple locations scattered around the globe," continued the technician.

"Is it a VPN (Virtual Private Network) masking the attackers' locations?"

"Yup. But what's weird is the influx of the supposed variable ISP locations is so random that it can't be."

"What do you mean?" Newland asked.

"L.I.S.A. was designed for just these types of cyber-attacks. She's saying that a variation of the same six-hundred ISP location portals are being used. It looks like whoever is trying this has programmed to shuffle the locations. But instead of a random shuffle, it's shuffling through the same exact 600 locations."

Newland listened and continued nodding. "Looks like their programmers didn't command an all known random sequence and is just randomly selecting from 600 different servers. But does that help us? Can we backtrack from those using the same logic?"

"Well boss, we can try. But look what L.I.S.A. is saying," the programmer said as he handed the X.O. a document.

After studying the data, Newland looked up. "Although L.I.S.A. can't backtrack to an exact location, the general area has been identified as China?" Newland explained.

"Yes, sir. And I don't think it's a coincidence. The prior hit regarding the military computer gaming software company DDD is also from China and the same province from where these attacks are originating from."

"Which one?" inquired Newland.

"Xinjiang."

"It's time to call Director Valdez," added Newland.

*　　*　　*　　*　　*

Susan Betts was hunched over her back office desk reading an encrypted message from one of her agents, Icarus. It was alarming. *"How could the DDD computer software company have uncovered an older version of the U.S. nuclear minuteman missile launch code formats?"* she thought. *"They must not realize what they've stumbled across. Otherwise, they wouldn't be broadcasting it to the entire world as one of the set-up options in this military computer gaming tournament."*

After visiting the DDD website, Susan downloaded the ICBM launch control panel proto-type. It was time. She needed to call the Director and give her a heads up. Using her Agency encrypted and secure SAT phone, she made the call. When the person on the other end answered, by the background sound, she must be flying.

"Valdez," answered Director Nena Valdez.

"It's Betts boss. Can you talk?"

"Hello Susan. Yes. We're in the jet now flying back to Camp Bonifas. We're over Indian airspace now. What's up?"

"I just received a report from Icarus. There's a Chinese computer software company, Dragon Digital Dynamics, DDD, that's holding an international military computer gaming tournament. Each contestant selects a specific format; ICMB, bomber, submarines or mobile rocket launchers. After several rounds of tournaments, the winners battle it out in China and the winners receive $250,000."

"My guys back home let me know about them earlier yesterday. What about it?" Nena asked.

"One of the ICBM format choices is the older version of the Minuteman missile launch command. I downloaded the sample from DDD's website. It's identical, except it's using the older 9 digit launch code authenticator."

"I didn't know about that piece of information," Nena said. After a brief pause, she continued. "They must not know what they have. Or else, they wouldn't be advertising it on their website and using it in their game."

"My thoughts exactly," replied Betts.

"Send me everything you got. I'll be on the ground later tonight."

"Sounds good boss," answered Betts before she terminated the call.

"*China, what the hell are you guys up to?*" thought Director Valdez.

*   *   *   *   *

After the long flight in from Germany, Director Valdez walked to her wing of the building. She glanced around her little part of the global Agency Empire tucked away inside Camp Bonifas inside the DMZ (Demilitarized Zone). It was good to be back. Since being promoted, not counting her weekend trips to visit her parents in the Philippines, this last trip was her longest time away as a Director. She'd been asked to step in for Director Gamboa in California. That assignment involved re-opening a closed Director's File that sent her team to Germany to tie up some loose ends. Aside from a quick triple hop on the modified Concorde to Washington D.C. the year before, her literal trip around the world from Seattle to San Jose, California, then off to Paris, France and then East Berlin, she'd travelled almost 17,000 miles. Unlike civilian life, she never collected rewards miles to spend on other things. She typically flew an Agency Jet.

Nena grew accustomed to her little neck of the woods. She loved her job, her permanent assignment location in S. Korea, and her team. Before she turned on her computer, she heard a knock on the door.

"Boss," said X.O. Newland as he stuck his head through her door. "Welcome back."

"Jim. How have you been?"

"Fine, boss. Long trip?"

"It was. Always nice to get home," she smiled. By the look on X.O. Newland's face, she could tell he had something urgent on his mind.

"So, X.O.," continued Director Valdez. "What's going on with the Chinese trying to hack into our nuclear facilities?"

"L.I.S.A. has picked up several events. My team is still trying to dig past the VPN connection that is masking the original location where the attacks are originating, but the software suggests that the majority of the hits are leading back to China, specifically, Western Xinjiang Provence. So far, none of our facilities have been compromised."

Nena listened and nodded while she scribbled some notes. She tilted her glasses back with her index finger and looked up at X.O. Newland. "I spoke to Betts. Some Chinese software company, a..." she glanced back at her notes, "...a Dragon Digital Dynamics. They're having an international military computer gaming tournament. The winners get $250,000 each."

"Did you say winners?" asked Newland

"That's right. They're running several platform options. Each group competes in several qualifying and elimination matches before the grand finale in Beijing all-expenses paid."

"Wow. Things sure have changed since I was a kid."

"There is another wrinkle," Nena added.

"What's that?"

"The software company is allowing the contestants to download prototypes of the launching command centers consoles for each format." Newland leaned forward.

"Are they very realistic? Accurate to what we're using today?"

"That's the wrinkle. One of the ICBM options is the splitting image of our older Peacekeeper missile launch code sequence."

"Really?"

"Yup. Even has a nine digit code design versus the modern twelve digits," added Nena.

"That's pretty damn creepy. It's one thing to have accurate cockpit simulators for commercial airplanes and jet simulator games. But nukes?"

"That's what I thought too."

"Do you think some ex-military personnel is consulting with the software company?"

"Maybe. But I doubt it. You know all the non-disclosure documents we're subjected to. I made some calls in route from Berlin. Those nuke guys have it even worse," Nena explained. They stared back at each other in silence. "Given the remaining missiles were removed during the Reagan Administration, I guess it's not really an issue."

"That long ago?" asked Newland.

"We should be good. As far as I know, there aren't any of the Peacekeepers left in our arsenal. It just bothers me that the Chinese have access to it. Makes you wonder."

Newland nodded in agreement.

"Let's keep an eye on the Chinese. Keep your guys digging around on those ISP locations. It would be nice to know exactly where they're originating from. You never know, it could be from one of the other enemies. Seems like that list keeps getting bigger."

"Ok boss. You're right too. It still could be someone else."

"By the way, did you give all our nuclear locations a heads up?" asked Nena.

"Yes, ma'am I did. First thing. They're all on high alert for a cyber-attack.

*   *   *   *   *

Mr. Fennu was annoyed. He hates being disturbed. Besides, it couldn't be anything important. He had long thought he was forgotten. He couldn't remember the last time anyone from home had contacted him for anything.

Fennu stared out the side window of the old Mercedes-Benz taxicab window. After World War II, he'd found his assignment in Hamburg appealing and opted to remain there permanently. Back then, things were busy. Germany was divided and the Cold War between the U.S. and Russia kept things exciting. But after the Berlin wall came down, and the U.S.S.R. dissolved, things had become quiet. Too quiet.

As Fennu studied the back of the taxicab driver's head, he wondered why Colonel Fangqi was so interested in old U.S. military bases anyway. *"What good could come from that?"* he thought.

Fennu rarely left Hamburg, Germany and was disappointed that the driver was taking him to the old east side of Old Berlin. They'd been bumping along an overgrown dirt road hidden by huge beech trees that blotted out the sun from the forest of branches and leaves. When the sunlight broke through the darkness, Fennu was taken aback to see a large white building surrounded by crypts and graveyard crosses. As the cab pulled behind the building, Fennu read the rusted metal letters posted on the façade – S A C H S E N H A U S E N the central Berlin concentration camp turned into a museum of sorts.

Fennu's stomach turned. Having to see the Lone Wolf again, after all these years, was one thing. But here? In this isolated dreary location? The sound of the crunching gravel beneath the taxi's tires echoed off the otherwise empty parking area. As Fennu stepped out of the cab, the first thing he noticed was the man's piercing blue eyes. He watched the Lone Wolf walking toward the cab. Van Aelst was still in good shape. Much younger than Fennu who was envious in contrast suddenly self-conscious about his own appearance.

"Ni hao?" which translated into "How are you?" in Chinese.

"Nice to see you again Van Aelst," replied Fennu.

Cornelius Van Aelst was a prominent semi-retired ex-Stasi agent hiding inside his remote underground Old East Berlin location. He flashed Fennu a controlled tight-lipped smile. Fennu's real name was Wang, the most popular surname in China. Van Aelst found it humorous that Wang used the name Fennu as his alias translated into "angry" in Chinese.

"Won't you come inside Fennu," said Van Aelst as he stepped toward the building's back door and pointed his arm in that direction. Van Aelst walked ahead, opened and held the door open for Fennu. "Your cab driver will wait outside and drive you back when we are done," explained Van Aelst.

They walked inside the first doorway that appeared. It was an empty medical examination room. As they entered, Van Aelst glanced at the opposite wall and recalled it being covered with blood. Through so much pain and suffering, he'd recruited the newest member of his team, Diane Klein.

"So Fennu, what brings you all the way from Hamburg? It's been a very long time since we've interacted," said Van Aelst.

"Well Cornelius, Beijing wanted to know if you had any knowledge from the old days," hinted Fennu.

"The old days? You need to be more specific, my friend," replied Van Aelst somewhat annoyed. The Chinese had a roundabout way of communicating. Remaining in control, Van Aelst raised his eyebrows encouraging Fennu to elaborate.

"Yes, it has to do with our old enemy the Americans."

"Oh, the Imperialist Capitalists. What about the Americans?"

"It's about their nuclear arsenal," Fennu said in a lowered voice just above a whisper. He glanced about as if fearful others were listening.

Van Aelst paused. So much for a simple request. Anything about the United States had its own risks. But to get involved with their nuclear weapons was something else altogether different.

"Fennu, Fennu," replied Van Aelst. "Such a subject. Like your Japanese enemy from the past once said, let's not wake a sleeping giant. I think it was General Yamamoto who said that. A prophetic comment," added Van Aelst as he directed his piercing eyes back at Fennu without blinking. After an awkward silence, Van Aelst pushed back. "What exactly are your friends interested in?"

"They're just searching for some political push back given the recent trade tariffs. They were hoping the U.S.

still had some older missile silos in the Far East. Something we could use to get some economic relief. We could leak the information through social media perhaps," improvised Fennu. He'd known that the Lone Wolf would ask. However, Fennu really didn't know why Beijing was interested in this information. In anticipation of Van Aelst's question, Fennu concocted this seemingly realistic response.

Van Aelst studied Fennu's face and was almost certain that he was lying. Yet, it made sense. Van Aelst rubbed his chin as he thought about the Americans and their nuclear missiles. Returning Fennu's scrutinizing gaze, Aelst spoke up. "I heard of one situation. But remember Fennu, it's been decades. Even if the rumors were true, it was a long time ago. The Americans most likely moved them by now."

Fennu raised his eyebrows and leaned forward. Van Aelst paused as they exchanged serious looks. After a prolonged silence, Van Aelst broke the silence.

"What do you remember about October 1962?"

Fennu thought. It took a moment before he replied, "Cuba? The missile crises?"

"That's it."

"My friend," chuckled Fennu. "They're interested in something closer to China not in the Atlantic," said Fennu in a condescending manner.

Van Aelst waited for Fennu to regain his composure before continuing. "Then you must not know," said Van Aelst.

"What?" Fennu said in a surprised manner. "*What does the Lone Wolf know?*" he wondered.

"On one of the islands in Japan."

"Which island?"

"Okinawa, inside their Air Force Base- Kadena."

Fennu was taken aback. He'd heard nothing about nuclear missile silos on Okinawa during the missile crises.

"Most people don't know what happened," said Van Aelst. "Let me explain."

4

Jeanne made her way through the University of Okinawa main administration building. She double checked her flyer as she glanced around the square. There were large color banners hanging from the façade- Dragon Digital Dynamics announcing the first round competition for the international gaming tournament. As Jeanne turned the corner, there were droves of people milling about.

Most were spectators. Based on their clothes, most wearing full military combat attire, she assumed they were the participants, and maneuvered around the crowd. She noticed that the participants were being herded into the sports arena. As she passed through the open double doors, she was surprised to find the arena almost filled to capacity. Seeing a single vacant seat in the front lower level, she scurried down the aisle and sat just as the lights dimmed.

"Good morning ladies and gentlemen," boomed an excited voice through the arena PA (Public Address) system. The introduction was repeated in Mandarin (the main Chinese language). The huge over-head hanging monitor was telecasting video clips that explained the tournament format, showing the bracketed sequence for future competitions. There were multiple tournaments held the next three weekends leading up to the Championship tournament in Beijing. As the voiceover's message echoed throughout the arena, the spectators focused on the action packed video display showing submarines racing underwater maneuvering through sea cliffs, mobile rocket launchers bounding over dusty hillsides, bomber planes floating through and disappearing into clouds, ending with a close-up of ICBM silos in varying stages of deployment. The video was synchronized with rock music. The pounding bass drum and electric guitars helped whip the crowd into a frenzy.

The overhead monitor display cut to supersized images of the elaborate trophies for each format followed by four $250,000 checks. A bright light cut through the dark auditorium and focused in on a sharply dressed executive wearing a black tux as he marched toward the podium. Fangqi found himself caught up in the excitement and joined the throngs of spectators clapping in unison creating a thunderous synchronized symphony of noise.

Fangqi had never been to such an event. The live video feed zoomed in for a close-up of the executive leaning into the microphone. His voice boomed out over the speakers. He sounded like the announcer Michael Buffer, the famous Las Vegas fight MC, as he yelled, "Let's get ready to rumble!!"

As if on cue, the spectators glanced about the arena. The volume inside ratcheted to even higher decibels as everyone, including Fangqi yelled. The concrete floor vibrated from all the clapping and stomping.

"Welcome to the first International DDD Military Computer Gaming Tournament. Today, each district winner will move on to the regional elimination tournament, followed by each countries' National Tournament. All finalists will be taken to China, on an all-expense paid trip to compete in the final championship match in Beijing. All final winners will be awarded the grand prize of $250,000 (U.S.)."

Colonel Fangqi glanced around the arena. He was awestruck and caught up in the excitement, but for another reason. It was as if all these people were rooting him on to achieve the impossible- to infiltrate a U.S. nuclear missile. Watching the announcer speaking from the front row of seats, he forgot any concerns he'd previously had over selecting this man as the announcer. As Fangqi scanned the multitudes, making eye-contact with his senior computer specialist brought everything back into perspective.

The oversized monitor began displaying live satellite feeds across the globe from twelve of the 100 different tournament locations. Each feed was being displayed concurrently, with twelve large boxed images; three rows of four.

"And let's welcome some of your competitors around the globe!"

"Hello Sydney!...Tokyo!...Honolulu!..."

As the speaker continued reading the list of city tournament locations, that city's live feed expanded taking up the entire area of the oversized screen. The noise washed through the arena like a tidal wave culminating with an ear piercing crescendo as each image changed location arenas on the overhead screen. After the last location was shown, the view changed to an overview map of this particular competition. Each area of the arena was highlighted in different colors depicting where each platform competition would be played; submarines, mobile-rocket launchers, bombers and ICBM's.

"Now contestants, look up to the overhead monitor. Locate your platform area and make your way there. Once inside, you will check in and be taken to your assigned computer station."

Staring out across the packed arena, the spokesman stretched out his arms. While flashing an ear to ear grin, he shouted his final remarks. "Participants! Let the games begin!!"

The crowd erupted one last time. This time, the noise of shouts and clapping was replaced by murmurings of people on the move shuffling out of the seated arena and fighting their way toward their assigned areas. For a brief moment, a thought ran through Colonel Fangqi's mind, *"I hope this works."*

*   *   *   *   *

Jeanne's concern over wearing her NWU (Navy Working Uniform) to the event was short lived. The wear rules were recently updated to improve the practicality of normal activities following or preceding a workday. Jeanne's deployment had literally just concluded. Unsure of the actual starting time, she went straight to the event. As the participants streamed out of the arena heading to the separate locations, she noticed that most people wore military clothing. It was easy to identify the civilians from the other active military personnel by their haircuts and obvious lack of attention to detail. From outdated uniforms, to generic home grown patches, the civilians tended to blend this attire with obvious non-military tennis shoes. While the active personnel stood out by being in perfect matching uniforms and appropriate footwear.

As Jeanne sidestepped across the aisle to maneuver to the Submarine Platform area, she saw another active military personnel from the Air Force branch. She assumed he was stationed at the AFB Kaneda. With knowing glances, they exchanged quick nods before heading to their designated areas. Given they both held similar ranks, no saluting was necessary. The Air Force man watched Jeanne enter the Submarine are, before he ducked inside the ICBM area.

As a member of one of the U.S. Air Force missile combat crew (CCC), he'd felt special. There was something unique having access to nuclear weapons. He wondered how accurate this computer software company DDD was when compared to the systems he'd trained and used. He was stationed at Kadena AFB. Although the existence of Kadena's underground launch facility was a secret, there were no special orders by his C.O. (Commanding Officer) and the base Commander, General Blair from participating. He was curious and thought, *"What was the environment and accuracy of the simulation? How realistic is the software?"* He'd heard from others that one of the on-line sample systems was eerily close to what they used at Kadena's launch control center. Knowing the winners would receive $250,000 took his curiosity to another level. *"Could I actual win?"*

As he walked through the large open double doors, the interior was overly air-conditioned bringing the entire ICBM area to a chilly 60 degrees. Displayed on another overhead projector were the images of three different missile launches as the bombs were rocketing out from underground; an American Minute Man II, a Russian SS-18 (nicknamed Satan) and an Israeli Jericho III. Each video clip showed a computer generated image close-up version of each missile surrounded by toxic gas clouds billowing about engulfing the rocket during takeoff.

He saw a long line of folding tables pushed up against the outer wall. He glanced around the crowd turning about making a 360 degree rotation to get a full view.

"Excuse me," said the attendant looking up from the chair. "Your last name please?" he asked with a cheerful smile.

"Oh, right. Owens. Brian Owens."

Searching the portable filing cabinets, the attendant flipped through the folders. While being processed, each participant was secretly filmed from three different hidden wall mounted cameras, as well as close ups taken from the attendant's lapel pins.

"There's a questionnaire inside. Please, take a few moments to fill it out," the attendant added.

While Owens read through the questions, the attendant studied his appearance. The jacket he wore definitely looked authentic. This close cut hair style and the way he stood and walked, further suggested he was an active military American. The questionnaire was designed to give the Chinese a better chance to capture each participant's physical characteristics and appearance. When the participant handed back the questionnaire, the attendant was surprised. It was fully completed every answer being provided.

"So, you're an active military personnel?"

"That's right," replied Owens.

With a bright smile, the attendant pointed toward the far right room. "Door number four. And good luck!"

Owens gathered his gear and walked toward the doorway. Certain Owens was out of view, the attendant pasted a silver star on the questionnaire and slipped it into a special oversized envelope with the others. Owens was the third one he'd found. The other attendants were busy processing the remaining participants. The registration for each participant was capped at 1,200. Otherwise, there would be too many people to track and evaluate. With a total of 100 locations, they hoped to narrow down their targets from the total 120,000 registered global participants. Even if only one percent were active military, that would give them around 1,200 possible targets.

The others waited as the attendant processed the next participant before being ushered off to the scenario rooms. Everything was going as planned.

*   *   *   *   *

"X.O. Newland."

"Yes, replied Jim as he maneuvered through the L.I.S.A. cubicles. "Whatcha got?"

"That's just it. All the Robo-pings that have been knocking against all of our fire walls. They just stopped. All at once. Like a spigot was turned off," explained senior computer specialist Joe Erbes.

X.O. Newland stared at the computer screen then back into Erbes' face. "I need a report, just the gross totals, of all the locations that were being attacked. "

"That's gonna be a huge number."

"But it's possible right?"

"Yes, sir. But it may take a while."

"Good. Get on it. Are you certain nothing's been compromised?"

"As far as we can tell. Nothing," Erbes said hoping nothing slipped through the cracks.

*   *   *   *   *

Buehler was finishing up at the underground complex, working on silo number four. It was almost ready for its decommissioning next month. They'd rotated out the rocket fuel, upgraded the communication software, along with a full state-of-the-art onboard computer. The changes basically upgraded the missile to match the other modern ones.

"It seems strange working so hard getting number four all dialed in just to disassemble it and swap it out again next month," offered Buehler.

"Yeah, well you know how everybody up and down the chain of command gets paranoid about evaluations. Getting too many demerits could be the difference between a promotional opportunity and your re-enlistment getting bounced just before reaching your 20 years. At least then, you're guaranteed a retirement of some sort," replied one of the senior technicians. The same technician paused long enough to give Buehler an obligatory wink.

"And it's even worse for us nukes. No one wants one with too many checks in the wrong boxes, know what I mean? I hope I haven't wasted the last two tours sweating it out over here in South East Asia for nothing. I put in for Colorado. It's time for some cold powdery snow for a change," added another technician as he tightened down the upgraded components.

"Okay gentlemen," announced the ranking officer in charge. "Let's test the connections."

As the crew closed up the missile siding and made their way back toward the launch control room, Buehler noticed a bay of old mint green CRT's (cathode ray tubes), the old-school boxy computer monitors. They seemed to be active. Being the new kid on the block, Buehler didn't want to draw any more unwanted attention to himself. He was already under heavy scrutiny.

As they walked by the wall of old computers, Buehler glanced about to see if anyone else noticed. He even raised his eyebrows as if asking the Lieutenant *"What's up with the monitors."*

The Lieutenant ignored Buehler's expression and pressed forward without glancing around. Looking straight ahead, he didn't notice the monitors. One showed a blinking white light at the bottom of the screen. That prompt hadn't blinked in decades. Everyone was focused on the missile. With all of the changes, the powers that be hadn't considered the ramifications of upgrading the communications systems without re-patching the linkage points to the modern secure server. That system was fully functional and had the top of the line most up-to-date security software and firewalls.

With a shrug of his shoulders, Buehler assumed *"it must be nothing to worry about."*

*   *   *   *   *

"Colonel," said one of the Chinese computer technicians.

"Have you found something?" asked Fangqi with an eager grin.

"We have. We've established a connection."

"Where, Colorado?   Is it Cheyenne Mountain?" asked Fangqi.

"No. We weren't so lucky."

"South Korea?"

"Okinawa."

"Okinawa? And it's a connection through a known nuclear routing network?" Fangqi asked incredulous.

"Yes."

The river of constant key stroke clicks that had been pounding away on the keyboards stopped. The room was quiet. No one moved. The technicians working the farthest away stood and began walking closer to the Colonel to listen to their conversation. In a whispered voice, as if afraid the Americans could somehow hear their conversation, Fangqi continued.

"Do they know we've gained access?"

The technician gazed back at his terminal and reviewed the data flow detailing the connection. Certain that no new activity or new software was trying to collapse the connection, he finally replied.

"It doesn't look like it." The technician glanced across the tables searching for a more experienced computer engineer. Seeing him, he waived him over.

Not missing a beat, the most experienced engineer was waiting, hoping someone would ask for his involvement. With an eager accelerated pace, he maneuvered around the expanse of tables while the others watched.

"Take a look," instructed the computer technician, while he stepped away from the console knowing the new arrival could validate his finding.

This most experienced engineer sat next to the terminal and accessed the ISP connection and began recording. He then searched for direct connections to this location. Based on what he could determine, it was an older connection that had no modern malware or firewall protection.

The engineer began reviewing this remote computer's prior connection history. He was stunned to see dates starting back in 1982. These connections were not cataloged as part of any program. Unlike modern computers, this one required the data be manually obtained.

"I'm going to install a very basic software package, like the modern "bird dropping" process used by ransomware hackers," the engineer explained.

After a few keystrokes, the program uploaded and dumped on the remote computer.

"As the end user starts interacting with the computer, this program will start pulling data. I'll be able to tell you where it's physically located," the engineer explained.

Colonel Fangqi didn't quite understand the process or exactly what he was doing. But based on their expressions, Fangqi gathered that so far, it was good news.

"How accurate will it be in terms of the location?" Fangqi asked.

"Very. It will give me the Global Positioning, accurate to four meters," replied the engineer.

"Excellent," replied Colonel Fangqi.

As the senior technician and junior technicians backed out of the remote computer, the entire room, that was packed with computer technicians and advisors, watched their every move. It was as if everyone was afraid their movement could alter the outcome and success of the mission. Only after the senior technician disconnected from the remote computer, did he turn away from the monitor and face the Colonel. In unison, the men all exhaled sending a strange gasp echoing through the huge makeshift computer lab. Without warning, the senior engineer stood and thrust his arms in the air and flashed an ear to ear smile and yelled, "We've done it!!"

The room erupted into a roar of cheers. Suppressing his excitement, Colonel Fangqi allowed only a slight smile to appear on his face. He wanted to encourage his men but knew they were a long way from reaching their goal.

"Where exactly is this remote computer located? And more importantly, was it really inside a working nuclear silo complex inside an American facility," thought Fangqi.

*   *   *   *   *

Buehler was the last one to exit missile silo number four. It was Friday, so everyone was eager to get back. Some staying on base, others heading to their off-base housing. Regardless where they were going, everyone was eager to start their weekend. With all the components checked and computer hardware and software upgraded, the team was ready for their first full system check scheduled for the following Monday.

Just before he turned off the lights and caught up with the others, Buehler heard a soft electronic tone. He glanced back at the bay of old computer monitors. The one that had the blinking mint-green square, that square had disappeared. Assuming that the screen saver just blinked the screen off, Buehler kept going. He didn't realize that these older CRT screens didn't use screen savers. Without giving it another thought, Buehler grabbed the metal handrail and started climbing the stairs.

*   *   *   *   *

Fangqi's people were busy monitoring each tournament around the globe. The initial elimination games were set up in teams, with groups across the globe fighting other teams from other qualifying tournaments. The teams that survived to the end, would advance to the next elimination tournament held later.

"Have we been slotting the active U.S. military into the nuclear launch room roles?" asked Fangqi as he studied the bank of monitors that displayed every tournament location. Each screen would flip between the four platforms; submarines, mobile launchers, bombers and ICBM's.

"Not quite. Many of the active military personnel have no contact or affiliation with their nuclear operations," explained one of his senior advisors

"How do we know?" asked Fangqi.

"We have our people surrounding the people that have admitted being active U.S. military. But we're guessing that a few chose not to disclose their involvement with the military."

"And how is this helping us make a better determination?" Fangqi asked.

"Our people are prodding them through casual conversations; commenting on their uniform and their use of military jargon to engage them; getting the participants to explain exactly what types of work they do," explained the advisor.

"I see."

"For these non-nuclear affiliated personnel, we're assigning them to support positions inside the game. Our goal is to locate active U.S. nuclear personnel. If we can place these people into the positions they normally work, we just might get a glimpse into what we're really looking for."

"The launch codes," whispered Fangqi as he stared off in the other direction.

"Exactly," replied the advisor."

"What if we succeed in locating these people and they are on a losing team? What if they don't advance to the next round?" asked Fangqi.

"That won't happen," explained the advisor. Seeing the confusion on Fangqi's face, he added, "We control everything. We'll make sure they win."

Fangqi turned toward the bank of monitors nodding in silence. "How many active nuclear personnel do we think we've unearthed?"

"None so far," answered the advisor. Sensing Colonel Fangqi's disappointment, the advisor elaborated. "Keep in mind, that number is for the Xingjian University tournament only. There are 99 other locations doing exactly the same thing."

"Right," nodded Fangqi. "How many total participants?"

"120,000, and the games have just started. I'm certain we'll turn up a few," the advisor added with confidence. "It's a mathematical certainty. And we only need one."

5

"**S**o, X.O., get me up to speed. How is the L.I.S.A. project working out?" asked Director Valdez.

"Well boss, last night L.I.S.A. was tracking thousands of what appeared to be automated Robo-attacks throughout our global computer networks. And then, simultaneously, it just stopped," explained Newland.

"All of them at one time?"

"Yes."

"Was it a localized power failure that disconnected the attacking computers?" Nena asked.

"We're looking into that. At that precise moment, there were 103 global electrical outages. We're cross-referencing those locations with any possible group or clustered IP activity," replied Newland as he scrunched his face. "But this assumes they're all housed under one roof or from a central location. They could be doing it from multiple locations," he added.

"True," answered Nena as she rubbed her chin, lost in her thoughts. After a brief silence, she asked, "Have we received anything suspicious from any of our bases?"

"Nothing. The L.I.S.A. team is archiving all email replies and plan to initiate calls to bases that haven't answered?"

"How many haven't answered their email?"

"37."

Nena nodded as she processed everything. "Should we bring anybody in to help bounce around some ideas?" Nena asked.

"Like Gibby and Carla Jo?" asked Newland.

"Exactly."

"It couldn't hurt."

"I'll call them in," confirmed Nena.

*   *   *   *   *

"Colonel Fangqi. We've done it!"

"Done what exactly?" asked Fangqi as he stared at the senior advisor from across the desk.

"We've hacked into one of the American's nuclear launch rooms," explained the advisor, unable to suppress his smile. He was more than pleased with his team and eager to give the Colonel the good news.

"Explain," pressed Fangqi, unwilling to get overly excited just yet.

The advisor slid a folder across the desk as he explained. "Our engineers uploaded a software program that allowed us to compose an encrypted message without communicating this information normally. The program included the physical IP address. We then used our other hacked American accounts not related to this mission and were able to upload another program designed to look like an update. That same software allowed us to utilize a localized GPS locator. We're 100 percent certain that the computer is located inside Kaneda's AFB. And, our sources say that Kaneda has a secret underground nuclear missile silo complex."

Hearing this last part, Fangqi allowed himself to feel elated. Then, he remembered. "Wait. There aren't any nuclear silos in Okinawa," said Fangqi in a disappointed manner. "At best, the Americans have mobile rocket launchers."

With raised eyebrows, the advisor replied, "Our sources have come across new information that suggests they do, and have had an ICBM silo complex since 1960," continued the advisor. Colonel Fangqi leaned back in his chair and raised his hand to the advisor encouraging him to elaborate.

"Apparently, during the U.S. and Russian stand-off during the Cuban Affair, the U.S. authorized them to launch their hidden rockets against Russia. This story has been floating around suggesting that official launch orders were received," explained the advisor.

"Really?" asked Colonel Fangqi incredulously.

"And this was before SALT (Strategic Arms Limitations Talks) so it was a multi-missile rocket. The word is there were 32 total bombs in the delivery package."

"What happened? How did the launch get stopped?" Fangqi asked.

"The Senior American Launch Officer saved the day. Only one of the launch tubes had a missile crew willing to launch. The others didn't believe the order. They assumed it was another training exercise, or a mistake. But this particular crew had received location targets for only Russian cities," continued the advisor.

The room had turned quiet. No one else knew the story. Everyone around leaned forward, on the edge of their seat, listening to his every word.

"Continue, please," urged Fangqi. "What happened?"

"It was a technicality really. Even with official verified launch codes, the American's protocol required the Defense Condition to be at DEF CON 1. Otherwise, regardless of the authenticity of the launch order, nuclear missiles cannot be launched."

The room was deathly still. Everyone imagined the world that would have followed had the missile launched. No one spoke for some time. Everyone seemed lost in thought, envisioning a nightmare averted.

"Even still, one silo's launch officer was prepared to launch. All his targets were inside the old U.S.S.R. He couldn't imagine why this order would be false."

"It was the Senior Launch Officer. He ordered that the launch be stopped and demanded the crew wait until a DEF CON 1 level was reached"

"What does DEF CON 1 mean?" asked another advisor.

"War," interjected Fangqi.

"That's right," said the senior advisor.

"Why did the officer wait?" asked Fangqi.

"Suspecting the crews' intentions, the Senior Launch Officer sent two armed airmen to that particular silo. Using the connected underground tunnels, it was only 30 yards away. Each silo had hard-wired connections to each other by regular closed circuit telephone system, utilized only inside the missile complex. He made a final call to that crew where he ordered them to stand down. Only after hearing the sound of the armed airmen's stamping feet arriving outside their silo did they abort the launch."

The advisor paused and looked around the room. Everyone waited, eager to hear each word.

"The Americans never changed the Defense Condition to one. The incident was over just like that. If it weren't for the actions of a few decision makers, they would have launched. The world would be a much different place today."

The men listening remained silent. No one said a word, absorbing everything. Until that moment, this game they'd been playing hadn't seemed real. It felt more like exploration, an intellectual curiosity. Their mission was just a game of cat and mouse, exploring a hypothesis. Posing a question that warranted an answer. It never occurred to anyone, even Colonel Fangqi the potential ramification of their actions. The unthinkable accidental collision course that could arise from their meddling.

Recognizing the somber affect this story was having on his team, Colonel Fangqi attempted to diffuse the negative energy.

"I'm curious. How did we get this information? It is very specific. Who is the source?" Fangqi asked.

"The Lone Wolf verified the story. He is a reliable source. An ex-Stasi agent still active in East Berlin."

"I've heard of him," replied Fangqi. *"Maybe there is some truth to the story,"* thought Fangqi. "What is the Lone Wolf's source? How can he be so certain? And with so much detail?" pushed Fangqi.

"One of his men was inside the silo. So, he claims."

"Incredible. A Russian or German?" Fangqi inquired.

"Neither. He was an American."

Everyone remained frozen processing the information.

* * * * *

Lieutenant Owens was eager to enter the underground silo complex. After clearing the security screening and passing through the body scanner, Owens flashed a smug smile before double timing it down the stairwell. As he wound around the metal staircase, he was happy to see a group of men gathering around the coffee pot.

"Gentlemen," announced Owens. "You're looking at one of the lucky and worthy players that gets to advance to the Regional DDD tournament."

"Woe, how cool is that L.T." replied one of the men.

"How many players were there?" asked another.

"A ton," replied Owens, unable to control his excitement.

"When's the next tournament?" asked another.

"Two weeks buddy! In Tokyo. I already put my leave request in. Dicky, I mean General Blair already approved it too."

"Good for you. That's awesome!"

Buehler was quiet just observing. He'd also advanced. Unlike Lt. Owens, he'd kept the information to himself. Nobody knew he'd even participated. For some reason, being the new guy, he didn't feel comfortable getting too chummy so soon.

Buehler hung back and followed the others down toward tube four. Out of curiosity, he glanced back at the old computer CRT monitor. A little green box was still displaying on the screen. This time, it was blinking.

*   *   *   *   *

Jeanne was disappointed. The tournament format and excitement were beyond her expectations. But to her dismay, just like that, she'd been eliminated. She hadn't made it out of the first round. She had no way of knowing that DDD had abandoned the pursuit of the submarine launch codes. The Chinese assumed that it was futile. Unlike the stereotypical perception that submarines remained out at sea hidden beneath the oceans somewhere, most of the time, they were tied up at dock.

After the Chinese identified Jeanne as a submariner, they purposely eliminated her from the competition. They wanted to focus on more viable options. That assumption cost the Chinese dearly. Had they spent a little more time and effort looking into submarines, things would have turned out much differently. It was a missed opportunity something Fangqi and his advisors hadn't fully appreciated.

*   *   *   *   *

"Colonel Fangqi, the General will see you now," announced the receptionist.

Fangqi stood and let a pleasant hopeful smile cross his face. His team did it. They'd hacked into the Americans' arsenal. They had uncovered a long list of active nuclear military personnel and gathered insight into the most likely launch code format that the ICBM silos used. Information gained by accumulating the behaviors of the participants was a treasure trove of data. It was human nature and the innate pursuit of personal greed. Knowing that the winners would win so much money, the nuclear personnel, as a collective group, in pursuit of their own self-interest, would begin to select the most accurate system set-up to what they currently use. In pursuit of fame and fortune, they would tap into their current real-life experiences in hopes of gaining some advantage over the competition. Knowing this insight would give them a huge advantage when programming the computers. The narrower the variables, the quicker the computers could locate the launch codes – theoretically.

With each step, Fangqi felt more and more confident. This meeting was his chance to remind the General about his promise. He was ready to leave the far Western Chinese frontier and head to Beijing. Being isolated in the rural countryside, Fangqi looked forward to being surrounded by 21 million other Chinese. After a quick salute, Fangqi sat in one of the available chairs in front of the General's desk.

"It sounds, from your report, that you've made great progress," stated Lee.

Fangqi was taken aback. Everything that was needed was in play. Short of proceeding to hack the Americans nuclear launch codes, from his point of view, his mission was complete. He was tasked with proving it was possible.

"Sir?" replied Fangqi in a surprised manner. "We've penetrated the Americans' secret silo in Japan. We've identified scores of active nuclear personnel from all four formats and manipulated their obvious addiction to greed, foregoing their security protocols, to gain insight into which console and launch code sequence they're most likely using. It's now no longer a game of theoretical possibilities. We've proven their vulnerability. The only thing left for us to do is to proceed." offered Fangqi in a frustrated manner.

General Lee leaned back in his oversized chair. He had no idea that Fangqi could make so much progress in such a short period of time.   The only response Lee provided was to raise his eyebrows followed by silence.

Confused, Fangqi pressed forward. "But, General," misunderstanding Lee's non-responsiveness, "if we proceed further, the Americans will undoubtedly discover our infiltration. For now, we have proven and uncovered access inside. Going forward, they will close down our access and all of our efforts would have been in vain. They may even, based on this understanding, be willing to re-invest in the code configurations making not only our current advantage useless, but any future potential access to their new configurations that much more difficult to attain. Our progress would become useless."

General Lee agreed. But he didn't want to directly challenge the Americans. From the onset of this mission, he'd thought that he was assigning Fangqi an impossible task. The truth be told, Lee didn't care for Fangqi. He intended on setting him up for failure then disposing of Fangqi by transferring him to some remote assignment.

An assignment that punished him for his failed efforts. He'd hoped Fangqi would be forever lost and forgotten in some desolate province. But now, it would seem that the assignment that was designed to ruin him would bring him just the opposite- accolades and a worthy promotion. Lee did his best to suppress his displeasure over Fangqi's apparent success.

"Colonel, I must say, you've made a lot of progress. I'm eager to see how your tournament turns out. How much farther you can go. Of course, you need to keep your actions hidden from the Americans. We don't want them to find out."

Fangqi studied Lee's face. He couldn't believe what he was hearing. General Lee wanted to proceed? He wanted them to continue to gather more information.

"But General, our next phase is to begin intense surveillance of these known U.S. nuclear personnel. Should I proceed?" asked Fangqi bewildered over the idea. Until now, this mission was theoretical. This next phase was altogether something else.

General Lee realized the dangerousness of proceeding. He guessed that actual surveillance would attract attention and increase the likelihood of being discovered. With the thought of Fangqi's actions being discovered resulting in retaliation by the Americans, a smile appeared on his face.

"Yes, Colonel. I want you to take your mission to the next level. Whatever you need," replied the General, "just let me know. And of course, don't get caught."

Fangqi sat frozen in disbelief. He was lost in thought, contemplating his next move. With a slight tilt of his head, Fangqi was certain they could do it.

"How far do you want me to go?"

"Your report indicates that we're only infiltrating a computer inside a hidden ICBM silo complex. What about the other platforms? The subs, bombers and mobile rocket launchers?" asked Lee.

"We've abandoned the submarines. It's just too difficult. How can we track them while they're hidden deep under the water?" replied Fangqi as he studied Lee.

Nodding, General Lee detected Fangqi's increased stress. The veins along his temples seemed more pronounced.

"We could definitely proceed with the bombers. Everything we need is available now," explained Fangqi.

"Good. Then let's proceed with the bombers."

Fangqi sighed. With an expressionless face, General Lee hoped that this phase of the mission would do the trick. He'd never imagined that Fangqi could have succeeded. Lee hoped he could achieve two goals; close down this dangerous game with the Americans and permanently ruin Fangqi's career.

*   *   *   *   *

The bomb ordinance technician's back was aching more than normal. While the blackjack dealer dealt the cards, he snuck a glance at his wristwatch. He still had a few hours before he had to leave. As the dealer turned over a king, he studied his hand. A sixteen. With pursed lips he chastised himself for not leaving when he had broken even.

"Hit me."

The dealer was fresh, having just replaced the prior dealer a few hands before.

"And a card for the gentleman," smiled the dealer. The bomb ordinance technician was the only one at the table playing. Not unusual for 4:00am in the morning.

The bomb ordinance technician flinched seeing the jack of spades. He flipped over the cards and showed the dealer his twenty-six. While the dealer swept away the cards, the bomb ordinance tech counted his small stack of chips. He had five hundred walking in and now had sixty bucks in colored chips.

After a deep exhale, he scooped up his chips. Exhausted, he practically stumbled toward the cashier cage. He needed the money for gas.

A man peeking out from under a baseball cap, watched the bomb ordinance tech stuffing money into his wallet. He'd never been to a casino before moving here from Russia. It amazed him how many Americans squander so much of it gambling.

He'd already followed several military personnel to verify their work locations. The Chinese were paying him good money to pass along the information. He'd taken the initiative and slapped on a GPS wireless tracking device and verified through Google maps the exact building on the Whiteman AFB. After a few hours of searching the military website created for the military personnel and their families, the Russian was confident that this man belonged to the bombardier squadron for the B-2 Stealth bombers.

Based on his research, the Russian guessed the man worked on aircraft armament systems, probably a specialist. Given the on-line requirements indicated that these people must be between the ages of 17 to 39, the Russian guessed this guy was in a senior position. Unless the Chinese asked for and paid for more detailed information, he decided no more snooping around was necessary. But, he was ready to move if the Chinese wanted more.

The Russian watched the bomb ordinance tech shuffle out the front doors and climb inside his truck. With nothing better to do, the Russian strolled over to the plate glass windows and watched the truck drive away toward the Interstate 29 on ramp South. He'd followed him enough times to know he would transition east on 70. Based on the GPS device used prior, it was exactly 73.1 miles from the casino to the front gate.

After watching the truck disappear from view, the Russian checked his cellphone. It was almost time for one of his girls to show up. Her date with a casino regular was about to expire. The Russian made his way to the bar. As he finished ordering a black coffee, his working girl exited the elevator and strolled over to the bar. With a deep sigh of boredom, the Russian waved her over. It was only her third date. The Russian glanced around wondering if any other regulars would call. Otherwise, it was going to be a slow night.

* * * * *

Burt's class was dominated by middle-aged Chinese men. The demographics stood in contrast to those he'd grown accustomed to at Harvard. But these Chinese students and the youthful foreign exchange students had two things in common; their intense concentration and copious note taking abilities. Burt recognized that fire in the belly. A desire to learn. At the end of his lecture, the class stood and applauded. The first day, it took him by surprise. Now accustomed to the tradition, he just smiled and gave a slight nod in appreciation.

Burt was distracted remembering he needed to pick up seed for his pet bird. A heavy double metal door slammed closed. The noise caught his attention. As Burt searched for the source of the sound, it opened again. Burt paused pretending to be reading his notes. While glancing over the top of his glasses, the door stayed open long enough giving Burt a clear view inside. What he saw stopped him cold. *"What are so many computers doing in this part of the university?"* he wondered. He was almost certain that that building was vacant. At least it was last semester.

Curious, Burt continued walking around toward the student union building. He lounged around finishing a coffee. Certain he wasn't being followed Burt doubled back to his previous location. With his back to the building, he opened his briefcase and propped his cellphone inside. After activating the camera, he aimed the phone and began filming. Having rotated the camera view, he watched the image as it recorded on his cellphone screen.

It didn't take long for the door to open again. After filming, he was eager to get back to his place and download the clip. From his desktop computer, he could edit the image. Gathering his stuff, Burt glanced about before tossing the empty cup into a nearby waste receptacle and left.

As he crossed the campus, Burt heard military boots echoing off the brick walkway. Not wanting to draw any attention, Burt focused forward and kept walking at a calm consistent pace. If the Chinese discovered him spying, he understood the ramifications. He faced corporal punishment and a bullet in his head. The Chinese have zero tolerance for such things. Listening more intently than before, Burt was certain there were two sets of boots approaching from behind. He felt his heart rhythm begin to race and beads of perspiration run along his collar.

"Over there," he heard someone yell in Mandarin. The distinct sound of their boots against the walkway confirmed that they began jogging. Fighting the urge to run, Burt took a deep breath and continued walking as calmly as possible. As the sound of the men's boots against the walkway approached, Burt tripped almost falling. Out of the corner of his eye, he saw a military officer in full dress uniform cut in front of him. The officer's shoulder slammed into Burt's back.

Startled, Burt stopped and wondered, "*Was this it? Had he been discovered?*" The soldier snarled into Burt's face. In a thick accent, he said "Excuse me" in a slightly apologetic manner. The man continued past Burt and entered the restroom door. The other soldier stepped up to the doorway, pulled out a pack of cigarettes and waited outside while the other soldier finished his business.

Burt regained his composure and continued walking in the same direction.

*　　*　　*　　*　　*

Janet checked her dormitory mail. When her handler needed to make contact, she delivered a special postcard

106

advertisement. It was advertising a pizza establishment that didn't exist. It looked like ordinary junk mail. Only upon closer examination, would someone notice there was no phone number, address or website. The Agency knew that most people never read their junk mail.

Janet's eyes focused on the coupon's expiration date. It was expiring the next day. There was also a cartoon like race car superimposed next to the pizza image. The race car had the number seven painted on its door. Glancing about, making certain she wasn't being watched, Janet tore the postcard in half and made her way back to her room. After entering her dorm room, she shredded the postcard into little pieces and flushed the pieces down the toilet.

She glanced at the clock and still had a few hours. She changed her clothes and wondered what her handler wanted. Since taking the assignment in China, she'd checked her mail daily. This was her first postcard.

She was a little nervous. During her orientation, she was told postcard drops were rare. The process was only used in emergencies. She was anxious to find out what happened. She'd have to wait a few more hours.

*   *   *   *   *

Director Nena Valdez and X.O. Newland waited in a nondescript restaurant. Like all off-site meeting sites, this restaurant was Agency run. Although it allowed uninvited foot traffic, there were no advertisements, no published

107

telephone numbers or television commercials. Still, patrons found their way in. In fact, on-line reviews were posted raving about the food. All the while, these regular patrons had no idea it was Agency owned. To discourage regular customers, the menu prices continued to increase. The Agency wanted enough regular traffic to appear legitimate without dedicating too many hours to keep up appearances. Most of the patrons were foreigners and tourists.

Newland was checking his wristwatch when he saw Gibby and Carla Jo outside. Their table was tucked in the far back corner. Disbursed throughout the restaurant, on the lookout for anything unusual, Nena's four-man security team was in position. X.O. Newland nodded toward the bullet proof windows. Nena glanced over and smiled. While holding open the door, Gibby's shoulder length hair flipped about as his head scanned from side to side searching the area making sure they weren't followed. As they entered the restaurant, one of Nena's men stood and directed them to the booth.

On cue, Gibby made eye-contact with Nena and X.O. Newland. Instantly, Gibby flashed his wide politician's smile while removing his sunglasses.

"Gibby," said Director Valdez as she and Newland stood. "...Carla Jo. It's nice to see you again. You both seem to have recovered from our trip to Germany!"

"Hello, Director," replied Carla Jo, "...and you too X.O. Newland."

"Evening, ma'am," said Gibby. Followed by just "Newland," spoken simultaneously with a quick nod.

After exchanging handshakes, everyone sat. Gibby glanced around still smiling.

"Hey, I remember this place," Gibby said.

X.O. Newland exchanged a puzzled look. After a brief pause, Nena nodded, "Right. We met here a few years back.

X.O. Newland still looked confused.

"You weren't here that time X.O.," added Carla Jo.

"I'm still jealous," added Gibby holding his arms crossed against his chest staring at Nena.

Nena smiled back. "Are you referring to the triple jump to the States?" asked Nena in a joking manner.

With a shrug, Gibby replied, "Yup."

The others laughed while a waiter began delivering their food. With raised eyebrows, Carla Jo and Gibby exchanged excited looks. This restaurant was one of the most expensive in town.

"We ordered ahead. Your favorites," explained X.O. Newland.

"So, boss. What's up?" Gibby asked.

"I'll let X.O. Newland fill you in," said Nena.

"Our newest warning system focuses on nuclear pre-warnings. It's designed to predict potential activities that could indicate an organized attempt to infiltrate any of our nuclear facilities," explained Newland.

Carla Jo and Gibby exchanged worried looks.

"We have nuclear missiles in Korea?" asked Carla Jo.

"Our system is a global network, so we are tasked with monitoring all U.S. facilities," added Nena.

"The acronym of the program is L.I.S.A. It stands for Launch Intelligence Sensory Application. We just call it L.I.S.A.," Newland explained.

Gibby and Carla Jo were stunned to learn that someone or some country was trying to hack the U.S. nuclear arsenal. After hearing the subject, neither felt like eating. They sat dumbfounded in shock.

"What idiot sees the wisdom in doing anything like that?" asked Gibby.

"Our thoughts exactly Gibby," said Nena. "Most people today weren't even alive when we dropped the bombs on Japan. It was over seventy years ago."

"The good news is we're only detecting concentrated cyber-attacks at the most basic access points. Whoever is behind it, has been systematically bombarding all of our known nuclear locations with robotic like frequency. Fortunately, they're only attacking basic email systems, for now."

"Just emails?" asked Carla Jo.

"As best we can gather," said Newland.

"Well, that's good news. I mean emails. Not much of a security concern there right?" Gibby asked.

"Well, emails aren't necessarily the concern. It's the fact that we've documented literally millions of automated pings across our entire nuclear network. Not a single known location has been missed. And then, for no explainable reason, the attacks just stopped," Newland explained.

Going around the table, they all exchanged concerned looks. With a tilted head, Gibby reached down, grabbed the silver plated chopsticks and maneuvered the utensils proficient enough to grasp a small leafy portion of Kimchi and tossing it in his mouth. After chewing, he broke the silence.

"All at once huh?"

Newland nodded.

"From all locations?" Carla Jo asked.

"Yup," Nena replied.

"Mighty peculiar," said Gibby. "What are you guys thinking?"

"It could have been a timed attack. It was designed to last for only a specific amount of time, that's all," said X.O. Newland.

"Or, for a certain number of attempts," added Nena.

Everyone glanced about the table measuring each other's reactions. Carla Jo and Gibby exchanged skeptical glances.

"Your thoughts?" asked Nena.

"So, the obvious question is," said Carla Jo. "...no one's reporting any form of compromise, right?"

"Correct," replied Nena.

"We've even gone to the trouble of contacting all known locations. No one shows any evidence of a breach and everyone has increased their security. Everyone is on full alert," added Newland.

"But why stop?" asked Carla Jo.

"Have we accused any one yet? Have we let anyone, even our allies know about these attacks?" asked Gibby as he glanced back between Nena and Newland. "And by allies, I mean specifically Israel and Germany?"

"No. Nothing," said Nena, "...to anyone."

The table went quiet while they processed everything. After a brief pause, Gibby again broke the silence.

"Then why stop?" Gibby said staring at Nena. With an intense expression, he continued. "If I had to bet, I'd say they got inside."

"That's what we're afraid of," replied Nena.

6

Fangqi stared at his computer screen. After a long sigh, he glanced at a stack of empty cardboard boxes. His move to Beijing was now delayed. General Lee wanted him to play this little game with the Americans a little longer.

"But why?" thought Fangqi. *"To what end?"* They'd already proved that the invincible Americans had a potential weakness, an apparent crack in their supposed impenetrable nuclear armor. With a snarl on his face, Fangqi jammed his index finger down on his telephone keypad summoning his secretary.

"Yes, Colonel?"

"Send in Huizhong."

"Huizhong?" asked the secretary.

In a frustrated sigh, Fangqi paused before replying, "Yes, Huizhong, the Senior Computer engineer."

"Yes. Right away Colonel."

While he waited, Fangqi stared at the empty boxes tapping his desk. He had a crazy idea. *"Who else would know? Who'd even suspect?"* But it was dangerous. Was it worth the risk? Frustrated, wanting to know why he was being asked to go beyond what made sense, Fangqi was grasping at loose ends. Maybe he could learn something; find some comfort over this new situation.

There might be something on General Lee's computer. Why had the General postponed his move to Beijing? Fangqi was concerned about pushing his luck with the Americans. Until now, everything had been done from a distance. This next phase was much different. It required making physical contact with active U.S. military personnel and pressuring them into cooperating. Fangqi rubbed his temples and envisioned the multitude of hurdles they'd need to safely traverse to succeed. This next level was very dangerous. For the first time, Fangqi felt a tinge of fear seep into his psyche.

The sound of footsteps approaching broke Fangqi from his trance. Huizhong would be able to access the General's computer without anyone knowing. Fangqi needed to know why the General changed his mind.

Betts watched the enhanced video clip several times. There was no doubt that the room was some kind of make-shift computer lab hidden inside the University. The video clip provided a view through the opened doorway. She saw several rows of computers set-up, side-by-side sitting on what appeared to be long folding tables. It was anyone's guess how long the tables ran. She knew she needed more information to make any sensible evaluation.

Susan glanced up at the wall clock. It was almost seven. The bar was quiet with only a few patrons present. It was mid-week and no American sporting events, or European soccer matches were taking place. As Susan finished drying off the glass, she spotted Janet coming through the front doors.

Janet glanced about as she made her way to the bar. She noticed her handler move toward the far back side of the bar. With a quick tilt of her head, Susan seemed to be signaling. Janet assumed Susan wanted her to sit at another bar stool.

"So, what will it be tonight Missy?" asked Susan with a casual unsuspecting tone.

"I'll just have a draft please," replied Janet.

"Sounds good," answered Susan. As she poured the beer, Susan scanned the bar area. She was certain that

Janet hadn't been followed. As she returned to deliver Janet's drink, Susan slipped a small pouch she'd hidden inside the wash rag. Susan made sure the pouch sat next to the glass. After making eye-contact, Susan raised her eyebrows in an exaggerated manner tilting her head toward the beer mug.

Catching her meaning, Janet saw the pouch. After a quick glance around, using both hands, she reached for her drink. Hidden out of view, tucked up next to the mug, Janet palmed the pouch sliding it off the bar with her other hand. Clenching the beer mug handle, she raised the glass to her mouth and drank. Her eyes darted about, peering over the top of the tilted beer mug, scanning the area. Under the bar, she slid the pouch into her pocket.

Having already walked away toward the opposite end of the bar, Susan watched Janet out of the corner of her eye. Certain Janet found the pouch, Susan ignored Janet the remainder of the time. Avoiding conversations, she paid cash for her drink and left never looking back.

*   *   *   *   *

"Herr Van Aelst," said an elderly retiree as he removed his beanie knit cap waiting for Van Aelst to make eye contact.

Turning away from the obituaries inside the Berliner newspaper, Van Aelst looked up. With a pleasant smile and unflinching deep blue eyes, he acknowledged the messenger.

"Yes, Comrade. How have you been? And your family?"

"Fine, Herr Van Aelst...fine. Sorry to interrupt your reading. But we just received this. It's a strange request," replied the retiree. With a concerned expression, he handed over the decoded note.

He read the entire note before looking back up. "This was sent via an encrypted and coded computer message?" asked Van Aelst.

"Yes, Herr Van Aelst."

With a slow nod, Van Aelst seemed lost in thought. Recognizing the sign, the retiree backed out of Van Aelst's office. As he was about to leave, Van Aelst spoke up.

"Thank you so much," and flashed a sincere thoughtful smile.

With a quick bow, the retiree cracked a satisfied return smile and closed the door behind him. Van Aelst re-read the message. It was years since he'd read his code name in any format.

"To the Lone Wolf:

We need help from your contacts near Whiteman AFB in Missouri and Barksdale AFB in Louisiana U.S.A. Are they still connected to our Russian friends and the casino?

The Hawk"

Reading those particular bases was a cause for concern. Every covert operative worth his weight in salt understood their importance. Whiteman housed the Americans' B-2 Stealth Bombers. Barksdale was one of the homes of the B-52 Stratofortresses.

"What do the Chinese want with the Americans who specialized in nuclear capable bases?" thought Van Aelst. With pursed lips, he thought back to his prior meeting with Fennu. The Chinese were after information about old secret nuclear bases in the Pacific. He'd mentioned the Cuban Missile crises and how it secretly involved Okinawa. This request is anything but coincidental. To reach out, contacting other organizations suggested something much more involved that some hypothesis being floated by the bureaucrats inside China's military.

The inquiries were specific. Too exact. It had all the feelings of operational awareness; the pre-planning phase. It had been decades since he'd felt such a jolt of concern. It reminded him of the nauseous sensation he'd felt just before the end of the Great War.

Van Aelst glanced at the closed door. His thoughts returned to events experienced decades ago. It was the last days of the war, when he and his other cohorts, despite their youth, helped evacuate the highest ranking Nazi officers out the hidden underground railway line leading to the coast and fleets of submarines. Lost in thought, he could almost see the Fuhrer's train and hear the rattling railway noises as the escaping train disappeared into the darkness. In fact, this corner office was the last building along this railway line before continuing underground for 50 kilometers that ended above ground just before the coast.

Van Aelst knew that the Chinese were up to no good. He decided it was time to make a visit. He checked his wristwatch and wondered if there were any direct flights from Berlin to Seoul, South Korea.

*   *   *   *   *

Hearing someone calling his name, Fangqi looked up from his desk. His bloodshot eyes and sagging shoulders matched how his exhausted body felt. The secretary paused, giving the Colonel a chance to regain his composure from another all-nighter. The secretary hadn't expected to see the Colonel again so early and planned on dropping off the sealed envelope on his desk. With Fangqi already there, he handed it directly to him.

"Your computer specialist wanted me to get you his report. He was specific that you should see it first thing," said the secretary before backing away and closing the door behind him.

After ripping the sealed envelope from the secretary's hand without so much as a "thank you", Fangqi tore it open. He read it out loud mumbling to himself. After skimming the entire document, he stared off in disbelief. As the information sank in, his sleep deprived exhausted state melted away. Having gained access to the General's personal notes and reports, the computer specialist uncovered the truth. General Lee never intended on him succeeding. It was a wild-goose chase, created to blemish Fangqi's military record. This entire mission was destined for failure. Speaking to an otherwise empty room, Fangqi's voice broke the silence.

"After all these years. After all his false promises. General Lee was trying to destroy my reputation, my career. He had no intension of promoting and transferring me back to Beijing."

After a deep sigh, Fangqi gathered himself. For some reason, he felt invigorated. Sitting up in his chair he straightened his crumpled uniform jacket. With intense squinted eyes, he puffed out his chest taking a full breath and leaned forward. With a resolute posture, he turned his attention to the report and whispered, "We'll see what happens next."

*   *   *   *   *

Nicholai glanced between the blackjack table and the elevator doors. He was anxious gripping his cell phone causing his fingertips to turn purple. One of his girls was supposed to be sitting next to the target. Seeing a security guard walking through the casino, Nicholai fed another twenty into the penny slot machine and pushed the minimum bet. He waited until the guard passed by before returning his gaze to the target.

Until he received a call from his boss, he'd marked this guy for an easy blackmail. Over the last six months, the target established himself as a frequent early morning gambler. Another new regular. All the dealers knew his name. His clean cut appearance and intense stare matched his military dress hidden by his thick down ski jacket. Technically, he was allowed to wear his uniform for appointments immediately preceding his duty time. But this exception wouldn't consider gambling an appointment.

Nicholai knew their target never drank alcohol while gambling. And only recently, had he shown up in his uniform under his jacket. Nicholai guessed that the deeper the target fell into his gambling addiction, the more liberal he'd become in terms of adhering to his military protocol. It was just another symptom of where his gambling habit had taken him.

Nicholai studied the target, watching the soldier reach for his wallet for the third time. The soldier paused, tilted his head toward the ceiling while removing his final two hundred dollar bills. With a deep sigh, he placed the money on the green felt. The dealer changed the money into colored chips, before stacking and sliding them in front of the soldier.

Nicholai specialized in gamblers. He'd learned to capitalize on people's addictions. Over time, these addicts predictably slid deeper and deeper into decline, doing anything to earn money to fuel their habit. Nicholai was about to check the time when he saw his girl exit the elevator. With a tilt of her head, she signaled to Nicholai and made her way to the target. She patted her purse checking to make sure the pouch was ready. She and Nicholai had this process down to a science. They'd done this to countless other gamblers. It was like a well-rehearsed choreographed dance. They'd followed the soldier the night before and had a good estimate of his height and weight. Unless he had some unknown reaction from ingesting the drug, he would become extremely susceptible to suggestions. It took them several prior attempts to get the proper mixture and quantities so that it did not overly inhibit a target's motor-skills. At least, not initially.

As soon as she sat at the table, she began patting down her purse.

"Oh, I lost my lighter again," she said leaning forward toward the target. With pouty lips, she stared at the target.

"Do you have a lighter?"

Caught off guard, the soldier reached into his jacket pocket and extracted a plastic butane lighter. She held out an oversized 120 thin menthol cigarette and leaned forward. While she looked into the target's face, she placed her opposite hand near his cup of black coffee. It was another one of his habits. He needed caffeine to stay awake.

After inhaling the cigarette's filtered end, she smiled back.

"Thank you so much," she said as she released a thick plume of smoke toward the soldier's face engulfing the table with smoke. During that precise moment, she emptied the contents from the pouch spiking his drink.

Nicholai watched from a nearby slot machine. He glanced about certain no one noticed anything out of the ordinary. Nicholai checked his wristwatch and began mentally calculating when his girl should make her move and coax him upstairs. He figured they had an hour. Having time, Nicholai wanted to cash his ticket. As he walked by, he glanced at his girl. After changing the ticket, he went to the elevator. Nicholai wanted to get the cameras set up before waiting inside the connecting room. It had become their standard operating procedure rotating between multiple casinos to prevent drawing attention to their scheme.

Initially, Nicholai was disappointed to discover the target was in the military. These guys were predictable but considered small potatoes. They usually focused on high-rollers and big shots. Until he received the call, he planned on moving to another potentially more profitable target. That all changed. While Nicolai rode the elevator up to the room, he wondered, "what do the Chinese want from this particular soldier anyway?" It didn't matter. The payment promised for the video clip was better than he'd normally extort from a high-roller anyway. Since arriving in America, his crew had capitalized on any opportunity that presented itself.

*　　*　　*　　*　　*

Janet locked her door then grabbed the chair. After adjusting the legs, she slid it under the doorknob. Certain the room was secure she placed the pouch on her desk. Inside, she found a small clear plastic box wrapped in cloth. Under the see-through container, was a computer flash-drive.

She attached the flash-drive to her Agency issued laptop computer, and studied the object wrapped in cloth. It looked like an oversized mosquito. There was only one file on the flash-drive.

"Weird," whispered Janet as she glanced back and forth between the clear container and the computer monitor. An enlarged image of the newest mini-drone designed to look like a mosquito took up the entire monitor's viewing area. Janet read the only words written at the bottom of the document. A sentence all in caps and bolded. It read: "**LOOK UNDER YOUR PILLOW**."

Janet turned her attention toward her bed. After a puzzled look, she wondered who and when someone entered her room. She walked over to her bed and lifted the pillow. Underneath, she found what looked like a remote control and a note that read, "YOU'LL NEED A LOT OF PRACTICE."

Janet, still holding the remote control, glanced back at the small plastic container encasing the mosquito shaped mini-drone and thought, *"What could this thing be for?"*

*   *   *   *   *

"General?"

Dicky's head was down reading what looked like a report spread out on his large wood desktop. When in fact, he was reading the NFL scores checking how his Patriots were doing. Peering up over the top of his glasses, he replied.

"Yes, Captain. What's up?"

"I wanted to double check with you about all of the leave requests we've already approved for mid-November," noted the Captain.

"Thanksgiving?"

"No, the week before. We've got several across the base. But what caught my attention was the Special Projects area."

Dicky raised his eyebrows at hearing that. The "Special Project Area" was the unofficial way of discussing the hidden nuclear launch silo complex. Without speaking, Dicky just nodded, encouraging the Captain to continue.

"We've got three different launch officers from different silo complexes that will be out at the same time. I just wanted to bring it to your attention now, in case we needed to rearrange and stagger their leave dates."

"What's going on? Why is everyone asking for the same time off?" asked General Blair.

"Word on the street is these men have been participating in a computer military gaming tournament. They apparently qualified for the International Finals," replied the Captain.

"You don't say?" replied Dicky.

"Yup, General. And the winner gets $250,000."

"If they win, somebody will be buying a lot of drinks at the Christmas party," smiled Dicky.

"Yes, sir."

After thinking it through, General Blair thought he'd let it slide. As long as there wasn't a sudden need to launch their nukes, he didn't see any reason to cancel their leave requests. And that wasn't going to happen.

"It should be fine. Let's let them all go and have their chance at the money," said Dicky.

"Yes, sir, General."

As the Captain left the General's office, Dicky returned his attention to the newspaper hidden under the monthly reports. He smiled, pleased that, even without Brady, the Patriots were still in first place and looking strong.

*   *   *   *   *

With a stiff neck and sore back, the soldier awoke in the front seat of his truck still in the casino parking lot. He started to panic before remembering he'd already finished his duty at Whiteman AFB before going to the casino. The sun was already up, but it still felt like morning.

The Russian girl had slipped a Rohypnol cocktail into his coffee. Over the years, Nicholai and his team of working girls had mastered this tactic. After getting them up to a room, they started feeding them alcohol to finish off the charade. In most cases, the targets couldn't remember anything. Without the video clips, they wouldn't have believed anything out of the ordinary took place.

The soldier rummaged through his pockets and was happy to find his keys and wallet. Other than losing most of his cash, everything else seemed in its proper place. He was about to slide the keys into the ignition when he spotted a bright pink flash-drive device attached to the keychain. With a confused expression, he wondered how it got there. It definitely wasn't his.

Using binoculars, Nicholai watched the soldier from the casino hotel room window. Seeing the target was coming to and staring at the pink flash-drive, he sent the

128

soldier an encrypted text message. Within seconds, an electronic notification echoed inside the truck. The sender's information was masked. Wondering what it was, the soldier opened the text. It was a picture of him sitting next to a young lady. More texts and photos followed. They all showed his mug shot with a stupid expression on his face. Even still, there was no doubt it was him. He looked drunk. After the last photo, came a text. It read, "Be sure to open the flash-drive before you go home."

The soldier snapped his head toward the key chain. In disbelief, he stared at the pink flash-drive before screaming, "Oh my God!"

7

Van Aelst released a deep sigh. He stared out of the business class window at the expansive emptiness of China below. Unlike Europe, the northern section of China, the area that borders Mongolia is unpopulated. The black emptiness below is a complete contrast from the metropolitan city landscape connecting towns and village in Europe. As the commercial jet continued east, a hint of lights below reflected out on the horizon. Van Aelst checked his watch. He'd already advanced the time eight hours to match Seoul, South Korean time zone.

He never imagined seeing the Agency Director again so soon. They'd first met a few weeks prior. She'd visited East Berlin to discuss the supposed removal of one of the Agency team members Diane Klein. That meeting was the Americans way of projecting power and global influence, especially for somebody as apparently inconsequential as an ex-Stasi agent and his band of retirees. Reminiscing would have to wait.

Having survived all these decades because of his instincts, Van Aelst felt guilty deceiving Nena and the Americans. Those feelings dissipated reminding himself that his motivation was honorable. Diane saved his grandson Curt from a certain death. With a satisfied smirk, Van Aelst straightened his thin black silk tie and continued sipping his drink.

Van Aelst had no way of knowing the Chinese intensions. He could only offer a hypothesis based on conjecture. When it came to nuclear issues, he understood that decisions along these lines, had a life all to themselves. His old sponsoring comrades from the now defunct U.S.S.R. still had their tentacles and influences to this day. Van Aelst felt a real sense of dread knowing how close the U.S.S.R. and the Imperialistic Americans came to starting World War III.

He'd shared the Okinawa story with the Chinese. But Van Aelst withheld part of the story. He purposely omitted the fact that the submarine that the Americans were depth-charging off the coast of Cuba in October 1962, was carrying operational nuclear bombs and torpedoes. Had they been attacked the submarine captain was given orders to launch against the Eastern Coast of the U.S.

It's been decades since he'd considered a conflict between U.S.S.R. and America. It seemed so unlikely that fifty years later, these same decisions, same automated systems designed during the Cold War could be somehow set into motion.

Those memories captivated his attention and he was lost in thought. He contemplated whether the U.S.S.R. scientists, who designed the automated system that guaranteed to release all of U.S.S.R.'s nuclear ICBM's, whether any one inside the U.S.S.R. were still alive. With a deep sigh, Van Aelst looked out the window and wondered whether *"the Americans knew about Russia's "Dead Hand" program?"*

This dangerous history still applied today. Through China's meddling, everything changed. It wasn't a question of loyalty. The fact was the "Dead Hand Program" should never have been implemented. He hadn't gone through everything, assembled and protected the members of his clandestine operation, provided all of the care for loyal Germans, including his most recent recruits, Diane and Curt, to see it all end over some hypothetical game the Chinese had no business playing. Van Aelst was one of the few living relics that knew first-hand the realities of nuclear wars, and the existence of this doom's day protocol. It was no legend or urban legend. The "Dead Hand Program" really existed.

*　　*　　*　　*　　*

"C.J.?" said Gibby as he peeked over the adjacent cubicle wall. Hidden inside Camp Bonifas, they worked with the L.I.S.A. project. The South Korean Agency base was situated along the DMZ that divided North and South Korea.

Staring up, Carla Jo replied, "What's up Gibby?"

"Have you noticed the satellite movements over Missouri and Louisiana?"

"Whose Satellites?" she asked.

"That's just it. I was able to identify it as a commercial bird. But when I start digging into the country of origin, I keep getting some multi-consortium for an upstart high tech company, some DDD. Have you heard of them?" Gibby asked.

"Nope," Carla Jo replied as she reached for a mouse. She accessed the Internet and brought up her Google browser. Staring at her screen, Gibby twisted his face.

"Really?"

Her search brought up DDD's website. With a twinkle in her eye, Carla Jo cracked a smile. Gibby offered a disappointing shrug chastising himself for not doing the same thing before bringing it up. He sat back down at his chair, followed her lead and started reading all about DDD.

They read the same information, describing DDD's inaugural International Computer Gaming tournament.

"Wow, pretty cool tournament Gibby. Are you reading this too?" asked Carla Jo as she projected her voice over the partition.

"Yeah. The championship tournament will be held in Beijing. An all-expenses paid trip for those that qualify," replied Gibby in an incredulous voice.

"Is either satellite piggy backing on some other shared commercial platform?" asked Carla Jo, more to herself than stating a question.

"Well, why don't we swing one of our birds over next to theirs and sneak a peek?" said Gibby as he peered over the top of the divider again. This time, only revealing his eyes and the top of his head. She imagined seeing Gibby's exaggerated politician's grin hidden by the partition. His bulging eyes seemed to pulse. Not getting a reaction from Carla Jo, he stood exposing the rest of his body. With a knowing smile, Carla Jo remained silent certain to aggravate Gibby more.

"You know, I could have one of ours over there within twelve hours," Gibby added.

He didn't need anyone's approval. But Gibby and Carla Jo worked well together regardless of constantly trying to one-up each other. It was a constant game between the two, trying to acquire the information or formulate the idea first. Even though Gibby technically out-ranked her, based on seniority and pay, they were still independent contractors. Although it was never brought up, they both knew that it was a card Gibby could play if he chose to.

"Make it so!" replied Carla Jo.

Gibby smiled and sat back into his chair while snorting under his breath. "Who made you Captain Pickard?" he whispered feeling slighted by Carla Jo's Star Trek reference.

"Did you say something Gibby?" she asked.

With a scrunched face, Gibby ignored her and started reprogramming one of the Agency satellites taking it out of a synchronized orbit to rendezvous with the DDD bird. They should cross paths somewhere over the Midwest continental United States. He replied, "No, I didn't say anything."

On the other side of the cubicle, Carla Jo smiled to herself. She'd heard what he whispered. She knew she got him with the Star Trek reference. Gibby hated when anyone else claimed the status as the Captain of the Starship Enterprise.

*   *   *   *   *

The senior North Korean agent watched his team from the safety of a rented SUV. A high ranking Chinese Colonel was making the calls. They sponsored and supported North Korea. For their efforts, the DPRK (Democratic People's Republic of Korea) offered what resources they could. In this case, it was access to sleeper agents inside Japan. Under the pretenses of a vacation, his small team was sent on a mission to secure detailed Intel surrounding Kadena AFB. Their goal was to find a way to covertly infiltrate a hidden missile complex.

A few crew members were playing golf on the course that ran adjacent to the base. They wore the newest fashion and carried top of the line golf equipment. Modified range finders were distributed. This part of their mission involved locating the most direct line of sight access point into the base. From this side, they saw an isolated small stand-alone building. While stationed in Seoul, S. Korea, all but one had learned to golf, and became real golf enthusiasts. South Koreans were fanatical golfers. There was one that had no desire or knack for the game.

Being mid-week, their afternoon tee times were perfect for their scouting mission. The senior agent watched each pair of golfers pass by. One hole ran parallel to the parking area. It was a perfect cover. There was nothing unusual about their behavior. In fact, they could stand out in plain view literally taking visual measurements without drawing attention. Part of golf included using range finders to acquire distances. Nor was it unusual for golfers to be seen writing down information.

Except in this case, the distances being measured and collected was the distance of the parking lot to the isolated stand-alone secure building on the far backside of the base.

The senior agent shook his head in disgust. Back in his country, the DPRK would never have allowed public access next to one of their military instillations. Under his breath, he whispered to his otherwise empty car, "stupid arrogant Americans."

*   *   *   *   *

Launch Officer Owens and Technician Buehler stared out across the base watching General Blair's jeep bouncing over the unpaved dirt access road leading to their isolated building. They'd been informed that the General would be dropping by for his monthly on-site inspection. As the General's jeep approached, the two men tossed their cigarettes on the asphalt parking lot and squashed the cigarette butts under their boots. In unison, they reached down, recovered the debris and slipped it in their pockets.

General Blair gripped the steering wheel as he raced toward the missile silo complex. With a deep sigh, he looked forward to decommissioning the oldest missile number four fondly nicknamed "Old Bessie". As the switch out date approached, everyone involved in that process understood that every protocol would be scrutinized. Careers may not necessarily be made during such processes, but many had been ruined as a result of them.

As the Jeep drove up, Owens and Buehler stood at attention extending smart rigid salutes.

"Afternoon, General Blair," said Lt. Owens.

Parking the jeep next to the men, General Blair flashed a knowing smirk, with his eyes hidden behind dark sunglasses.

"At ease gentlemen," responded the General as he swung out of the doorless dull green jeep.

"No driver sir?" asked Buehler.

"No. Getting and keeping one that maintains such a high security clearance, in and of itself, draws attention," replied the General.

"That makes sense, sir," added Lt. Owens.

"It's about that time Lt. Owens," said the General.

"You mean the nuke inspections, sir?"

"No," replied General Blair as he smiled and glanced across the field toward town. It took a while before Owens caught the General's meaning.

"Right! Yes, sir. That tree should be decorated for Christmas in the next few weeks sir. All those wires and ornaments would make for a difficult climb to the top, sir."

"Not a problem Lieutenant. Only a minor distraction. Something any Hotshot worth his salt could maneuver around," replied the General with a sarcastic grin.

As General Blair stepped toward the doors, the reflection off something glinted across the empty field casting a bright light into his field of vision. The General paused and stared out across the barren field. Buehler noticed the General staring toward the golf course out on the horizon barely in view. The three men stopped and stared. They could just make out several golf carts maneuvering on the plush green fairways. With a nod, General Blair turned and pushed through the doorway. Lt. Owens and Technician Buehler followed him inside.

*   *   *   *   *

Colonel Fangqi stared out from the window. Unbeknownst to any of his team, he'd set up a secret office in an old cottage on the edge of the frontier. From that point, one could literally walk out and keep walking until they reached the next country Kazakhstan. Due west an old radar base was designed to protect the Western Chinese border. Seeing his laptop's Internet establish a connection, brought a sigh of relief. The last thing he wanted to do was bring a computer technician here. The less anyone knew of its existence the better. For now, he swept the floor with an old broom and unloaded supplies.

*   *   *   *   *

Mr. Davies, Director Valdez's pilot, met Van Aelst at the gate terminal.

"Mr. Van Aelst, sir. Do we need to pull your luggage?"

"That won't be necessary. I travel light," replied Van Aelst as he raised a small leather Dopp kit that carried his toiletry items. With a nod, Mr. Davies led Van Aelst through the adjacent doorway, down the stairway and straight onto the tarmac. Holding the chopper door open, Van Aelst climbed inside. Without waiting for instructions, Van Aelst snapped the safety belts into place and adjusted the headset. By the time Mr. Davies made his way inside, Van Aelst was waiting and holding up the headset jack ending.

"Should I connect to input one or two?"

Taken aback, Mr. Davies replied, "Two. I get number one."

While Mr. Davies went through his pre-flight check, he asked Van Aelst, "So, is this your first trip to the DMZ?"

With a direct unflinching stare from his clear blue eyes, Van Aelst said, "This will be my first official visit, yes."

With a subtle nod, Mr. Davies thought to himself, *"He's been there before."* And warned himself to be careful what he said. The Lone Wolf was still connected. As he received radio clearance to take-off, Mr. Davies maneuvered the helicopter's controls and raised the specialized Agency helicopter off the tarmac. Van Aelst wondered if this was the same person that performed the flyby in East Berlin not so long ago. Probably. Van Aelst's natural curiosity took over. He began playing his favorite game; espionage cat and mouse bombarding Mr. Davies with not so innocent questions. Questions that would suggest he knew much more about most everything.

"So, Mr. Davies, what other aircrafts are you capable of flying?" asked Van Aelst.

With a side-ways glance, Mr. Davies knew the Lone Wolf was searching for some sort of confirmation. Knowing the game, Mr. Davies dodged the question.

"Well, you know. I'm old school. Most of my ratings are on retired planes," offered Mr. Davies.

"Is that so?" replied Van Aelst in an incredulous voice. "I was hoping you knew something about modified KC-135 Stratotankers, F-16 Eagles and F-15K Slam Eagles. Or maybe even a modified Concorde or SR-71.

Trying to keep his composure, Mr. Davies acted like he had no clue what Van Aelst was referring to. With a knowing smirk, Van Aelst turned his attention out the front windshield. He was certain that he'd struck a nerve.

Mr. Davies maneuvered the Agency Airwolf helicopter out of Inchon International airspace heading north toward the DMZ. It was disturbing and beyond a coincidence that Van Aelst mentioned the very planes Mr. Davies used in his most recent missions. Unfazed, Mr.

Davies remained expressionless concentrating as he descended. Flying into the DMZ required pilots to fly the nap-of-the-earth (NOE). Traveling just above the ground. This form of aerial approach into Camp Bonifas was the safest way. The DPRK were known, out of boredom, to take pot shots at their aircraft.

Mr. Davies glanced over at Van Aelst. With a slight nod, a smile broke out on Mr. Davies' face. Van Aelst wasn't the least bit scared. With his bright blue eyes wide open, leaning forward in his seat, and an excited expression, Van Aelst was enjoying the ride.

*   *   *   *   *

General Blair bounced along the dirt road heading back to his base office. He waited at a stop light to turn green. Having just come back from the underground missile silo complex, he looked forward to refitting "Old Bessie". Getting ready for its decommissioning took a lot of his time. A definite distraction from his normal duties. Having to face the eventual scrutiny about his past handlings and control over the nukes weighed on his mind. As the commanding officer of the base, everything was ultimately his responsibility. With a heavy sigh, he contemplated the wisdom of keeping those weapons operational. With the submarines and bombers, Blair questioned the necessity and feasibility, not to mention the added expenses and resources it took to maintain their readiness. Regardless, that decision was way above his pay grade. That was Washington's responsibility.

The sound of screeching tires and the smell of burnt rubber brought General Blair out of his trance. A pick-up truck pulling a trailer carrying long metal piping had turned onto the road heading the wrong direction. No one was injured, but the road would be jammed for a while.

As the traffic light turned green, General Blair drove past the accident. The truck's four doors opened, and several Asian men exited. Hearing them speaking Korean, Dicky thought he knew what happened. In Korea, cars drive on the right side of the road. In Japan, they drive on the left. Glancing back in his rearview mirror, General Blair saw the men standing between the vehicles talking. The other driver was a marine, still wearing his uniform. As the marine stepped up to address the group of Asians, General Blair noticed a stark difference in heights. The marine literally towered over them. With one last puzzled glance, Dicky redirected his attention forward through his front windshield. The last thing he wanted was to cause another accident. As Dicky sped away, something bothered him about the car accident.

His thoughts returned to the ICBM, and his suspicions vanished. Those sixth sense feelings can be fleeting. Almost like dreams. If one doesn't make a conscious effort to recall and analyze what they just experienced, the memory could be forever lost. In hindsight, that little accident could have been the event that prevented everything from happening. Unfortunately,

General Blair would make the connection too late. Well after the ICBM's launched. By then, it would be too late.

*   *   *   *   *

The North Korean agent stood in the road staring up at a huge American soldier. He forced himself to remain calm purposely avoiding eye contact with the senior agent who was watching from another vehicle.

"I'm so sorry," replied the North Korean agent as he stretched out his hand.

The marine remained respectful but was clearly annoyed by the accident.

"You're on the wrong side of the road," said the marine.

"I know, I know, my apologies," said the North Korean agent in perfect English. "It's an adjustment from Korea to Japan. Are you injured? Is your truck damaged?"

The marine glanced at the front of his Ford truck. Watching the truck as it entered the wrong side of the road, the marine anticipated the collision and stopped well in advance. The North Korean agent had slammed on the brakes. If it weren't for the over-loaded trailer, it could have stopped in time. Even so, there was no damage. The bumpers only touched.

"No, it looks fine. Hearing the screeching tires made it sound worse," said the marine.

144

"I think you're right," replied the North Korean agent. With raised eyebrows, he added, "Are we good?"

"I think so," replied the marine. "But make sure you drive on the left side of the road next time."

With a quick nod, the North Korean agent and the other men walked back to their truck, got inside and slammed the doors shut. Glancing about the intersection, he backed up maneuvering into the proper lane. With a disgusted look, the senior agent glared at the driver and waited for him to pass before pulling out behind and following them back to their hotel.

Under his breath, the senior North Korean agent said, "Gae Sekiya (meaning bastard in Korean)".

*　　*　　*　　*　　*

The South Korean Agency Director Nena Valdez came from a military family. Only after being recruited by the Agency did she learn that her father also worked for the Agency. Her desk was busy the last few years.

The year prior, she'd orchestrated the downing of an underground invasion tunnel built by the DPRK. That feat was supposed to be secret, but most of the global clandestine organizations knew about it. She'd just returned from a temporary assignment State-side babysitting the South Western Agency, while Director Gamboa recovered from injuries sustained by the North Koreans in retaliation for destroying their tunnel. Hearing

Mr. Davies' helicopter, Nena glanced up. From her desktop monitor, she watched it land. Leaning forward, she waited until she saw the side helicopter door open and watched a tall thin older gentleman slide out. As the rotor blades stopped spinning, the man brushed his fingers through short cropped hair putting it back into place. Nena shook her head in amazement contemplating the virility of Mr. Van Aelst. He had to be in his eighties.

Nena continued watching Mr. Davies and Van Aelst walk across the tarmac. As their images disappeared from the screen, Nena turned her attention to the front door of her office. It was only a few weeks before that she'd met Van Aelst. It required flying an alternate route back to Korea with a quick stop over in Berlin. For some reason, he'd reached out, urging to meet again as soon as possible. On cue, she heard a wrap on her solid steel door.

"Yes, come in," said Director Valdez.

The door opened. Before walking on the descending concrete hallway, her guards had cleared Van Aelst using the full body security scanner. There was only one way in and out of the Director's bomb proof shelter-like bunker complex. Nena heard one of her guards speak.

"Boss, do you want me inside?"

"No, that won't be necessary. Please close the door behind you," she replied.

With his striking blue eyes, Van Aelst stared back at Nena. With a slight smirk, he walked toward her desk and glanced around, openly inspecting its contents.

"Nice place. It reminds me of places I've worked in the past," alluded Van Aelst.

"Mr. Van Aelst," said Nena. "I never imagined we'd be meeting again so soon. It's almost as if we met just a few weeks ago," Nena added as she stood stretching out her right hand.

"Please, Director call me Cornelius. With everything we've been through, we should be on a first name basis," replied Van Aelst. After shaking hands, he sat in one of the chairs positioned in front of her oversized wooden desk. He waited for her to sit before continuing.

"And I must apologize. It seems our meetings are destined to be out of necessity. Maybe someday we will meet under normal social circumstances," explained Van Aelst.

"Has something happened in Berlin?" she inquired. Nena studied his expressions and waited for a reply.

"Oh no. Nothing whatsoever to do with Europe." Van Aelst paused and seemed to be searching for the right words. Sensing his reluctance, Nena offered her reassurances.

"This room is cleared for listening devises daily. In fact," Nena pointed at a small metallic box. "That machine scrambles all known frequencies. It's impossible to listen, transmit or record anything inside this facility. Our suspicious neighbors to the north are always trying though."

With a nod, Van Aelst seemed convinced the conversation would remain private. Inching forward in his chair, Van Aelst leaned forward. "I think the Chinese are up to something."

*   *   *   *   *

As Colonel Fangqi entered the make-shift computer lab hidden inside the University, he glanced about in paranoia. Walking through the aisles of folding tables, he was grateful none of the computer technicians looked surprised to see him. If the General suspected anything or discovered he'd hacked into his computer, he would have started an investigation and been removed from the mission. Just as Fangqi passed his secretary, he saw one of his senior computer technicians waiting outside his office.

"Colonel, someone is waiting to see you," announced the male secretary,

The senior computer technician held several folders against his chest, sitting in front of Fangqi's desk as if siting at attention. By the expression on his face, Fangqi guessed he had found something. With a quick pause, Fangqi made eye-contact with the man.

"Humph," grunted Fangqi. With a quick nod, he shuffled inside but left the door open. The man stood and scurried toward the door. Without asking permission, he shut the door and returned to the metal folding chair in front of the Colonel's desk.

"Colonel, we found several agents that fit the parameters perfectly," smiled the senior computer technician.

The Colonel kept his face calm and unexpressive. He felt a sense of relief wash over him as he realized this visit had nothing to do with his secret office set up in the abandoned cottage.

"What have you discovered?" Fangqi asked.

"We've been monitoring two military personnel; one located at the B-2 Stealth bomber base and one at the B-52 base," answered the man as he read from his notes.

"Where exactly are those bases?" asked Fangqi.

After flipping through his notes, the man looked up. "The B-2 Stealth bombers are out of Whiteman AFB, located about 70 miles outside of Kansas City, Missouri. The B-52's base is at Barksdale AFB in Louisiana. As luck would have it, they're both located close to casinos," he explained.

"Casinos?"

"Apparently both of these men have gambling problems," he explained.

"Right," nodded Fangqi. "And our Russian friends...they've got everything under control? They're ready at a moment's notice?"

"That's correct, Colonel. They are just awaiting your word."

Fangqi nodded and rested his chin in his hand. *"We're almost ready,"* thought Fangqi.

*   *   *   *   *

Gibby and Carla Jo moved out from the L.I.S.A. area to one of the Agency's satellite conference rooms. They both saw the simulator controls positioned in front of a large wall to wall and floor to ceiling screen. They assumed correctly that the controllers were used during a past mission when they helped drop a North Korean built invasion tunnel dug under the DMZ. This time, the images shown on the huge screen were coming from over the U.S., transmitting from the repositioned satellite.

"I think you're right Gibby," explained Carla Jo. "They don't appear to be watching Whiteman or Barksdale."

Gibby studied the GPS data. Using the Agency satellite, they were able to confirm what DDD's satellite was zeroing in on. Using the coordinates extracted from the DDD satellite, he made a breakthrough.

"Well, that's what they're watching," said Gibby as his index finger tapped against the monitor screen. "Two specific houses."

"That's strange," added Carla Jo. "I was thinking it had something to do with the military bases."

"Me too," said Gibby. "I would have bet a few hundred that they were spying on our B-2's and B-52's."

With a deep sigh of confusion, "Let's go update X.O. Newland and Director Valdez. I think it's time to get boots on the ground," said Gibby.

With a nod, Carla Jo stared at the computer monitor. "Wonder who lives there?"

*   *   *   *   *

 Nicholai stared out across the casino floor. Like clockwork, he watched the bomb ordinance tech from Barksdale AFB shuffle across the casino floor heading toward the black-jack tables.

"Before he sits down, give him this," said Nicholai.

The attractive Ukrainian girl grabbed the flash-drive as she stubbed out her thin 120 cigarette into an ashtray. Without speaking, she strutted across the plush carpeting. Her walk accentuated her shimmering sequin mini-skirt while smacking her lips chomping away on several sticks of chewing gum. The bomb ordinance tech saw her just before he reached the black-jack area.

"Here," she said and handed him the flash-drive. Without waiting for a response, she continued walking past toward the High Dollar slot machine section.

The bomb ordinance tech glanced about to see if he was being watched. Feeling it was clear, he examined another pink unmarked flash-drive. With a deep sigh, he stuffed it into his jacket pocket and walked to the nearest black-jack table. Stepping forward, he took out a small wad of cash from his front pocket and spread out $255.00 on the table; it was the maximum amount available for a payday cash advance loan. He'd stopped by one of the stores that lined the road leading to the casino.

While the card dealer changed the money into colored chips, the bomb ordinance tech stared at Nicolai at the bar who was watching him. What could he do now? The video of him and the girl was damning. Since then, he'd gone so far as to accept a $1,000 loan from Nicholai and felt beholden either way. The introduction of Nicholai pushed his ability to cope even farther down this rabbit hole. But none of that mattered. His gambling addiction started bleeding into his everyday thoughts. He couldn't help himself. During his prior visit, while driving to the casino, he made every green light. He didn't have to stop once all the way to the casino parking lot. He'd even found a parking spot right up front, the closest spot to the front door. He'd thought, *"Today is my lucky day."* That's why he approached Nicholai and asked for the loan.

As he looked at his cards, a smile came across his face. A king and ace. With a quick flip of his wrist, he turned the cards and flashed the dealer a big smile. "Blackjack." While the dealer paid the hand and retrieved the cards, the bomb ordinance tech had already forgotten about the flash-drive and Nicholai who was still there watching. After several more hands, the Russian shook his head in disbelief. Their target was so addicted to gambling, he'd showed no concern over his situation. He didn't seem to care.

As Nicholai walked away, he checked his gold Rolex wristwatch. It was almost time and started walking toward the hotel lobby elevators. One of his other girls should be finishing her date any minute. He needed to get to her before she had a chance to find a slot machine. She had the same vice as the soldier.

While he waited by the elevators, Nicholai wasn't concerned. He knew the soldier would watch the video clip. He'd been predictable. In preparation for the "real" goal of this long orchestrated song and dance, Nicholai thought it was time that they had the target's full undivided attention. He'd gone to great trouble when making the clip. He was certain it achieved the desired effect. It was a continuous stream, uninterrupted shot of his house with a close-up of the street numbers posed on the side of his house. But the masterpiece came at the end. The last few seconds was the money shot. He'd spliced in a close up of his neighbor tied in ropes and gagged laying inside the trunk of his car. For effect, he'd cut in another shot of his neighbor's home and children and wife arriving. They were oblivious that their loved one was inside the trunk of his car. As his family parked in the driveway, a final close up of the man's face was taken.

Later that day, inside his parked truck, the soldier would watch the clip. As he stared in disbelief at the man's face stuffed inside the trunk of that car, he understood there was no escape from his situation. He recognized the man. It was his neighbor. They were friends and had lived next door to each other for the last 3 years.

*   *   *   *   *

As Director Valdez entered the conference room, everyone stopped talking. Gibby and Carla Jo leaned toward each other, exchanging sideway glances. Everyone's attention was on the tall elderly gentleman walking behind her. He was wearing a dark charcoal two-piece suit with a thin black silk tie and long sleeved white shirt. If he'd been wearing dark sunglasses, he would have looked like the stereotypical spy as shown in most Hollywood movies.

With a confident grin, the man sat next to Nena. With a tight lipped smile, he glanced around the table making certain he established eye-contact before moving on to the next person.   It was like a silent greeting. Director Valdez broke the silence.

"People, I'd like to introduce one our ally contacts. I realize that this is very unusual to bring an outsider into our building.   The issue at hand is urgent and requires a break in protocol. I'd like to introduce Cornelius Van Aelst, an associate from our Berlin Agency.

While Director Valdez spoke, Carla Jo had scribbled something on her note pad. Tapping her pen on the paper, she waited until she'd gotten Gibby's attention. It read, "The Lone Wolf?"   Gibby glanced up at Carla Jo before redirecting his attention at Van Aelst.

Not missing a beat, Van Aelst waited for Gibby's attention. His piercing bright blue eyes darted around the room. "It's my pleasure to meet you all. I've heard so much about this place, as well as your recent successes. From the North Korean invasion tunnel destruction to the recent removal of a mole inside one of your other U.S. Agency offices. Your team, Director Valdez, has earned much distinction within our secret clandestine world. It's one rightfully earned."

Unfazed at his words, Nena deflected his obvious attempt to unnerve her team with access to TOP SECRET information.   "If we could go around the table, please introduce yourselves," said Nena staring at Jim to get things started. In a rapid fire, quick introductions, each person spoke.

"I'm X.O. Newland."

"Senior Satellite technician, Elliott. My friends call me Moon Dog."

"Lt. Kyle Benjamin, the newbie in the group."

"Michael Gibson, independent contractor."

"Carla Jo Hutchison, independent contractor."

Without replying, Van Aelst nodded and returned his gaze to Nena waiting for her to proceed.

"I wanted everyone to hear the information directly from the source. What he has to share might answer some of our earlier questions. If you want to ask a follow up question, I need you to hold your question until Mr. Van Aelst has had the opportunity to explain everything. Cornelius, please proceed," explained Director Valdez.

"Thank you, Nena. Ladies and gentlemen, my prior associates, those relationships created by the World War II alliances between Nazi Germany, put me in a unique situation. I have reliable sources on many sides of many different conflicts. Because of my fortunate longevity, many secrets and relationships were maintained under the belief that I would have passed away years, probably decades, ago. To the disappointment of many, on both sides of this clandestine game we play, here I am, still alive," explained Van Aelst. After a brief pause, he continued.

"I imagine that what I've experienced and the things I know, make me valuable to both sides. Having this universal utility keeps me safe. For now, anyways," he added while raising his eyebrows.

"It seems like our Chinese Comrades may be trying to balance their lack of nuclear weapons by creating instability. Potentially, by gaining access to the United States' ICBM launch codes, could diminish their apparent inferiority complex caused by not possessing a larger arsenal. What they seem to be missing is the inherent dangerous consequences that could arise from this type of meddling. I fear this concern is something that the Chinese don't fully appreciate.

"I can certainly attest to, having lived through the Cuban Missile crises, that this type of espionage has global implications. If history has proved anything, it's that you Americans are predictably unpredictable. But when it comes to nuclear weapons, you also hold the world distinction as the only country on the planet that's launched not one, but two of these weapons against unarmed civilians. So, the world understands that your government and those in power, at least back during that time in history, had gone through the mental gymnastics, analyzing the costs and the benefits. Using another American euphemism, even after great contemplation, the U.S. chose to cross the line, so to speak, yes?"

Without thinking, Gibby replied, "Let's not pass criticisms about decision making processes made during World War II, Mr. Van Aelst. I seem to recall Germany having some unique 'ultimate solutions' of its own." Unable to take back those words, intended to be thoughts kept to himself and not to be blurted out, Gibby's face grimaced showing his regret for speaking his mind. With a scrunched face, Gibby turned his attention to the center of the table and avoided seeing the disappointed expressions being flashed around the table.

"You are so correct, Mr. Gibson. We Germans have a lot of unpleasant dirty laundry as you Americans say." After a brief pause, Van Aelst continued.

"My concern is the Chinese are nosing around your older, somewhat dated missile silos. The Chinese, although well-experienced in the art of computer infiltration, are inexperienced in these types of matters. It seems that some of their recent cyber-attack victories have resulted in a lack in good judgment. Anyone else recognizes the recklessness of their actions. Their tunnel vision, focusing on your computer vulnerability only, doesn't address the potential diabolical opportunity that, even if the Chinese saboteurs have no actual intention of malice, by shining light on your country's weakness, exposes the United States vulnerability to others that truly seek this type of threat. This opening is my biggest concern."

"Others?" asked Director Valdez.

"A rogue State or worse, a small disgruntled faction inside China. It only takes one fanatical person that has access to your arsenal to start things in motion escalating into something beyond anyone's control."

The room went silent. If they weren't so focused, they would have noticed the increased rhythmic inhales and exhales as everyone was lost in their thoughts. It resembled the sound inside a dormitory at night; hearing the soft echoing sounds of people sleeping.

X.O. Newland, sensing Van Aelst was finished, spoke up. "Hypothetically, if what you're saying is accurate, there wouldn't be any fears on our side. Hypothetically, there are no older outdated ICBMs remaining in our nuclear arsenal. At least not in the U.S. arsenal. Potentially, inside our allies and most likely Russia. Well...hypothetically, not inside the U.S."

Around the table, everyone exchanged sideway glances. Without speaking, based on everyone's expressions, it seemed to be a unanimous consensus. After a long pause, everyone's attention became redirected to Mr. Van Aelst. Without hesitation, he spoke.

"Unfortunately, that's why I'm here. There's a saying that is evident and clear. It only arises when people are caught off-guard, unaware of a particular fact. This missing piece of information lulls people into a false sense of security," explained Van Aelst

"And what saying is that?" asked Director Valdez.

"You don't know, what you don't know," answered Van Aelst.

8

The senior North Korean agent relied on his technicians. Although he was the leader, designing an EMP (Electromagnetic Pulse) was beyond his understanding and expertise. He brought a different set of necessary skills for this mission. He spoke perfect English and specialized in organizing teams and planning missions. He was a logistics specialist. He was the details man.

As he studied the device, the other team members watched in silence. After reviewing his notes, making sure each step in his plan was checked off, he broke the silence.

"Very good, Comrades. Is everyone certain that their particular job is complete? Is there an issue that I should be focusing on that I've missed?"

The leader made eye-contact with each team member. Going down the line, each person nodded then glanced to the next person in line. This process was completed until everyone acknowledged their part of the mission was complete.

"We live and die as a Team. Our country is depending on us. We cannot fail and bring shame to our great country and our supreme leaders. It's time we show our value to China and reward them for supporting our small nation all these years. We need to bring honor to the National People's Republic of Korea!"

With a deep sigh, he glanced at the wall clock. "We go in two hours."

*   *   *   *   *

Launch Officer Owens waited outside General Blair's office. They were shorthanded going into the holiday. Thanksgiving was the number one day in the military where planned and approved leaves were granted. This year, it was even more so. Several additional members were away participating in a computer war game tournament. To his surprise, a few of his team had advanced to the international finals in Beijing.

"The guys were rightly excited over the all-expense paid trip and a chance to bring home $250,000. I'd hope I could have won my way there too," explained Lt. Owens.

"Okay, so that's what's happened," replied General Blair. "Staffing wise, are we good to go? No issues over at the shed?"

"Yes, sir. Next week, the nuke decommission team will be here to swap out 'Old Bessie' for the new one," smiled Lt. Owens. "All of its peripheral systems have been updated and tested. It's probably in its best working condition since it was originally installed."

"Sounds good."

As Lt. Owens stood and prepared to leave, he turned back and flashed a crooked smile. "I saw the Douglas fir yesterday, sir. All the decorations are being dusted off."

As if on cue, they both glanced over at a large wooden plaque over his back credenza. There was a pair of metal spike-like contraptions with leather ankle straps.

"What are those called again?" Owens asked.

"Hooks," replied General Blair with raised eyebrows. "When I left the Hotshots, my crew surprised me with the plaque mounted hooks. It was a little memento."

Lt. Owens leaned forward with his hand on a chair. He wanted to get the full story this time. As if re-living those days, the General's eyes glossed over as he remembered those days.

"Yeah, those were some crazy times L.T. I was a Squad Boss, lead sawyer. Before joining the Hotshots, I did some logging in Wyoming. I really enjoyed using those set of hooks climbing trees," Dicky said as he pointed at the plaque. "Had to do that from time to time. Sometimes, during a fire, I'd climb up to determine the best angle to go at the on-coming fire, or which area to harvest next when with the Forestry."

"Why'd they mount them on the plaque?"

"This one time, we were fighting a major 'Rager' forest fire in Idaho. I'd hauled the Superintendent's truck up to the top of the ridge. My crew was setting up a back-burn. But before we did, I grabbed those hooks," again pointing at the plaque. "...and scampered up the tallest tree. I wanted to get a birds-eye view of what was coming."

"Luck would have it. I was up there at the right time. The wind turned and started pushing the fire our way. The recent droughts made that area extremely dry. The fire began moving back in our direction and jumped from tree to tree picking up speed. From my perch, I saw a gully leading toward a small lake."

After a pause, General Blair continued. "My crew and I hustled it down the ravine, waded into the lake up to our chests and waited it out. Those hooks saved our lives."

"Wow! So, you weren't exaggerating about climbing the Douglas fir and signaling me with Morse code, were you?"

With a stoic expression, General Blair shook his head.

"As long as your Morse code is still sharp, we're all set, huh?" joked Lt. Owens.

General Blair started tapping his desk. As he finished, Lt. Owens paused. With his eyes dancing from side to side listening to the tapping. With a twisted expression, Owens said, "Was that STOP?"

"Yup."

They both laughed. Within 48 hours, this little Morse code exchange was a dry run for what was to come. It was the only thing that could prevent the launch of Old Bessie, the last operational old-school ICBM in the U.S. nuclear arsenal.

*   *   *   *   *

Susan Betts checked the clock on the bar wall. It was mounted next to a flat screen television screen. With the NCAA Football Bowl games being played, she expected more people.

"Where is everybody? The games are about to start," asked Susan as she glanced around the empty chairs and tables.

"It's that computer tournament," replied one of her regulars still nursing his beer trying to pace himself throughout the day knowing he would be drinking non-stop for 12 hours.

"Really? Since when does computer nerd stuff trump football?"

"Ever since the winner gets a quarter million," the same patron replied as he peered over his tilted half-full beer mug.

"That would do it," Susan said as she continued drying off a glass.

*　　*　　*　　*　　*

Burt remained diligent. Since he'd uncovered the location of the hidden Chinese make-shift computer lab, he'd contemplated other non-conventional means to see what was happening. He had an African Grey pet parrot. Most people don't realize how smart these birds are. They live up to 80 years, possessing the intelligence of a four year old human, adult chimp or dolphin. Burt took his pet with him on most of his international assignments.

While teaching at George Washington University, they approached him. The excitement of working for the Agency and living in Washington D.C. felt more like a movie than his real life. It took a while to adjust. After a few Agency assignments, his visions of being the next American James Bond evaporated. Using academia and

166

teaching as a cover, his occupation as a professor allowed him greater access to locations. Even still those visiting countries had no illusions that some of these foreigners were there to spy.

Training his pet parrot for surveillance missions was originally a running joke. But after moving to Chevy Chase, Maryland, the home he purchased was situated along Cedar Parkway. Rock Creek meandered through the area and emptied into open land near his backyard. Burt began acclimating his parrot to being outside. First in a cage and it progressed from there. To help his parrot feel more comfortable to his outdoor surroundings, on a portable hand-held boom box, he played Beethoven's Fur Elise. After weeks of being outside, the parrot began associating home with the music. It acted like an auditory homing signal.

To test his theory, Burt began taking the parrot outside of the cage. To prevent the parrot from flying off, he had a custom body suit made. It was a sturdy vest with a metal attachment latch. He hooked the parrot's suit up to a long leash. Over the following months, he extended the length of the leash. After each flight, the parrot was rewarded with his favorite fruit- fresh mangos.

Over the next year, Burt decided it was time to see if his parrot could be trusted to be set free without any leash connected. Burt was reluctant knowing there was a possibility that his pet bird could fly off never to return. He opted to keep the parrot strapped into his custom vest.

This time, he used a short 2 foot heavy gauge twine hoping that from the prior conditioning, the parrot would believe that he was still leashed preventing him from going too far away.

That first solo unattached flight proved a success. Hearing that distinct piano music piping out from Burt's back patio deck, combined with the reward of fresh sliced mangos upon his return did the trick. That was 14 years ago. He still wears a body suit and listens to Fur Elise, as well as the reward of sliced mango upon his return.

Over the years, Burt took the training to a new level. The parrot started looking for particular objects that were placed about the back yard. Using similar positive reinforcement tricks, his parrot learned to search and locate objects he'd memorized from photographs. Prior to going out, first thing in the morning, a photograph of the image was placed in his cage. Presumably, the parrot would be forced to see this object up close and personal non-stop for several hours.

Over time, the parrot mastered the game. With unfailing patience, Burt continued training his parrot to the point that he could recognize many different kinds of objects; boats, towers, even locations like a park, lake or particular building in the area. As technology progressed, Burt started attaching a light-weight micro Go Pro camera on the parrot's body suit. The food reward began increasing in size to account for the amount of energy he was expending, as well as to reinforce his successes. Burt modified the training by encouraging the parrot to fly around the general area where the object was discovered. Each time the parrot returned the initial food reward was given. While the parrot ate, Burt retrieved the camera and they watched his surveillance video clip together.

Every time the parrot flew about the area as opposed to flying in direct straight lines, Burt would give verbal praise and replay the video clip reinforcing that the circular repetitive viewing was what was being rewarded. A different type of fruit and physical attention in the form of scratches, petting and hugs followed. Using only positive reinforcement, he'd trained the parrot to locate, hover and survey a target. Using the new technology, the parrot was able to video document everything he saw.

Burt glanced across the living room and called out, "Are you ready?"

"Ready," replied the parrot in a sing-song manner.

Burt reached inside the cage and removed the oversized photo. The parrot had stared at Fangqi's face, non-stop all morning. Burt repeated, "Go find him! Go find him," while holding up a large uncut fresh mango. Burt double checked the body suit and camera. Certain they were secure, he opened the cage and walked to the sliding glass door. Swinging his arm in an arc toward the opening, Burt pointed outside. The bird knew the drill and leapt up out the cage and landed on Burt's arm. As if saying goodbye, the parrot stared into Burt's face before flying out the open door.

Over the last few days, they'd been tracking Colonel Fangqi at the University make-shift computer lab. For now, the parrot would fly to the campus and perch himself on a street power line just outside. Tonight, was different. The parrot knew that he received bigger rewards for being more adventurous. For some reason, the parrot found himself especially hungry and was very much looking forward to the mango reward waiting for him at home.

*　　*　　*　　*　　*

Fangqi stood in front of the panel of monitors. The make-shift computer lab had been transformed. The center row of tables was removed. They no longer needed all of the computers. They'd served their purpose trying to access any U.S. nuclear facility location. Just as planned, the computer military gaming tournament sponsored by the shell DDD company, utilizing the internet, web-browser ads and the high payouts to the winners, attracted enough contestants and the highly sought after active U.S. nuclear military personnel. Using the preliminary matches, Fangqi's team took advantage of the opportunity and dug deep into these key participants. Fangqi wanted to make one-hundred percent certain that these guys, were who they thought they were.

"You're certain about their backgrounds? You have no doubts about their current job and assignments?" asked Fangqi. The pronounced veins on his neck confirmed his anxiety. His emotions were being transferred to the team. The senior computer specialist could see that the Colonel was wound up tight. Today, with the final DDD tournament championship underway, he was even more so.

"We're certain Colonel. We synchronized each key person and have been surveying them from assigned satellites. We even went to the trouble of sneaking them into U.S. airspace and assigning each person with their own satellite. We've been tracking their every move for the last two weeks."

Fangqi knew all this. He'd watched the images over his computer technicians' shoulders. On his orders, they'd tracked them down following them from their houses to their job site. In some cases, taking them to known missile silo complexes. After scouring through their personnel records, social media accounts, there was a 99.9 percent probability that these participants gave them their best chance at hacking into an U.S. nuclear launch room.

After all these months, his team had learned to read his mood, judge his reactions. Knowing how Fangqi handled past stressful situations, they'd come to expect him to ask rhetorical questions out loud, directed at no one in particular. It was his way of coping with stress.

The other men in the room did their best to remain focused on the DDD tournament. With all the money on the line, the Chinese hoped that each active U.S. military personnel would utilize some part of their current nuclear assignments seeking some advantage. The thought was they would select the system and the launch code format closest to the real thing. Given how much they stood to win, it was a likely possibility.

"Do we have all eight contestants' systems linked and on screen?" asked Colonel Fangqi.

"We do," replied the senior computer technician, doing everything in his power to control his emotions and not scream, "of course we do look at the monitors!"

"The contestants are about to set up their systems," explained another systems tech.

"What is contestant number 1,964 picking?" asked another computer technician. The Chinese had a side pool, betting which of the eight Americans would get them inside the launch system. As each contestant began selecting the system they would use for this final competition, Fangqi, along with the full room of his team of computer specialists, leaned forward and watched as it unfolded.

*   *   *   *   *

Contestant number 1,964 glanced around the huge auditorium. It reminded him of the NBA Finals. There was even a large 4-sided overhead screen that flashed live images of the other contestants. As he studied the arm patches on those images being shown above on the big screen, he saw an American flag patch on his arm. Wanting to see the contestant's face, he diverted his eyes up. He was startled to see his own face staring back at himself. A huge ear-to-ear grin washed over his face as the adrenaline of the moment kicked into high gear.

Several of Fangqi's men exchanged knowing glances. It was their idea to have the cameras purposely capture close-ups of each of the American contestants. This extra attention might be what pushes them to abandon their better judgment and choose the most accurate system and launch code set up.

Contestant number 1,964, like his other seven active U.S. military personnel had never been treated so well. They'd traveled first class and flew to Beijing together as a group. They were purposely placed side-by-side on China's newest wide body 777-300 ER commercial jet. The seats were more like luxury office cubicles with a small desktop, lamp, large screen monitor and adjustable chairs that could fully recline.

Upon arrival, they were picked up curbside by stretch limousines and taken on a tour around Beijing through the scenic route before arriving at the Rosewood Beijing Hotel; the most expensive one in the city. Each contestant was assigned a suite; living room with a window view that overlooked the multi-lane street below.

The Americans were purposely kept together placed in the same hotel wing isolated on an entire floor. A group dinner was arranged for all contestants. To further reinforce the competition between each other, they received detailed statistics gathered during the qualifying tournaments ranking each participant against each other. The statistics were fabricated and designed to further increase their competition.

At Fangqi's insistence, a clear acrylic padlocked suitcase was brought into the dining area and passed around the tables. Inside were stacks of banded one-hundred U.S. dollar bills, totaling $250,000. The Chinese needed the Americans to pull out all stops.

As contestant number 1,964 saw the overhead large screen change images, he felt his heart race as the camera switched to other contestants. During those few moments, he wasn't surprised to see each of the Americans' faces splashed across the big screen in succession. The Chinese played into their weakness for attention, recognition and ever increasing social-media trend of self-promotion.

The tournament was about to start. With the music blaring out across the packed arena, crowded by predominantly young male Chinese computer game enthusiasts. In all prior tournaments, the active U.S. military personnel purposely avoided selecting a particular set-up option. It looked too much like the real thing. In each past tournament, they felt pressure through a sense of loyalty and secrecy which prevented them from making that selection. For some reason, they each felt that doing so was somehow dishonorable; indirectly revealing a secret that they were entrusted with keeping.

All of the manipulation by Chinese was working: the hype, the excitement over potentially winning the money, the bragging rights, the close-up images displayed on the over-sized screen for everyone to see, the VIP treatment at every level. But the final carrot brought the desired effect- the acrylic suitcase full of cold hard cash.

Regardless of their collective prior decisions, each active American did something that none of them had done prior. They each selected the same set-up options. As the Chinese computer technicians began confirming their selections, everyone inside the make-shift computer lab watched it unfold. It was clear, today they were witnessing something different.

"Sir!" yelled the senior technician. Turning his head toward Fangqi and flashing a huge smile, "Every one of them. They're selecting the same option."

The make-shift computer lab was packed with advisors, computer technicians and specialists. At seeing what was happening, they all turned and waited for Colonel Fangqi's reaction. With a stern unexpressive face, and both arms rigid as his hands gripped the armrests of his over-sized chair, Fangqi curbed his excitement. In a shaking voice, veins in his neck pulsing, he finally spoke.

"Have any of them ever selected this option before?"

"No, sir."

With a quick rotation of his neck, Fangqi glanced at the senior technician. "You're certain. There are no doubts?"

"No, sir. Never. We've been monitoring each of the selections and tracking their selections during every tournament."

Hearing the news, Colonel Fangqi's demeanor changed. He stood up and raised both his arms over his head and yelled "We've done it!!"

Everyone inside also stood. In unison, they cheered and clapped. Some even threw their caps into the air. An outsider would have thought it was a graduation ceremony. As they began to regain their composure, they redirected their attention to the DDD computer tournament and their assigned contestants. For that brief moment, they'd lost the fact that they were located inside a University. The other students in the surrounding buildings heard all the noise and wondered what was happening.

As the muffled cheers echoed through the hallways and across the campus, not only had thousands of students looked up away from their studies, but some of the professor's paused during their lectures. One inconspicuous bystander was hanging onto an electrical wire just outside the make-shift computer lab. Burt's parrot flinched as the loud cheers rang out. With a gentle bob of his head, the parrot adjusted his grip on the wire and glanced about. Perched high above the ground, no one heard him speak in his high pitched sing-song voice, "Uh oh."

* * * * *

The North Korea team woke early, ready to initiate their most bold and direct attack against the Imperialist Americans. His Supreme Excellence was eager to exact retribution for the destruction of their most ambitious invasion tunnel into South Korea. With the support and encouragement from Beijing, this mission was being monitored through Chinese satellites.

"Comrade, the device is in place," said one of the team members.

"The senior North Korean agent glanced up from the restaurant booth. The streets were empty. Like most U.S. military bases, most of the traffic in and out started early. By mid-morning, Kadena's front and back gates were clear. The long lines of cars had already passed.

The senior North Korean agent saw the modified metal tube mounted on a trailer attached to the pick-up truck. Triangular cones were staged around the area while several team members looked busy around the coned off area. Hidden inside the long perforated metal piping was

177

the EMP (Electromagnetic Impulse) device. The exterior piping was approximately 24 inches wide and twenty feet long. It narrowed toward the back to prevent others from seeing the devise hidden inside.

"Has the EMP been aligned?" asked the senior agent.

"Yes, comrade. It's calibrated and is aimed at the main door to the remote building."

Hearing this confirmation, the senior agent dialed his other agent who was sitting in a golf cart holding a mini-drone remote control. He wore a single lensed binocular eyewear. It was similar to a one-eyed night vision goggle. This adaptation allowed him full access to both hands. Hearing his phone ring, the agent put the call on speaker phone while watching the miniature drone through the eye piece.

"Yes, comrade?"

"Are you ready? Is the drone in place?"

"I'm ready. No one is around so I've placed the drone in a hover just in front of the building near the entrance door. I've got an unobstructed line of site. The control signals are strong and clear."

"No static or interference?"

"None, from either camera. We'll have to wait and see if the drone's transmission is affected inside."

The senior North Korean agent looked at his SAT phone. Everything was in place. He stared at the mint-green satellite phone screen and waited for Colonel Fangqi to give the order.

*　　*　　*　　*　　*

Fangqi stood at the base of his elevated chair. In preparation for this moment, his team built a platform and arranged the tables into eight separate circled groups that surrounded Fangqi. This formation allowed him to pivot from one location and see each groups' main monitor screen and speak to each team with ease.

The last part of the plan was devised to reduce the amount of time they needed to hack into one of the U.S. ICBM rocket controls. Getting inside the launch room was an achievement, but not the end goal. The mission was to tap into and override one of the missiles. The Chinese felt that having this capability reduced the imbalance of power. Even though the U.S. possessed thousands of ICBM's, by interfering with their nuclear infrastructure, hijacking the rockets neutralized the balance of power. If China could use America's own missiles against themselves, ownership and possession of these weapons of mass destruction became a disadvantage rather than a strategic advantage. This capability leveled the playing ground.

Rather than committing resources toward research, development and maintenance of these ICBM's, China could exploit the situation by using the weapons against its owners. This ability meant China was no longer beholden to the old-school arms race mentality. It no longer became a game that was won by the country that possessed the most weapons of mass destruction. The tables would literally be turned against the Superpowers. Maintaining and possessing ICBMs made the possessors more susceptible to attack by others capable of hijacking their own weapons.

"Get ready comrades," said Fangqi while surveying his group of computer specialists.

Each team watched as the Americans began programing their tournament ICBM consoles. As part of the process, each competitor was required to select and set up their weaponry system. The active U.S. military personnel were accustomed to this process. During their actual real military jobs, setting, inputting, verifying and protecting launch codes was an everyday occurrence. To not include ICBM nuclear missile launches as part of the gaming tournament would have seemed inauthentic and awkward. None of the Americans suspected anything. It was natural.

"Here they go," said the tournament announcer as his voice boomed out across the arena floor and echoed inside the make-shift computer lab speakers. "It's time to load your passwords. Remember, if one of your competitors hacks into your system and disables your launch, you lose," explained the tournament announcer.

Each team was gathered around a central oversized monitor and watched as their assigned contestant entered their unique code.

"Eleven digits!" yelled out one of the Chinese computer specialists. "Numbers and alpha letters only. All caps. No lower case and no special characters."

"Copy that! We have the same thing here," replied another team.

"Same here," said another.

"Me, too. Numbers, alpha letters, all caps, no special characters."

"Copy that. Same thing here!" answered the last team.

Wasting no time, Fangqi yelled, "Lock that search criteria: Eleven digits, all alpha letters in caps, numbers and no special characters!"

The room fell silent as everyone watched the senior computer technician program the search criteria. Knowing the exact perimeter drastically reduced the live search time needed to obtain the launch code. This entire charade, the creation of DDD and the tournament was implemented to acquire this precise information.

Part of the equation was knowing that once they infiltrated the U.S. ICBM missile, they only had a limited amount of time before their presence would be detected.

Every second they saved during this process increased their odds of success.

"Colonel, it's done. We're ready," said the senior computer technician.

Every eye turned to Colonel Fangqi. The room went silent. As Fangqi reached for the SAT phone, everything seemed to move in slow motion. Fangqi bent his thumb and depressed the pre-programmed number. It took the call a few extra seconds to connect. When the call connected, Fangqi broke the silence.

"Comrade?"

"Yes, Colonel. We're all ready," answered the North Korean senior agent.

"Initiate the EMP attack."

"Yes, sir."

The North Korean senior agent reached out across the small aluminum restaurant table and glanced out the plate glass window toward the Kadena AFB's back gate. All his team's equipment and communication devices were modified to include special lead protective plating to assure that their equipment would be unaffected by the EMP burst. He slid the remote trigger to the center of the table and depressed the single button on the remote key. Just like that, it started.

*   *   *   *   *

Technician Buehler and Launch Officer Owens were inside the silo complex bay. "Old Bessie" just completed her final check. Every system was operational. All available modern enhancements were added; remote wireless access points; reinforced housing plates to reduce the vibration during atmospheric re-entry and an abbreviated targeting package. Rather than allow for re-targeting each missile, Old Bessie would stick to old-school missile protocol using pre-designated target packages. In this case, they had two options- A or B.

Buehler looked up at Owens. "So, Lt., your call. Option A or option B?"

"Where do they go?"

"Moscow or Tehran?"

"Let's pick our long-time nemesis. It's only fitting right?" replied Owens.

"Sounds appropriate. It never gets old dreaming about bombing the Russians," Buehler replied with a grin.

Buehler set the target package. The location was GPS specific and aimed at the center of the Kremlin. A metal plate was screwed down over the instrumentation locking the selection. With Option A selected, it couldn't be changed without re-opening the missile, removing the plate and then unscrewing the plate to access the selection panel. Using his cell phone, Launch Officer Owens leaned down and took a picture. That photo would later be transmitted as confirmation. Upon receipt, the information was archived off-site and cataloged in the national registry maintained deep inside Cheyenne Mountain's NORAD complex. With this part of the process complete, Buehler welded the panel shut. After Buehler shimmied out of the crawl space, Owens handed him the final refit documents. With everything now complete, Buehler took the pen from Owens and signed the paper. Owens took a final review before signing and dating the document as the witness. After checking his wristwatch, he added the completion time.

Buehler removed his leather gloves and touched the missile's cold metal skin. Old Bessie had never been in better shape. It was ready to fly and perform its duty, should it ever be called into action. Buehler patted the missile before stepping through the large access panel. Just as he was about to shut and lock the maintenance access panel, an eerie vibration pulse, like a soundless shockwave came barreling inside the silo complex. Everyone physically reacted to the pressure change, with some of the guards' eardrums popping. The feeling was similar to the sensation felt when driving a car up a mountain road. Without warning, the power to the entire silo complex stopped. Without power, everything went dark.

From the loss of power, the system switched to the battery back-up auxiliary power. The emergency powered lights flickered awake and gave the subterranean interior silo structure a mint-green glowing like tone.

"What the hell?" said Owens.

Distracted, Buehler turned and followed Owens up the stairwell and forgot to close Old Bessie's maintenance access door. As they arrived in the lobby, the other guards were gathered crowding around the front door. Buehler pushed the front door open and propped it open allowing the natural light inside increasing the visibility inside.

The mini drone was hovering outside waiting for this opportunity. Wearing his binocular eyewear, he saw the door open. Using the remote control, he maneuvered the mini-drone through the open doorway. Because the door was propped open, the Chinese satellite connection remained strong not having to work around the interference created had the door been left closed. Unnoticed, the mini drone flew about.

Back in the makeshift computer lab, Fangqi and his men waited for the connection.

"We're in Colonel. I'm detecting an available wireless connection. It's from an unknown origin. Based on what I can tell, it's one of the ICBM missiles. It's too soon for the U.S. computer networks to be back on-line. It will take them at least two hours to restore a connection, maybe longer."

"Wait, I'm seeing an array of other wireless devices. But these others all have sophisticated firewalls. We don't have time to hack into those," explained another specialist.

"Go for the first one," ordered Colonel Fangqi. "Hurry! It may represent our only chance."

The decoding team engaged the mainframe with a train of linked desktop computers working in concert to obtain the launch code. It started running through all of the various possible matches. For now, it was all up to the computers and time.

*   *   *   *   *

Nicholai watched his crew escorting the active U.S. bomb ordinance technician toward the cargo van. The soldier's head hung with slumped shoulders. As he stepped up into the back loading doors, two other crew members waited inside and helped him up. Being surrounded by Russians, the soldier recognized the futility of resisting. Besides, the Russians had proved their determination by murdering his neighbor. When their leader, Nicholai shared photos of his family, as well as a detailed schedule for each including their locations during any given day, the soldier understood what was at stake. If he wanted to protect his family, he had to cooperate.

Nicholai slid the side cargo door open. The bomb ordinance tech's hands were tied behind his back with plastic zip ties synched up to his wrists. Nicholai leaned forward and waited for the soldier to make eye-contact.

"Are they loaded?" Nicholai asked.

"Yes," replied the soldier.

"And was the deployment cone left ajar?"

The soldier closed his eyes. After a sullen sigh, he answered, "yes."

"You're certain? Everything was left as instructed, there were no deviations?" pressed Nicholai.

"Yes, everything. Exactly as you requested."

"You know what happens if you didn't?" asked Nicholai.

"Yes. Of course, I do! What choice do I have?" replied the soldier.

"Everyone has a choice. I just want to make sure that you're cooperating. If you love your family, then you made the correct choice. But one never knows in these types of situations."

Nicolai continued staring at the soldier. After a few moments, he was convinced that he was telling the truth. Even still, he pressed on to further gauge his truthfulness. Turning toward one of the crew, Nicholai spoke loud enough so the soldier could hear.

"Keep him alive until the mission is complete. If he didn't do what he was supposed to, I want him to watch as we deal with his family. We'll start with his daughter."

187

The soldier kept his composure. He'd contemplated all his options. The Russians had him under 24 hour non-stop surveillance. He knew that if he deviated, his family would be killed. The soldier rationalized that by just "loading" the B-2 Stealth Bomber payload with nuclear devices wouldn't make them useable. The bombs had to be manually armed and activated. Just putting them on board wouldn't make that happen.

What he didn't know, was the brains behind the mission planned another means to access and remotely activate the bombs. As the van's cargo side door slid closed, the crew members wrapped a cloth handkerchief around the soldier's head covering his eyes, then muzzled him. One of the crew adjusted the cloth so the soldier's nostrils were uncovered so he could breath. Finally, he placed a plastic goggle spray-painted black to prevent him from seeing where they were taking him. They'd learned the hard way how desperate their victims could get. Once one got loose and jumped out the moving vehicle.

The soldier knew his fate. As the van rumbled down the road, the soldier spent his last minutes scared and alone. He never saw the outside of the van alive again.

*   *   *   *   *

X.O. Newland read the latest L.I.S.A. report. With a tilt of his head, he was perplexed by the multi-page report. It appeared to be a laundry list of random bullet points listing individual events. For some reason, L.I.S.A.'s analysis indicated that these events, when taken together suggested a heightened nuclear threat. He was lost in thought shaking his head when Director Valdez interrupted the X.O.'s concentration.

"Jim, what's the problem?"

Turning away from the report, "I just don't see how some of these things are relevant. Like this one," said X.O. Newland as he pointed at the report. "What does a vehicle accident near the Kadena AFB have to do with our nuclear readiness? Or this one, an increase in the number of personnel out on personal time?"

"Where is the analysis section?" asked the Director.

"Gibby and Carla Jo are working on it now. That's what our meeting is about," explained X.O. Newland as he looked at his wristwatch. "They should be coming through the doors any minute."

Director Valdez, X.O. Newland and Moon Dog sat on one side of the conference room table, while Van Aelst sat next to the three empty chairs. The sound of the doors opening broke the silence. Gibby, Carla Jo and senior computer analyst Joseph Erbes walked through each carrying thick binders. Gibby's typical care-free manner was gone replaced with a stern look of concern. Everyone, even Van Aelst, noticed the change.

Not waiting for the new arrivals to sit, Director Valdez spoke up. "What's wrong Gibby?"

Placing their binders on the table, Gibby leaned forward supporting his weight with his two outstretched arms and braced himself against the table. "We've got some problems, plural. Something's up at the Whiteman AFB."

"Where the B-2 Bombers are housed?" asked Moon Dog.

"Yup," replied Carla Jo.

"And that's not all," added the new-comer Erbes. Erbes and Gibby were long-time friends. They'd met at UC Irvine. Erbes went to Stanford, then MIT where he received a master's then PhD in Computer Science. His security clearance allowed him to be present at the meeting.

"This is my good buddy Joe," announced Gibby. We needed him to bounce some of the stuff L.I.S.A. has been reporting."

"Hello, everyone. It looks like some Russian gangs, with the co-operation of a commercial Chinese satellite, have been tracking several active U.S. nuclear ICBM launch technicians."

With stunned expressions, everyone glanced around the table trying to gauge each other's reactions.

"It gets worse," interjected Carla Jo. "We just scanned a group of B-2 bombers heading out toward the

Pacific on a training mission to Kadena AFB. They are emitting a radioactive signature. We had it analyzed and at least one of the planes is carrying nukes."

"What?" asked X.O. Newland.

Director Valdez glanced across the table and thought it was time to excuse Herr Van Aelst. This information was beyond the need to know exception that he was being extended. This territory was now beyond sensitive and confidential. Just as she was about to say something, Van Aelst spoke.

"It wouldn't be the first time."

Van Aelst glanced at Director Valdez before continuing. With a quick nod, Nena encouraged him to continue. For some reason, she wasn't surprised that Van Aelst would know. He had a knack for being one step ahead and having an inside track on information. She was curious what he knew and how accurate his information was.

"Back in 2007, following your Labor Day holiday, some nuclear weapons were accidentally placed on a group of B-52's and flown from North Dakota to Louisiana."

The room was quiet. It was disturbing to hear one of your allies briefing them on something that only a few at the table knew about.

"Is that true boss?" asked Gibby.

With pursed lips, Nena looked at Van Aelst. "What else do your sources say Herr Van Aelst?" Nena asked.

"We believe there were six nuclear devices loaded on the wings. The planes were parked overnight that way, before flying over your country," said Van Aelst.

The others sat around the over-sized oval table exchanging questioning looks. Everyone wondered how Van Aelst seemed to be on the pulse and in the know about most things. He never displayed any arrogance, just a confident matter of fact expression.

"Boss?" asked Gibby. "Is that true?"

"It is," replied Nena without turning her attention from Van Aelst.

From the side room that lead to the L.I.S.A. project area, a loud constant high pitched beep started blaring. Within seconds, another team member from the L.I.S.A. team hurried inside.

"X.O. Newland, Director, my apologies for interrupting, but something is happening in Japan. L.I.S.A. is recommending a drop in the overall global DEF-CON (Defense Condition)."

"Tokyo?" asked Nena.

192

"No," replied the team member as he glanced around the room reluctant to say anything. Sensing his concerns, Nena responded.

"It's fine. Everyone here is cleared to hear this information." She made a point at staring at Van Aelst.

"It's Kaneda AFB."

9

Colonel Fangqi continued his vigil perched over the computer specialist's shoulder. Sitting in the elevated chair, he scanned the make-shift computer lab as everyone waited for the computer to decipher the launch code. They knew there was only a short window of opportunity. The Americans would isolate the problem and swap out the energy sources for generators or link to the naval vessels to re-energize Kadena AFB. Their clock was ticking. The Chinese continued to monitor social media and international news agencies. So far, no one was reporting the EMP attack. There were a few mentions about being unable to access Kadena. Most commenters assumed it was just a power outage. Once the word gets out what really happened, things would change.

Colonel Fangqi reverted to the predictable way he dealt with stress. He started barking questions to another group of technicians tasked with surveying the social media and news agencies.

"Anything?" Fangqi asked in a rushed voice.

"No, sir. Everything seems to be normal. No new concerns being raised. It's being reported as a power outage."

Fangqi leaned forward in his perched chair as if urging the computers to work faster. The computers kept working behind the scene searching through trying to crack the launch code. The computer technicians exchanged glances nervously waiting. There was nothing else they could do.

*   *   *   *   *

"L.I.S.A. is suggesting a change in the DEF-CON," announced X.O. Newland.

"What's changed?" Nena asked

"There's a sudden unexplained power outage at Kadena AFB. The entire island of Okinawa has been affected," replied Lt. Kyle Benjamin.

"X.O. Let's get a call to the commanding officer at Kadena. Who is it?

"That's Dicky...I mean General Richard Blair," replied the X.O. as he exited the room.

"Kadena?" asked Van Aelst with raised eyebrows.

Everyone looked around the table exchanging curious looks.

"Boss, what about L.I.S.A.?" asked Gibby.

Before Director Valdez could reply, Kyle pushed through the heavy double doors holding a tear sheet from the L.I.S.A. group.

"Excuse me Director. This just came in," said Kyle as he handed Nena the papers.

While she read the report, the room was still. "People, we have yet another seemingly coincidental nuclear issue," explained Nena. "Our satellites are picking up a second group flying over the continental U.S. that is definitely emitting radio-waves consistent with nuclear weapons.

"Ours?" asked Gibby and Erbes in unison.

"Yours" whispered Van Aelst in an incredulous tone.

"Kyle, have we isolated the aircraft?" asked Nena.

"Yes, ma'am we have. This second group is a group of B-52's that left Barksdale AFB," replied Kyle.

"This makes the second group of our bombers, flying around loaded with nukes," said Carla Jo.

196

As the group processed this newest piece of information, what Cornelius Van Aelst said next took everything to an altogether different level.

"This doesn't look good. How will Russia or China interpret this news?" asked Van Aelst.

"Okay people. I have a meeting with the National Agency Director in exactly 45 minutes. We need to organize our thoughts and provide a brief detailing everything that's been happening. From all indications, our newest program L.I.S.A. has connected the dots based on these seemingly unrelated situations and suggests we change our Defense Condition," said Nena.

Although it was unusual to allow Van Aelst to remain in the meeting, because he seemed to have access to intelligence that no one inside the U.S. knew about, he was considered essential and a vital asset under the circumstances. He also provided a direct insight from an Eastern European and Socialistic ideological perspective. Things were happening so fast having immediate access to this perspective was invaluable. Under the current situation, there just wasn't enough time to pursue other opinions.

"People, in preparation for my meeting with the National Agency Director, I'd like to introduce two of my counterparts; Director Jon Moore from Dallas and Wes Fleming from Chicago. Gentlemen, normally I wouldn't put this conversation up for my team to hear.

Unfortunately, time and protocol are not on our side. I have a hard deadline to brief our Boss, the National Agency Director in less than 45 minutes. I need everything you two can provide about the two flights. One left Whiteman AFB and the other from Barksdale. Who's ever ready, proceed."

"I guess I'll go first. Hello everyone. My name is Wes Fleming. I manage the Chicago Agency. Hearing about the radiation signatures from the B-2 bombers, we chose to let them proceed in route to their training mission. The powers that be have elected to keep the pilots in the dark. The last thing we need is for someone to panic and go rogue and attempt to off-load the payload somewhere fearing a remote detonation."

"Director Fleming, this is Michael Gibson," said Gibby. Where exactly are they now? And second, where are they heading?"

"They just cleared the West Coast of the U.S. over San Diego. They 're heading to Kadena AFB on Okinawa," replied Fleming.

Hearing Kadena again, everyone at the South Korean Agency inside Camp Bonifas exchanged concerned looks.

"Has anything turned up on the maintenance and bomb ordinance duties at Whiteman," asked Nena.

"So far, everyone is checking out. We're interviewing all personnel as I speak to determine if this is just some accidental load. Apparently, that's happened in the past. However, they're adamant that precautions and procedures were implemented to prevent this from happening again."

"What types of precautions were taken?" asked Carla Jo.

"Well," continued Fleming, "back in the day, the special ordinances were kept in the same location. Since then, they've been physically separated and stored and maintained from different facilities."

"So, if they are really carrying 'specials', it wasn't an accident?" asked X.O. Newland.

"Correct. It would be very unlikely."

"Anything else?" asked Nena.

"Whiteman AFB is having trouble locating one of the bomb ordinance techs. He never showed up for duty this morning." Fleming added.

"Were the aircraft prepped yesterday?" she asked.

"Affirmative," said Fleming.

"Has this guy done this in the past? Failed to show up?" asked Gibby.

"Negative."

The table and talking heads got quiet. It was no coincidence. Something was happening. But what?

"Could you benefit from some reverse satellite analysis from his last known location?" offered Nena.

"That would be extremely helpful. As you know, we can't utilize that technology in the States."

"Understood Director. I'll have some of my people get on it," said Nena as she nodded at Kyle and Moon Dog. "We'll need his last GPS location and time."

"That's all I've got, Nena," said Director Fleming.

"Jon. What have you got?" asked Nena directing her question to the other Director.

"Nena, we have a similar situation here," replied the Dallas Agency Director Jon Moore. "Unfortunately, it seems to be much worse."

"What do you mean?" she asked.

"One of our B-52 squadrons was supposed to participate in the Pacific Training. They're heading east and are over Africa as we speak. They were going to meet up going the other way to Japan. Similarly, our European counterparts have confirmed a radioactive signature presence detected on at least one of those planes."

"What's different?" asked Director Fleming. "They sound almost identical."

"One of the Barksdale AFB bomb ordinance techs also went AWOL (absent without leave) yesterday. We just received a call from the local Shreveport PD. They found him along the Red River. His hands were secured behind his back with plastic zip-ties. A single shot to his right temple and a double tap to his chest."

"This can't be a coincidence," said Van Aelst.

The room went silent. Nothing from anyone on the wall monitors, nor from those sitting at the table. Everyone's brains were spinning through all the possibilities. X.O. Newland and Specialist Erbes, working on the L.I.S.A. project, having dealt with the subtle apparent random pieces of information over the last few months put them ahead of everyone else. And L.I.S.A. was proving her worth today. Another report was generated that advanced the analysis allowing meaningful insights that would have taken weeks to accumulate and analyze.

"Director Valdez," said X.O. Newland. "I think it's time we clear the room. What I have to say is for L.I.S.A. personnel and Director's only."

Without waiting for additional discussion, everyone even Van Aelst, stood and exited the room. As soon as the double doors closed, X.O. Newland spoke.

"We are way behind the curveball on this one," explained Newland. "L.I.S.A.'s been churning out lists of related events. Until now, I would never have believed it possible."

"What do you mean, Jim?" asked Nena.

"The fact that two separate bomb squadrons missions both mysteriously involve unexpected nuclear ordinances loaded; two missing bomb ordinance techs from two different nuclear equipped bases. And now, an electrical outage at one of our main Asian bases Kaneda AFB on Okinawa, Japan."

"If we couple this data with the reduction of nuclear personnel at all three of these locations, that coincidentally are attending the same inaugural computer military gaming tournament, it should come as no surprise that all of these things somehow lead back to China. The championship is even being held in Beijing. This is no coincidence," offered Joe Erbes.

"What's L.I.S.A.?" asked both Directors Fleming and Moore at the same time. Their voices echoed through the conference room inside Camp Bonifas.

"It's a new software designed to detect all potential events that could affect our nuclear readiness. It's an acronym that stands for Launch Intelligence Sensory Application. We just call it L.I.S.A." explained Director Valdez.

Turning her attention away from the two Directors projected on the wall monitors, she addressed X.O. Newland and Specialist Erbes.

"You're suggesting this is all related?"

"Yes, ma'am," replied the X.O.

After a brief pause, Specialist Erbes added, "I think it's time to get our first line of defense ready to launch."

"And what is that, exactly?" asked the Director Valdez.

"Part of the L.I.S.A. project requires us to have a last minute contingency plan to down any launched missile threats. With all the problems and concerns we've had with North Korea one team is placed at Seoul. The other is in Berlin," explained Erbes.

"What does this contingency plan entail?" asked Director Moore.

"We have our next generation SR-71 Blackbirds. They're classified as hypersonic jets that travel Mach 20," replied the X.O.

"Technically, they're called SR-72's. But everyone is familiar with the SR-71 Blackhawks," added Erbes.

"Are you thinking that some other country may be preparing to launch against us?" asked Director Fleming. His tone made it clear that he felt that possibility was beyond likely.

"Not a launch from another country, Director," explained the X.O. "Rather, a potential unauthorized infiltration into one of ours."

The room became quiet. Each Director nodded in unison as they thought through this possibility. Nena was the first person to speak.

"Does L.I.S.A. protocol involve shooting down one of our own planes?"

"Technically, that would be one of our options. But not the initial goal," explained Erbes.

"So, why deploy the SR-72's?" asked Director Fleming.

"The SR-72's are the fastest jets in the world. Their top speed so far has been clocked at 13,000 mph. They've been touted as our newest spy planes. When in reality, our satellites and drones are more than sufficient to handle our surveillance needs," expounded the X.O.

"Have the SR-72's been modified to down ICBM's?" asked Director Moore.

"They have. But like so many modern technologies, we no longer rely on an old philosophical approach that involves physically destroying the missiles," said the X.O.

"How then?" asked Nena.

"We disable them," said Erbes.

For a second time during this meeting, the room became quiet while the Directors contemplated how this was accomplished.

"And how does that happen?" Nena asked.

"All ICBMs can travel great distances. To do this, they actually exit the atmosphere and rise up to 1,200 miles above the earth. We nerds call this distance Apogee. Okay...TMI (too much information). Most missiles travel 15,000 mph. However, in order for the missile's nuclear package to arm, it must re-enter and then reduce its speed to about 1,988 mph. At this rate, the missile is much more stable with less vibration. This stability allows the ICBM to properly self-arm and detonate on its target," said Erbes.

"Who pilots these SR-72's?" asked Director Fleming.

"No one," explained the X.O. "They're UAVs (Unmanned Aerial Vehicles)."

"They're drones?" asked Fleming.

"That's correct," confirmed the X.O. as he looked at Director Valdez.

"Okay? Then, who flies the UAVs?" asked Fleming.

Still looking at Director Valdez, the X.O. paused as he anticipated Nena's comments.

"Let me guess," said Director Valdez with a slight smirk. "It's Moon Dog and Kyle."

Looking down avoiding eye contact, the X.O. replied, "That's correct, ma'am. They've been practicing on the simulator for the last 90 days. Ever since they returned from Berlin. Until now, we figured it was just a temporary job function. We always assumed we would recruit a special group of pilots permanently assigned this duty. But the L.I.S.A. project is in its infancy stage and we assumed we had time to worry about that later. Today, they are our best options to pilot the SR-72 UAVs. Other drone pilots haven't been training on racing these jets up close and personal with ICBMs. Our current drone pilots around the world could take off, land and fly straight, but asking them to rendezvous with a nuke as it returns to earth and then disable it, that's a tall order."

"In the near future, given this situation, we will encourage the DOD to implement this position and start the necessary training. But for now, under our immediate needs, they are the most qualified," added Erbes.

*   *   *   *   *

"Hey, Gibby," said Carla Jo as she jogged over holding up a piece of paper. It was the GPS location for the missing bomb ordinance tech from Barksdale, AFB.

"I thought Moon Dog and Kyle caught that assignment?" replied Gibby.

"I guess they got pulled for some UAV duty," replied Carla Jo. Gibby puckered his lips as he thought about flying. Prior to being an independent contractor for the S. Korean Agency, he'd planned his life around flying jets. After being medically disqualified Gibby opted for sniper school in the Marine Corp. If he couldn't fly jets, he didn't want to be anywhere near a plane. He felt that he couldn't handle the constant reminder of what could have been.

Carla Jo thought Gibby's eyes looked glazed over with a distracted expression. Working side-by-side for many years, she recognized that look. Knowing his past, she gave him a few seconds to clear his thoughts. With a deep sigh, Gibby reached out and took the printout.

By the time he read the time stamp and GPS location, he was back on task with a laser focus. Carla Jo sat next to Gibby as he began inputting the data.

"Let's pull up the satellite and drone images and find out what happened to our bomb ordinance tech," said Gibby.

*   *   *   *   *

Colonel Fangqi paced behind his computer specialist. The array of computers uncovered three of the nine digit launch codes. They only needed six more.

The obsolete ICBM missile housed in silo four was the last vulnerable nuclear missile in the entire U.S. arsenal. Without inside help, all others were properly protected equipped with modern advanced computer malware and firewalls, with redundant infiltration prevention programs that did nothing but search for and isolate potential programming issues even "Trojan Horse" malware. In the new modern missile complexes, the introduction of such invasive software would automatically shut down the site, unable to return to active status until all issues were resolved. The outer hatches would literally shut and lock in place, followed by power being cut. Multiple authorizations would be required before the missile complex was brought back on-line.

The U.S. nuclear arsenal was massive and relied on redundant backups. Losing hundreds of missile complexes at once had no effect on its ability to properly protect and defend the nation. The Kadena site was different. The politics of Japan, having been the only country to experience the effects from the nuclear bombs dropped on Hiroshima and Nagasaki, created a culture that hated anything to do with nuclear bombs. Following the destruction of three nuclear power plants at Fukushima, the Japanese began dreading anything related to nuclear reactions. Inside Japan, the Americans took a "don't ask don't tell philosophy". Meaning no one could confirm or deny the presence of nuclear weapons. The Japanese and the rest of the world believed the U.S. had nuclear weapons there. They just wouldn't admit it.

Most of the computer specialists inside the make-shift computer lab stood about wringing their hands. All of their hard work, programing and logistics, was accomplished. Now, it was a waiting game. The computers ran through trillions of computations searching for the launch codes. Time was the variable that they could not control. Everything depended on finishing the search before the Americans detected the breach and shut it down. There were other potential stumbling blocks to avoid; the propped open front door or missile access door could get shut; bad weather could interrupt the satellite relay. Many factors play a role in the success or failure of their mission.

"We got another one!" yelled one of the programmers. There's only one left!"

A bolt of electricity vibrated across the floor. The rumbling and energy subsided as they continued waiting. Everyone watched their computer monitor and listened to the sudden silence as time dragged on while the computations marched on trying to decipher the last digit. As long as the connection wasn't interrupted, it was a mathematical certainty. They were getting close.

*   *   *   *   *

"What's that sound?" asked Launch Officer Owens.

Turning back and looking through the open door, Buehler replied, "It's the generator. The silo complex is switching over."

On cue, the interior lights blinked back on full strength as the power was automatically re-routed from the back-up batteries to the gasoline powered generators.

"What about the air conditioning?" asked one of the guards.

"It has to be manually switched back on. Keep the front door open while I get it going. It's pretty stuffy down there right now without the circulation," said Buehler.

Owens held the door open for Buehler and had one of the guards bring a large rock to prop it open. The contrasting bright outside lighting compared to the dark underground complex played with his vision. Buehler made his way down the stairwell. The unusual sounds, while trying to restart the air-conditioning unit, was enough of a distraction that he didn't notice the open maintenance panel.

It was a perfect storm. The Americans had several opportunities to disrupt the unobstructed wireless connection starting from the ICBM through the open maintenance door, up to the mini-drone, and then out the open doors to the satellite above. If either door shut, the connection would stop.

Buehler continued making his way to the main corridor. Bending over, he stretched his arm, reaching for the circuit panel behind the air-conditioning unit. With his free hand, he aimed a flashlight down and saw the breaker switch had flipped. Using his thumb, he pushed against the lever. With a loud thud that echoed back up through the stairwell, the air conditioning kicked back on. The intake fan began turning and the air began to cycle through.

Buehler raised his hand in front of a vent and smiled as the cool air washed against his palm. As he glanced about looking for the other vents, something caught his attention. He thought he saw something hovering above the stairwell. What caught his attention was the constant blur created by the spinning propellers. With a quick tilt of his head, he thought, *"What's that?"*

*   *   *   *   *

Carla Jo shook her head in disbelief. Back tracking the video satellite surveillance made their work easy. They'd used the same process on several prior cases. The most recent one involved tracking down Curt Anderson's journey across the U.S. eventually ending in Germany.

Carla Jo and Gibby tracked the perpetrators back to a nearby casino. By backtracking from known locations, it was a simple matter of either rewinding or forwarding through the clips. Eventually, they'd tracked the van to a remote area and saw a body being dumped. She copied the GPS coordinates and presumed that this is where they would find the other missing bomb ordinance tech from Whiteman AFB. Gibby was working on the AWOL (absent without leave) from Barksdale AFB. So far, one soldier had been found.

Gibby stared over the cubicle divider at Carla Jo. "I'll let Director Moore know where to locate their missing bomb tech."

"This is beyond coincidental," replied Carla Jo. "It's the same process for both soldiers."

"Yeah, and both Perps are working out of a local casino. What are the odds of that?" added Gibby. "Have you had any luck with the casino surveillance tapes to identify them?"

"Director Moore and Fleming have brought in the FBI. They have agents scouring through the casino surveillance tapes now. It should be quick order. We have the time stamps when they left and arrived. They should be able to go straight to those time signatures to see what was happening," added Carla Jo.

*   *   *   *   *

Nena waited in her office reviewing her notes. Over the last few years, she'd seen more than her share of the National Director. More than all her prior years combined. The destruction of the invasion tunnel into S. Korea and her temporary assignment substituting for her California counterpart were the most recent. Until now, destroying the invasion tunnel mission was her crowning achievement. The implications of what L.I.S.A. is suggesting has over-riding implications over the entire U.S. nuclear defense program. This unique cyber-infiltration angle could flip the academics' and strategists' protocols and assumptions on their heads.

The National Director (NATD) was appointed by POTUS. This NATD held his position through several administrations and was the only boss she'd known. NATD was a calm steady influence. He was a rebel in his own way ignoring the unwritten rule that Directors didn't wear facial hair. He sported a full beard making sure it was well-groomed. His ego didn't require coloring away the patches of gray on his head and beard. It was a badge of distinction only available to those fortunate enough to live that long. He wore wire framed glasses which matched his demeanor.

He received his undergraduate degree in History from CSU Chico before catching the attention of his superiors. He was recruited directly into military intelligence and was assigned to the nearby Beale AFB. Most people didn't know that during World War II, German prisoners of war were kept there. That base was also home to the now famous U2 high altitude reconnaissance spy planes. He cut his teeth analyzing the film taken during those flyovers.

NATD moved to Sacramento, the Capital of California and continued his career at Mather AFB while attending CSU Sacramento where he received his master's also in History. His demeanor and attention to detail caught the attention of others. He was soon approached by the Agency where he enjoyed assignments around the globe, with continuous promotions until appointed the National Agency Director by President Obama.

"Ma'am," said her male secretary over her telephone intercom.

"Yes," replied Nena.

"It's the National Director Allwardt on the line."

"Pass it through, please." After hearing the call come through, Nena spoke. "Director Allwardt. We speak again."

"Nena," replied NATD Allwardt in a soft almost whispery yet friendly voice. His demeanor stood in contrast to most of her counterparts. "It sounds like we have a potential powder keg situation involving the Chinese?"

"That's correct, sir. And if things keep going as they seem to be heading, we'll need to involve POTUS and all the DOD (Department of Defense)."

"That serious?"

"I'm afraid so. It's probably worse than that, sir. Our newest nuclear software defense program L.I.S.A. is recommending a change to DEF CON 3. L.I.S.A. is anticipating an inevitable change to DEF CON 2."

The line went quiet. In order to change the country's defense condition to three, meant the current overall situation warranted an increase in force readiness. But going to DEF CON 2 meant the situation had escalated to the point that the next step is nuclear war.

"What specific facts have we uncovered? No speculative analysis yet, just facts?" asked NATD Allwardt while still speaking in a quiet controlled manner.

"The Chinese have been seeking intel about our nuclear silo locations, specifically the older ones," explained Nena. "We also have confirmation that a newly formed Chinese computer software company that specializes in military games has created its first international tournament. The tournament competition is completely based on nuclear weapons of all types."

"What's the company's name?" asked Allwardt.

"DDD. It stands for Dragon Digital Dynamics."

"Never heard of them."

"Me too, until now."

"Proceed," urged Allwardt.

"We've confirmed that two of DDD's commercial satellites were doing more than facilitating better real-time transmission to enhance the tournaments. They used these same satellites to perform aerial surveillance over two active bomb ordinance technicians. Both techs worked inside our nuclear capable bomber divisions, one from Whiteman AFB and one from Barksdale."

This second set of facts spiked NATD's attention. "That's where our B-2 Stealth and B-52 bombers are housed, correct?" Allwardt asked.

"That's affirmative, sir. I just spoke to Directors Fleming and Moore. Both bases reported a bomb ordinance soldier going AWOL. One was found by Shreveport PD. He was murdered execution style. Using our S. Korean satellites, we back-tracked from where the soldier was found and have located and confirmed via satellite and on-ground video surveillance footage who the perpetrators are. Local FBI are working with Agency members as we speak."

"That's a lot of dots that seem to be connecting," said Allwardt.

"This other information is even more concerning."

"Worse than what you've already told me?"

"Unfortunately, yes."

"Proceed."

"Our satellites are detecting the presence of special ordinances being carried by two separate training runs. It's no surprise based on what we now know that the training originated from the same places; Whiteman and Barksdale. Both groups took off earlier this morning. We let them proceed out of the continental U.S. airspace and have each group flying around in circles; the B-2's over the

Pacific and the B-52's over the South Atlantic. We have multiple refueling tankers staged so we can keep them airborne indefinitely if need be."

"Good thinking, Nena. I'm doubtful that someone could infiltrate those bombs and remote detonate. But let's not take any chances," said NATD. "Based on what you've outlined, I need to get in contact with DOD bigwigs. POTUS will certainly be brought in. Has any of your foreign counterparts reached out yet?"

"Not as of yet, sir. But with our planes flying around in circles and the staged refueling tankers, it won't take long."

"Who do we have working on it?" asked NATD Allwardt. This time, his voice was elevated as he spoke in quick bursts.

"My team, with the new L.I.S.A. personnel, as well as Director's Moore from Dallas and Director Fleming from Chicago. Only my S. Korea Agency team is working the satellite surveillance, so we're handling everything on the up and up," explained Nena.

"Excellent. Is there anything else?"

"Yes, sir. It seems somewhat related only because L.I.S.A. says so."

"What's that?"

"There's a power outage at one of the bases."

"Which one?"

"Kadena on Okinawa, Japan."

The line went quiet. Nena knew something was wrong.

"Sir?

"Did you say a power outage in Kadena, AFB?"

"Yes, sir Director."

"I need you to move one of your satellites over Kadena ASAP! Is General Blair still the Base Commander?"

"Yes, sir."

"Is there a contingency plan in place that your L.I.S.A. program has implemented?"

"Yes, sir. We have access to the new SR-72's. It's the only detailed protocol that's been developed. But I'm not certain it could help us now," explained Nena.

"What purpose do they serve?"

"The SR-72's can travel Mach 20 hypersonic speed. They provide us a means to disable an inbound ICBM," said Nena in a defeated tone. Implying that their contingency plan couldn't be of any help in their current situation.

"And you have access to the SR-72's now? Are the pilots trained?"

Confused, Nena replied to his question, but unsure how they could help. "Yes, sir. We have two of my team members that have been flying the simulators and drones for the last 90 days."

"Are they pilots?"

"No, sir. These jets are currently only in the drone, UAV stage of development. However, one of the pilots flew the modified refueling tanker we used a few years back during the invasion tunnel issue in North Korea. You may recall watching it unfold on the Washington D.C. screen?"

"Yes, I remember. Perfect!"

"I'm confused, sir. Why should we activate the SR-72 drones in the first place?"

"We have a secret ICBM silo still hidden at Kadena AFB. In fact, Kadena houses the last old-school ICBM in the U.S. arsenal. It is literally scheduled to be decommissioned in the next few days."

"Sir?" asked Nena still unsure what it all means.

After an awkward pause, NATD Allwardt explained, "We think an EMP weapon may have been unleashed there. All cell towers and computer connections are non-responsive. Nena, I'm afraid the Chinese are trying to remote launch one of our ICBM's. We've been trying to contact Kadena for the last 10 minutes. Nothing. No communication either way in or out."

*   *   *   *   *

Colonel Fangqi stared at the wall monitor. He kept glancing back and forth between the computer screen and the wall-mounted monitor, hoping that one would display the last digit to the launch-code. The room was still. Not a sound. They were down to the final digit in the launch code number. Then, just like that, it happened. The search just stopped. In its place a prompt appeared. It read: "Do you wish to proceed?" The senior technician translated the sentence reading it out loud for the entire room to hear. Afterward, he turned to the Colonel. "We've done it, sir!! We have people in place awaiting your orders."

"You're certain that by proceeding, the missile won't be launched?" Fangqi asked. Pulling up his arms against his chest and crossing his legs, his body language confirmed his reluctance to do any more.

"Yes, sir. The missile requires a pre-ignition protocol. Once all the systems are synchronized, the outer doors will open. The missile will internally authenticate the pre-launch readiness and wait for additional instructions; launch or to stand-down.

"And after that, what happens? What if we don't choose either option?"

220

"After 30 minutes, if a missile option is not chosen, it automatically places itself on pause. A new launch code must be entered to re-start the process again," explained the senior technician.

"How do we know this information is accurate?" pressed the Colonel still retracted into himself, cradling his chin and looking at the man through squinted eyes.

"We have one of the software engineers for this part of the launch protocol working for us. He was one of the most recent additions, a new hire inside the Cheyenne Mountain Complex. It's the United States' NORAD (North American Aerospace Defense Command) now their main missile warning center."

Hearing this information, Fangqi glanced over at his senior advisor, second in command.

"Is our contact available by SAT line now?"

"Yes, Colonel," he replied while holding up the phone.

Fangqi grabbed the satellite mobile phone out of the Captain's hand and raised it toward his mouth to speak. "Comrade?" asked Fangqi in a quiet controlled manner.

"Yes, Colonel," replied the North Korean senior agent.

"Do you have direct visual sight of the silo area?"

"Yes, Colonel. My men are all watching from different angles. Several are also filming everything for later analysis," he replied.

"Okay, stand by. I'm putting you on speaker phone. I want everyone to hear everything. Once the missile is readied, I want the documentation saved and immediately uploaded."

"Understood, Colonel," replied the North Korean senior agent.

Fangqi placed the SAT phone on the table. By his expressions, he seemed to be lost in his thoughts. With a deep sigh, he shook his head as if trying to clear his mind. Finally, the Colonel stood, scanning the room. The computer technicians, specialists and advisors waited in anticipation. Fangqi's voice cut through the silence. Today, they were making history.

Raising his arm and shaking his fist in the air, he spoke, "Comrades, finally, all our efforts are paying dividends. Today, we prove to the world that China is also a superpower. We've used our intellect to outsmart the imperialists, outwitting them at their own game. We've proven that we are capable of using their own weapons of mass destruction against themselves!"

The men were mesmerized and watched his every move. They were oblivious that they were inside a make-shift computer lab hidden inside the university. Caught up in the excitement, as a unified group, everyone shouted.

Their muffled roar behind closed doors echoed out across the otherwise peaceful campus grounds. It was nearing sunset, so most of the classes were concluded.

The sudden noise startled several birds perched on a nearby power line that hung in front of their building. The pigeons bolted from their perches flying away in opposite directions. A single bird held its ground. It was a larger bird that looked out of place. If anyone took the time to study its appearance, they would have realized it was a parrot wearing some sort of vest. The parrot lifted a leg to regain his balance, startled by the shouting and the pigeons' sudden departure. After gaining his composure, the parrot glanced back at the doorway below and continued his wait.

*   *   *   *   *

Fangqi's face seemed unrecognizable. Most of his men never saw him smile. This was a different occasion. With an ear-to-ear grin, the Colonel scanned the room and waited for the crowd to calm before continuing.

"Comrades, now, after today, the world will appreciate the wisdom in not investing in research, construction and the maintenance for these weapons. The small arsenal we possess is enough to deter others. But now, we've proven that we can neutralize the Americans' advantage. What good is it having more missiles if others can neutralize them this way?" yelled Fangqi as if he were speaking directly to America, chastising them for their mistake. This time he raised both arms and shook both his fists.

Another roar erupted. The North Korean senior agent smiled as he listened to the Colonel's speech. Seeing the Americans being tricked brought a sense of retribution for what they did to their recent tunnel, but more for the decades prior for meddling in Korean affairs. If it weren't for the U.S., the two Koreas would have unified years ago.

"Comrades mark your calendars. Today will be remembered as yet another milestone in our illustrious history!"

Colonel Fangqi stepped down off the raised platform and walked to the senior programmer's workstation. Without any more fanfare, he grabbed the computer mouse, slid the cursor over the "LAUNCH" icon and clicked the mouse button initiating the pre-launch protocol.

10

Director Valdez stared out the backseat cockpit of the ROK's (Republic of Korea's) modified F-16. Her pilot Mr. Davies was one of the few pilots assigned to Agency Directors. These pilots were trained to fly most planes, jets and helicopters available in the U.S. and allied forces. Having access to a wide range of aircraft disciplines, proved useful. It provided flexibility and unpredictability during missions and emergency situations.

Nena struggled to see her cellphone through her helmet's acrylic face cover. Kadena AFB and South Korea were on the same time zone. There was no need to add or subtract to figure the current time. As she moved about, she was grateful knowing Mr. Davies had disabled all but the telecommunication switch inside her section of the cockpit. Looking about, she found and depressed the intercom.

"Mr. Davies, how long until we touch down in Kadena?"

"Only 15 more minutes, ma'am. The communications are all still down there. The EMP knocked out all communications. The satellites are functioning normally, so we're guessing the local hardware was fried," replied Mr. Davies.

"Does this present any problems for us landing?"

"No ma'am. Protocol restricts outbound flights to an emergency basis. Even the computers are off-line throughout Okinawa. I'll do a flyby to announce our arrival and intent to land," explained Mr. Davies.

"Sounds good."

Nena glanced down. She would feel much more comfortable being over land.

*   *   *   *   *

Director Fleming stared at the middle of his oversized wooden desktop. He could only imagine what was going on around the globe. His part of the mission was bad enough. He'd never been involved in a nuclear issue. Something serious was happening and it was on his watch. Many careers were made and ruined based on their response to emergency situations. Hearing his secretary's voice interrupted his thoughts.

"Director Fleming," boomed over his intercom, "I have the St. Louis PD Captain on the line, sir."

"Put him through."

"Director Fleming?"

"Yes, Captain. What did you find?"

"We went to the GPS coordinates you provided. His body was dumped in the river along the road. It drifted downstream to an undeveloped small island, a sandbar really, on the Mississippi state's side. We used Fish and Game to gain access. It's a sanctuary for birds. I explained that you guys needed to get to the bottom of this problem with urgency. They got the message and cut through the normal bureaucratic red tape," continued the Captain.

"And the soldier," asked Director Fleming cutting off the Captain. "Did you find him?"

"We did. As you anticipated, it didn't end well for him," he explained in a subdued voice.

"How did he look?"

"A single round to his right temple at point blank range, followed by a double tap to his chest. Based on the forensics, he was already lying down on his back. Definitely execution style. He was most likely gone from the headshot. Whoever did it, just wanted to make sure he was dead. No signs of a struggle, no defensive wounds. His hands were still secured behind his back with a plastic zip tie."

"I have my own crew in route. Can your people keep the area secure until then? No media. Are there any Lookie Loo's?"

"No, Director. It's a remote area. There aren't any structures either."

"I appreciate your assistance and cooperation Captain. This situation is classified. I'm authorized to prohibit you from filing any written reports of any kind. I hate to pull rank and jurisdiction, but this is one of those situations. It's something you and your career could never recover from if something happens. Are we good Captain?"

"I totally understand, Director."

"Nothing in writing," repeated Fleming.

"There's nothing to report sir. In fact," the Captain paused before continuing. "I don't even know what you're talking about, Director," he added in a sarcastic voice.

"Thank you, Captain," answered Fleming as he ended the call.

*   *   *   *   *

"Director Moore, we're all set," replied his field Supervisor.

Director Moore stared out across the casino parking lot. Louisiana was in the Central Time Zone, 18 hours behind Korea and Japan. It was mid-night in Bossier City and almost sunset the next day in Kadena.

Using the satellite Intel provided by Gibby and Carla Jo, Moore was able to backtrack the perpetrators that murdered the soldier from Barksdale. The video tapes confirmed that after dumping the soldier, the van drove to the casino. It was still parked in the same spot shown from the satellite surveillance videos taken hours before.

Director Moore parked at a 7-11 convenience store parking lot across the street along Barksdale Blvd. He had three A-teams from his Dallas Agency parked in various locations surrounding the van. This casino was small and had no hotel. It closed daily at 2:00am and re-opened at 6:00am. To avoid media and the attention of others, the plan was to take them down as far away from the Casino as possible.

With the help from Shreveport FBI, and using the casino security tapes, they had close up photos of all the perpetrators that came out of that van. Several FBI agents were staged inside posing as gamblers prepared to follow as they left. A voice echoed inside Director Moore's parked car.

"Director, they're coming out," said the Agency Supervisor.

"Everyone, keep back," replied Moore over the shared communication line. "We don't want to spook 'em."

As the four men walked through the front casino glass doors, they had no idea several of the other people leaving were from the FBI and following them.

"Man, why do we come here?" asked one of the men.

"Let's head over to Harrah's?" suggested another.

"Sorry boys, we have a busy day tomorrow. Let's head home," instructed the crew leader. As he approached the van, he double clicked his remote key. The van's parking lights flashed on and off accompanied by an electronic sounding chirp. Trying to look casual, the agents made their way to their parked cars. The A-Teams waited ready to follow the van.

More patrons exited the casino. It was the weekend. It seemed to be the general time when most people went home. The crowds knew the drill and were distracted thinking about the money they'd lost. Creatures of habit, none of the patrons noticed anything unusual and made their way to their parked cars. With so many people leaving at the same time, there was a slight traffic jam waiting for the light to change.

"Keep back and disburse between the cars," ordered Director Moore. "There's enough of us that they won't be able to get lost in the shuffle."

Preparing to turn onto the previously empty Barksdale Blvd, the van proceeded without realizing three FBI agents were ahead and four others behind all strategically spaced. As the light changed, most cars turned left while the van turned right. As the van passed the 7-11 convenience store, Director Moore watched the unsuspecting van continue south unaware what lies ahead. After traveling a few miles, it turned right onto Ash Point Road. The van continued past Moon Lake on the right then turned into an isolated home at the end of the road that faced the lake.

"Let's take them here," ordered Director Moore. The van drove into the driveway and parked. The Russians didn't notice the vehicles. As they entered the sub-division, the Agency and FBI teams fastened their night vision goggles before turning off their headlights. To catch them by surprise, two cars drove straight across the front lawn while some circled around the back to prevent anyone from escaping. Having just come from the casino, no one was armed. After crushing a pink plastic flamingo propped up in their front yard, the lead car skid to a sudden stop.

The Russian crew leader was taken aback unable to react to what was happening around him. The Agency and FBI cars turned on their high beam lights before jumping out of their cars aiming 9mm pistols at the men. Other agents rushed forward with their weapons also drawn.

"What the hell?" said the crew leader in a thick Russian accent.

"Keep your hands raised!" announced the Agency A-team Supervisor. Without resisting, the crew was handcuffed each taken away in separate cars. Over the shared communication line, the Supervisor said, "Director, I've got the leader. I'm bringing him to you now."

Director Moore started his black Crown Victoria and parked in front of the house. The A-team Supervisor grabbed the front passenger door and shoved the crew leader into the front seat. With his hands cuffed behind his back, he lost his balance and fell face first into the dashboard. Leaning backward, he struggled to a sitting position.

"He's clean boss. No weapons and his cuffs are nice and tight. I cuffed him myself."

"I'll meet you at the place," replied Moore. The Supervisor slammed the front door shut and Moore sped away doubling back onto Ash Point Road, heading to Barksdale Blvd.

"Where are you taking me?" asked the Russian.

"We have a nice room waiting for you on the Barksdale Base," replied Moore. "I suggest you get your story straight."

"No story straight," replied the Russian in choppy English. "What's this about? I have rights. I want lawyer."

"You've been watching too many movies. And you got into the wrong car for something like that," responded Director Moore.

*   *   *   *   *

Colonel Fangqi stared at the telephone on his desk. After proceeding with the pre-launch, he had an idea. After gathering two of his most experienced computer programmers and advisors, he moved them into another room well beyond the main make-shift computer lab. It was set up as over-flow and functioned on the same platform and access points. Fangqi wanted them away from the others while that area was clearing out. That mission completed, they planned on letting the time expire so that the missile would simply shutdown on its own. In the meantime, in case they couldn't access the ICBM, Fangqi contemplated another side mission. He knew it would be a long shot.

"Have you been tracking the bombers?" Fangqi asked his second in command.

"Yes, Colonel. The planes have been circling in two areas; the South Pacific and the South Atlantic."

"Good. Let's focus on the Atlantic group," ordered Fangqi. "You two, I want to initiate the same process we did in the main computer lab."

"A second ICBM location?" asked one of the programmers. Fangqi shook his head.

"The bomber group?" asked the other.

"That's correct. It's a secondary training mission. Given our success with the ICBM we wanted to see if this technology could translate to another platform. However, before we initiate that, I need you to access a computer," improvised Fangqi.

The senior programmer followed Fangqi to his office. Like before, the programmer infiltrated General Lee's computer. Only using the ISP numerical location, this other senior programmer didn't know he was hacking into the General's computer. Given all of the covert things they were doing, he never considered it. Inside the Chinese military, such traits did not co-exist well. Curiosity could result in a firing squad with the cost of the bullet billed to the person's family.

"It's all set, sir."

"Thank you. You may go back to the secondary lab now and assist with our efforts to infiltrate the bombers," ordered the Colonel.

Fangqi had achieved the goal. General Lee thought this assignment impossible. Now, having achieved success, Fangqi wanted his just reward. Accepting the assignment to the far western Chinese frontier was a far cry from where he wanted to be. The attraction was being promoted. Under the circumstances, being able to move to Beijing was worth the sacrifice.

He'd learned a lot from the General's emails. He understood the mission was a wild goose chase. Now, having succeeded, achieving what appeared an impossibility, left Fangqi justified. General Lee should have a change of heart. If nothing else, now he could appreciate his hard work and dedication. Regardless of the General's initial intent, it was still possible for him to follow through and keep his original promises. Everything could be all forgotten, swept under the carpet. In Fangqi's mind, how could the General hold back his promotion now? It was clear that through his leadership and drive, he'd achieved what no other country had accomplished.

It was time to confront the General and demand he be promoted back to Beijing. Fangqi grabbed his phone and dialed the General's direct line.

*   *   *   *   *

The sun was just setting. Burt stared out his back door. Normally, he'd have looked forward to another colorful sunset. Tonight, he was concerned about his parrot. He'd already set up the exterior speakers and was playing

Beethoven's Fur Elise, the homing call that helped the parrot make his journey back home.

Burt scanned the sky worried that a hawk or other bird of prey could get him. Burt settled into his lounge chair and sipped another glass of dry cabernet. It was going to be a long night.

*   *   *   *   *

Buehler stood on the top stairs. His eyes fixated on a blur that seemed to be hovering above. He couldn't imagine what it could be. *Were his eyes playing tricks on him?* Given the unexpected nature of the day, he wasn't quite sure. Just as he was about to ask the others to come and take a look, a green light emitted from the blur. It blinked on and then off. The blur turned swinging a tight semi-circle before darting away toward the open front door. Buehler flinched as the "thing" disappeared. *"Maybe it was a hummingbird,"* he thought.

Without warning, the silo bunker complex started vibrating. A loud hiss echoed below. Launch Officer Owens recoiled in shock with a confused expression. Rushing to the open door, he leaned his head outside and saw steam venting out escaping from one of the underground silos.

"Soldier hold open the door!" ordered Owens, staring at the closest guard.

The soldier scurried over and grabbed the door frame and watched Owens sprint past and around the corner. Owens almost fell as he slid to a stop. He couldn't believe what he was seeing. He'd only read about it. In that moment, his mind flashed back to those grainy black and white photos from his training days. But this was real.

Owens' attention was drawn to the ground. It seemed to be moving. Without warning, a subsurface circular impression formed. Then, the surface dirt and rocks seemed to come alive as the debris danced jumping in the air. A twenty-foot diameter hole appeared in the ground. In an abrupt moment, a huge metallic object pushed up through the hole. Its top splitting into two identical semi-circles while rotating inward separating into two halves. Each half turned inward away from each other until an elongated cylinder leading below ground was visible.

Owens' eyes bulged as he watched the cylinder rising through the opening. This was it. He would never have believed it if he weren't watching. He'd trained most of his career for this very moment. But nothing was going as planned. *How could this be happening?* He hadn't initiated the advanced set-up stage. Nor had he been asked to authenticate and key in the two-person launch code. Was NORAD initiating a remote launch from Wyoming? Then it hit him.

How could he have missed it? It wasn't a power outage. It was an EMP attack! It's the only thing that made sense. Someone was trying to remote launch the missile.

"Oh my God," whispered Owens. He turned toward the base. On the horizon, the tall Douglas fir stood above the area and caught his attention. *"I need to authenticate this launch. But how? All lines of communication are not working. Even our cell phones,"* thought Owens. He turned and sprinted back through the open door. From Owens' expression, the soldier knew something was wrong.

"Does the phone work?" asked Owens.

"No, sir," replied the soldier sitting behind the front desk.

"What about our computers?"

The same soldier turned toward the desk top computer and jiggled the mouse and shook his head. "Nothing."

"Lt. Owens, what's wrong? What's happening, sir?" asked the soldier standing by the open door.

Owens glanced back and forth between the guards. Trying to catch his breath, Owens' hands were on his hips. "One of the missiles is starting up. It's initializing in preparation for launch."

"Which one?" asked the other soldier.

"Old Bessie, number four," replied Owens.

For a brief moment, they all stood motionless not believing what was happening. Owens broke the silence.

"We have 30 minutes until it can launch. Where's Buehler?"

Having heard the commotion, Buehler was standing at the top of the stairwell. "I'm right here," Buehler replied.

"You need to get to General Blair. With the missile in pre-launch, I can't leave my post. Did you ride your motorcycle?" asked Owens.

"I did. What do you want me to tell the General?"

Launch Officer Owens' eyes darted about thinking it through. "I need the General to confirm whether we've been authorized a launch. Without direct orders from the Base Commander, I cannot manually abort the launch. From my perspective, it looks like Kadena has suffered an EMP attack. Otherwise, this launch could be for real. But we need to make 100 percent sure."

Owens checked his wristwatch. "We only have 27 minutes to sort this all out."

Buehler also checked his wristwatch. "It will take time to find him. What if the General isn't in his office? Should I find the second in command?" asked Buehler.

"No! Only General Blair has the authority to make this happen," explained Owens.

"There's not much time," explained Buehler as he checked his cell phone. There was no service. "It's still not working," holding up his cellphone looking at Owens. "Without phones or computers, how can he communicate anything to you?"

The missile silo complex became quiet. Owens had to think through is options. Just as his mind was drawing a blank, about to overload from the stress and frustration, on the verge of panic, he remembered. "The tree!!"

"Sir?" asked Buehler. "The tree? What tree?"

"The Christmas tree in the center of the base the Douglas fir! Tell the General to send me his answer with Morse code. It's almost sunset. I'll be able to see his message. He'll know what I'm talking about! Hurry! We're running out of time!" urged Owens.

As Buehler ran out the front door, Owens stared back toward the stairwell thinking, "This can't be happening." He just realized that if it is an EMP attack, the entire base may have lost communications. How was the General going to contact NORAD? After a deep exhale, Owens walked down the stairwell and stared at "Old Bessie." A thought started to form. He may have to manually disable the missile without the General's orders. He stared at the open maintenance door and wonder if that was even possible.

*   *   *   *   *

"General Lee. I wanted to be the first to inform you of our success. We did it, sir. We've not only infiltrated one of the U.S. nuclear missile complex but were also able to initiate its preparation start-up sequences. Technically, we could force a launch. I'm certain they're scrambling as we speak," explained Colonel Fangqi.

"You're certain?" inquired General Lee. His tone was incredulous and his personal disdain for Fangqi reflected his skeptical tone.

"It's been verified, sir. We have a team on the ground that is video documenting the opening of the missile outer door and its tube has extended. Also, steam is billowing out the hatch confirming the rocket is initializing. For your reference, I've sent you an image taken by one of our satellites. It's in your email as we speak."

General Lee's computer email box was mirrored onto Fangqi's. The Colonel could see everything the General was seeing. Fangqi's heart raced as he watched the General's cursor slide over and open the email. Watching the General double click over the image file brought a smile to the Colonel's face. The satellite image that appeared was perfect. It was magnified looking down an open silo missile hatch opening. Even the steam plume was visible.

"Amazing Colonel. And this is from inside Japan? On the American base Kadena?" asked the General.

"That's correct, sir." After a brief pause, Fangqi continued. "We did it!"

"Colonel, I must say, I never thought it possible. In all sincerity, your efforts and results will help China decades into the future. My heartfelt thanks for your achievement Colonel," said General Lee.

Fangqi felt a change of heart. It seems things now placed him in the General's good graces. Did he dare revisit his promotion back to Beijing? Sensing the General's present attitude, Fangqi decided to push for it. With everything still fresh on his mind, he felt he stood the best chance of success.

"General, if I may. You'd promised me a promotion back to Beijing should I succeed. I wanted to know if that was still the plan. Do you expect to make that decision a reality?" asked Fangqi.

The line went quiet. Fangqi questioned the wisdom of pushing the issue now. Given the General's good mood, he wanted to capitalize on this apparent attitude change. Was the General sincere or were these just words, hot air spewed from a high ranking bureaucrat?

"Colonel, you're right. I had promised you that promotion. You've held up your end of the bargain. You've earned this right. You've earned the privilege and promotion to Beijing. I'll put in the paperwork. It only requires an email to get the process started," explained the General.

"You are serious?"

"I am."

"If I may be so bold, and if it isn't asking too much, while we're speaking, could you send the email? It would mean so much knowing that everything is resolved. I know how busy you are. This way, I won't have to worry about bothering you making sure the transfer was initiated."

"Colonel… Comrade, you are being so forward," the General pushed back in a disappointed tone.

Sensing the General's apprehension, Fangqi tried to temper this unusual request. Fangqi understood that this line of questioning and pushing his superior into action was considered rude and out of line. But having the opportunity to spy on the General's email was his only way to know, with certainty, Lee's true intentions. It was the risk Fangqi felt compelled to take.

"My apologies, General. It must be all the stress I've experienced from this mission. Being isolated in this far Western Province, working day and night, battling the Great Imperialist Americans, I seem to have lost my etiquette. Although I apologize for being so forward. I was just hoping," explained Fangqi reminding the General of his efforts.

He could hear the General typing on his keyboard. The clicks came through clear on the telephone line. Fangqi's heart fluttered in anticipation. His eyes bulged as he watched through the mirrored computer screen and saw the email being formed. To Fangqi's delight, he watched the General type "INITIATE COLONEL FANGQI'S TRANSFER" in the subject line

"When do you want the effective date?" asked the General.

"This year, the New Year falls on February 12. Let's use that day. I can start the new year back in Beijing," replied Fangqi in an optimistic tone.

The Colonel's pulse quickened watching the General type in "EFFECTIVE DATE FEBRUARY 12". Fangqi held his breath, unable to suppress the grin of excitement as he watched the General compose the message. As the General specified "HEILONGJIANG PROVINCE" not Beijing his heart sank. He was sending him to the northern most province, a mountain range bordering Russia. Without any more discussion, the General sent the email.

"There. It's done. Your request has been submitted. You'll have a new commanding officer at that location," explained General Lee. His tone remained calm in a higher pitch as if trying to project optimism.

All the good will that the General had fostered came crashing down. It was clear that even still, after pulling off this huge victory against the Americans, the General had no intention of recognizing and rewarding him. In fact, this next transfer was a step down, like a demotion.

"Congratulations again Comrade on your success and efforts," said the General.

Without waiting, the General ended the call. The dial tone echoed through the telephone. Colonel Fangqi clutched the plastic handset. As each second passed, Fangqi's grip tightened until his knuckles turned white. With a deep sigh, Fangqi set the telephone handset back onto the hook. With slumped shoulders, he stared at the General's mirrored computer screen. Fangqi walked back to the make-shift computer lab. A sense of warmth washed over his body. He sensed that this feeling was like the calm before the storm. When in fact, Fangqi knew it was more like the eye in a hurricane.

The only thought that dominated his mind was, *"There will be hell to pay!"*

11

General Blair stood next to the jeep. He was parked next to the tarmac and waited for the South Korean ROC F-16 to land. One of his officers reported seeing the jet making multiple flybys in an apparent effort to notify the tower of their intent to land. Given their inability to hail the tower, and lack of air traffic for one of the busiest airfields in the region, the pilot's message was clear. The disturbance created by the F-16's F110-GE-129 engine created a rumble that dominated the entire area. The General could feel his shirt and pants vibrating.

After landing, the jet maneuvered toward the waiting General. With an abrupt deceleration, the front nose dipped toward the ground before stopping. As the engine began shutting down, General Blair stepped back covering his ears. He watched the two-seat cockpit open. To his surprise, he saw Director Nena Valdez, from the South Korean Agency waving.

"Nena?" asked General Blair.

"Dicky." Realizing she was addressing the base commander, and under the circumstances, followed with, "I mean General Blair." Nena removed her helmet and made sure she didn't touch anything, especially the red ejection bar.

General Blair stepped next to the ladder that the ground crew wheeled up next to the parked jet. "What brings you to Kadena?" asked Blair with an elevated curious tone. Nena descended the ladder and maintained a stern serious expression.

"General, this is my pilot, Mr. Davies," said Nena while pointing at Mr. Davies. "Unfortunately, this isn't a social visit. We have an unprecedented situation. Is there somewhere we can talk in private?"

Dicky paused processing what she said. He wondered if the unusual power outage was something more serious. He'd been receiving reports confirming every telecommunications device on Okinawa was fried. They were still unable to re-establish connections even with their dedicated geo-synchronized satellites.

"The power outage?" asked Blair.

247

"I wish that were the only thing," replied Nena.

"Hop in my jeep. Let's go to my office," said Blair as he helped Nena into the doorless jeep. "Better buckle up," he added with a smile. As he started the jeep, Nena leaned toward him. To be heard over the outside noise, she raised her voice.

"Dicky, we have credible information indicating that Kadena has been attacked using an EMP designed to disable all electrical devices, specifically your communications."

"For what purpose?" he asked.

"We believe the Chinese, in concert with others, are trying to remote launch one of your ICBMs."

General Blair gave her a concerned sideways glance. He knew that this information was classified TOP SECRET and wondered how and why Nena knew about his ICBMs. He contemplated how to proceed knowing that this subject was on a need to know basis. Sensing Dicky's reluctance to discuss the matter further, she continued.

"Until an hour ago, I didn't know about your secret underground missile silo complex. But the National Agency Director Allwardt filled me in. As we speak, POTUS along with the Joint Chiefs of Staff are being brought up to speed Dicky. It's been a while since we've dropped our Defense Condition. I think it was during the last Gulf War."

"Nena, this type of game is beyond dangerous. It's been our worst nightmare. Having nukes is a double edged sword. Back in the day, attempting such a stunt wasn't even a remote possibility. The limited technology prevented it. It would have been a fool's errand. Until today, I still thought it was technologically impossible."

"Knowing that you have limited communications, we're moving a specialized communications satellite that will remain geo-synchronized over Kadena until we fix this. We've also contacted the Navy. Because the submarines are submerged and encased by thick metal housings, we're hoping their communication systems are intact. You can piggy-back onto their systems to increase communications as well," added Nena.

General Blair nodded as he maneuvered the jeep through the base heading back toward his office. As they passed the tall Douglas fir Christmas tree, a modified motorcycle with a custom painted gas tank, driven by a helmetless soldier dressed in fatigues came roaring in their direction. He was exiting the General's parking lot. Blair scowled in displeasure seeing the soldier driving so recklessly without wearing a helmet. Dicky had to turn the steering wheel and pump the brakes to avoid an accident. Rather than turn away to avoid the oncoming jeep, the soldier appeared to swerve into it.

"Soldier!! What in the world are you doing, son?!" yelled the General.

Maneuvering the motorcycle, he pulled up next to the jeep. Buehler skid the bike to a stop and turned off the engine. "General, sir! Launch Officer Owens sent me to find you, sir. One of the ICBMs is automatically initializing for an unauthorized snap-shot launch, sir!" Buehler explained while trying to catch his breath.

"You're certain?" asked General Blair.

"Sir, yes, sir! I saw the outer doors open and the steam billowing out. Lt. Owens believes that the power outage is a result of an EMP attack. He speculates we're either being overridden by NORAD in Cheyenne Mountain, or some bad guys have hacked inside and are trying to initiate a remote launch."

Their eyes darted around trying to process everything. Buehler was the next one to speak. "Sir, Launch Officer Owens needs to know if NORAD is trying to launch. Apparently, you're the only one authorized to abort a launch, General."

Dicky turned to Nena. "Do you have an SAT phone?" She patted her jacket pocket.

"Right here, Dicky."

"Good! Let's get to my office. I have the direct NORAD numbers. I pray to God they didn't authorize a launch," explained Dicky. Turning back to Buehler, General Blair continued, "Soldier, how much time do we have?"

Buehler checked his wristwatch, "Twelve minutes, sir."

With a puzzled expression, General Blair asked, "Why is your watch still working, soldier?" The EMP didn't take it out?"

"It's old school, sir. An old Timex wind up. My dad gave it to me. Nothing about it is high tech."

"Right. Let's go!" said Blair.

Buehler depressed a button on the handlebars to restart the motorcycle. He burned a donut as he sped the bike in a 180 degree turn and followed the jeep back into the parking lot. The General came to a sliding stop setting the jeep in a crooked angle between the lines. Nena struggled out of the safety-belt and ran following Dicky toward his office. Buehler drove right up onto the lawn and parked his motorcycle next to the front door and fell behind Nena as she entered the door. The force of the door being thrown open startled the men inside.

"Sargent, I need the direct phone number to the CIC NORAD, now. Hurry son. As if all our lives depend on it," ordered General Blair.

The Sargent flipped through his desktop rolodex looking for the number. "But sir, all of our phones and computers are down, sir," replied the Sargent still ruffling through the index cards.

"Sargent, the benefit of being a General is you get to have special friends. And my special friend here is Director Nena Valdez," replied Dicky as he pointed his index finger at Nena. "She comes bearing an important gift son- a SAT phone!"

Nodding his head, he smiled up at the General holding out the index card. "Here it is, sir. It's great to be a General, with all those friends, sir," joked the Sargent.

Grabbing the index card out of the Sargent's hand, General Blair winked at Nena. "Let's go to my office."

Dicky held the door open for Nena and Buehler. He handed Nena the index card. "Make the call Nena. I don't know how to work your SAT phone." Turning his attention back to Buehler, "How much time do we have left?"

"A little over ten minutes, General," replied Buehler.

"Here's the call Dicky," said Nena as she handed him the SAT phone. "It's ringing."

Just as the General raised the phone to his ear, someone answered the line. "NORAD CIC," answered a man in a calm authoritative and controlled voice.

"This is General Richard Blair, Base Commander for Kadena, AFB in Okinawa, Japan. I need immediate authentication on whether NORAD initiated a remote launch. I repeat a remote launch. We believe we've sustained an EMP attack and are in the dark. I'm calling on an Agency SAT phone. One of our ICBMs has initiated a pre-launch countdown. We are inside ten minutes. I repeat we're inside ten minutes to launch!"

"General, I need to get your verbal authentication code, sir."

General Blair closed his eyes and took a deep breath before repeating his ten-digit alpha numeric code from memory. Afterword, he placed the call on speaker.

"Your identity has been confirmed," replied the man in the same even tone and calm manner. After a brief pause, the man continued. "General Blair, that is a negative, sir. No one at NORAD nor any one inside the Strategic Command has authorized or initiated a remote launch. I repeat negative, sir!" For the first time, the man's voice rose in his excitement.

"Do I have NORAD's approval to abort?" asked Dicky.

"Affirmative. Abort! Affirmative, Abort!!" repeated the caller. "Do we know the pre-set target package, General?"

Dicky looked at Buehler knowing he was part of the decommission team. With raised eyebrows, Buehler replied, "Moscow, sir. The missile was initialized for 'Old Bessie', sir. It's our oldest one in our arsenal. Was to be decommissioned next week."

General Blair repeated the target, "The rocket is targeting Moscow, NORAD. It's Moscow."

"We're redirecting our satellites over Kadena. At the conclusion of initialization, I need a verbal confirmation from you General. We're trying to see if we can abort the launch from our end as well."

"NORAD, this missile is our last old-school bird. I'm not sure if that's possible with 'Ole Bessie.'"

"We're running out of time, Dicky," said Nena in a concerned voice.

"I'll get back to you NORAD," said Dicky as he ended the call. He then looked at Buehler.

"We've only got 8 minutes left sir."

General Blair seemed to be talking out loud to himself saying, "There's no time to get all the way back to the silo complex."

Hearing his words, Buehler remembered. "Owens said something about the Christmas tree, sir. The Douglas fir. Somehow you could send him Morse Code," explained Buehler with a confused expression uncertain what it meant.

Dicky turned to the plaque and smiled.

*   *   *   *   *

Fangqi sat in the elevated chair overlooking the now empty makeshift computer lab. He had a dazed expression as if lost in thought. From across the room, the side door opened and one of the senior programmers stepped inside. They were still trying to access the in-flight bombers.

"Sir, we've isolated one of the bombs. It's the only one with an open plate. We're not having any luck though. The firewall system is much different. The only positive thing is the plane is circling in a small area in the Atlantic. We've been able to use one our satellites and maintain a good connection. Unfortunately, it will take much longer to access its launch code. Much longer than we used to obtain the in-ground ICBM, sir."

Fangqi stared at the senior programmer. "Keep trying, Comrade," ordered the Colonel.

"Yes, Colonel," he replied as he stepped back outside and shut the door behind him.

With a deep sigh, Fangqi turned toward the monitor below. He knew that if nothing was entered, the ICBM they accessed would reset forever closing his access to the nuclear weapon. He stared at the icon that read: "READY TO LAUNCH". Fangqi's eyes darted about as he wondered if he had the courage to do the unthinkable.

*   *   *   *   *

It was almost completely dark. Now alone, the parrot was still sitting on the wire. All the other birds had long since left for the night. He'd thought his target would have come outside. Earlier, a stream of soldiers filed out the building. But none resembled the picture. Besides, the man's red car was still parked outside. Unfazed, the parrot busied himself preening his feathers and continued his vigil.

*   *   *   *   *

Launch Officer Owens was bent down with his upper torso hidden from view. Only his legs were visible. His head felt puffy. As if full of blood that accumulated from hanging in this awkward upside-down bent position. The two soldiers watched Owens reposition himself until he stood from a bent-over position shaking his head to clear his vision. He looked exhausted using his arm to wipe the sweat from his forehead.

"If we don't get the General's authorization to abort, I will have to do it manually," explained Owens as he struggled to his feet.

"Can you do it, sir?" asked one of the soldiers.

"I think so," explained Owens. "This underground access point was designed just for such occasions. It will lock the stabilizing arms against the missile casing. By delaying the missile, we could force the rocket to expand more fuel. Even if we only delay the launch a few seconds, that wasted fuel could prevent it from reaching its necessary altitude. If it holds and burns enough fuel, we could interfere with the timing. Theoretically, the trajectory and velocity could prevent the missile from reaching its necessary height. These bombs are equipped with a fail-safe feature for ICBMs. If the bomb, for whatever reason, doesn't meet the trajectory requirements to hit its specific target, it will not arm. In which case, it would act more like a falling object or gravity bomb. However, in this case upon impact, there would be no explosion, just the physics of the missile impacting the ground. Theoretically," explained Owens.

"So, if we can prevent the rocket from reaching its required altitude, the missile won't arm?" asked the other soldier.

"Correct. It's a crap shoot, but our only chance. These rockets possess so much thrust, I doubt these housing brackets are strong enough. They weren't replaced during the refitting. I'd prefer the General's authorization code to abort the launch. Entering his code would guarantee it!" added Owens.

After a few more adjustments, he was done. "We're set here," announced Owens. He clutched the oversized flashlight with both hands. Staring at the flashlight, he hoped it would work. It was the only way to communicate and confirm the General's authorization code. "One of you guys, follow me. And bring a pad of paper and pen," said Owens as he rushed out the door.

*   *   *   *   *

Nena stood at the base of the huge Douglas fir tree staring up at Dicky. With his "Hotshot hooks" strapped to his boots, he was scaling the tree and working around the branches. Clutching the SAT phone, Nena worked with her team in South Korea. They needed to be prepared for the worst.

"Moon Dog, just in case, I want the SR-72's airborne ready to go. Do we need to modify the software before they go up?"

"No, ma'am. It is pre-programmed with all versions of our ICBM rockets. These babies were designed just for this purpose," replied Lt. Elliott.

"How many hours do you and Kyle have using the simulator? Enough?"

"We've been working with these SR-72 UAVs for the last 90 days. We've had countless different intercept scenarios around the globe as well as night-time real time flights. We're ready. If it comes to that."

"I want Gibby and Carla Jo working with you guys," said Nena.

"I agree. I'll put Carla Jo with Kyle and I'll take Gibby," confirmed Moon Dog.

"I want you on the navigation piece. Kyle can focus on disarming the missile. Redirecting the missile will take more time. It's more complicated. You've got more live experience doing this sort of thing," said Nena referring to the mission when he flew the modified refueling tanker UAV over the DMZ.

"Yes, ma'am. I was thinking the same thing. Is this for real? One of our own rockets is about to launch against Russia?"

"That's what it looks like. Unless we can stop it before it leaves Kadena."

"Why don't we just blow up the silo?" asked Moon Dog.

"We thought about that. But if something goes wrong and we only end up damaging it, we could lose the SR-72 option. Besides, the last thing we want is another nuclear accident in Japan. That is not an option," explained Nena.

"We're getting close, boss. Too close."

"No choice. The EMP fried all normal lines of communication. For now, this SAT phone I'm speaking to you on is the only working phone on the island. We also have the Comm's from our F-16 jet, as well as Navy ships that are being recalled as we speak to help re-establish communications. Things are happening so fast. We're making decisions on the fly."

"Boss, God forbid. What if the General can't stop the launch? How much time until it could take off?" Moon Dog asked.

"Once it launches, we're estimating the ICBM will be airborne between 30 to 45 minutes depending on the efficiency of the rocket engines and weather conditions. Once it goes, we'll be able to get live data and narrow that estimate to within a minute. The other variable is this missile was recently re-fitted in preparation for decommission. No one is quite certain how "Old Bessie" will perform."

"Old Bessie?"

"That's what they call it."

"Great," said Moon Dog in a sarcastic concerned manner.

"Once you and Kyle get the SR-72's airborne, I want you to head straight to Moscow. Our friend Van Aelst is greasing the Russians as we speak. He's asking them to wait until the last minute before trying anything. If they interfere and only damage the missile, it may prevent us from disabling or disarming it. It takes a lot of trust, but it gives us the best chance of success."

"Understood, boss. Once we're up, I'll let you know. I'm sure you'll be very busy. I'll text your SAT phone. Let's hope it doesn't come to that," added Moon Dog.

"Likewise, Lt. Elliott. Out." With that, Nena ended the call and continued watching Dicky climbing the tree. It reminded her of Spider Man with boots and an oversized flashlight tied to a tool belt. Nena hoped Dicky's Morse code message was received in time. For a split second, she chastised herself for not flying in on the Harrier. It had vertical take-off and landing capabilities and could have flown the General over to the missile silo area. The F-16 needed a runway and all the helicopters were on the other side of the base. With no communications, they couldn't get ahold of them in time.

Nena stared up at Dicky scaling the Douglas fir hoping everything worked. It had to. The alternative was unthinkable.

*   *   *   *   *

While standing on the step ladder leading to the SR-72 simulator cockpit, Gibby glanced over at the oversized wall monitor. Looking down inside at the instruments reminded him of his days in flight school. With a deep sigh, he wondered what his life would have been like if he hadn't been forced out due to an unexpected medical condition that surfaced just before graduation.

"Hey, Gibby!" yelled Carla Jo as she stood next to the desk and computer set between the two SR-72 simulator cockpits. Hearing her voice, Gibby snapped back into reality.

"This is way cool. I'm patching in," said Carla Jo as she tapped her headset with her index finger. "Come on, stop day dreaming, buddy. Let's get dialed in with a Comm's check before things start getting crazy."

"Sorry about that. I got lost in my thoughts. You know me and jets," replied Gibby as he descended the ladder.

The two SR-72 simulators were placed side by side. There was just enough space between them for the two workstations. As Gibby approached his work area, Carla Jo handed him his headset.

"I'll be hooked up with Moon Dog," said Gibby as he sat and acquainted himself with the keyboard and adjusted his chair and then monitor.

"Roger that," said Carla Jo. She'd arrived earlier and was all dialed in. "I'm with Kyle," she added with a smile.

"So, our purpose in this mission is to ride shot-gun until it's time to start the program while they maneuver the jets alongside the ICBM?" asked Gibby in a deflated tone.

"Yup," replied Carla Jo in a positive snappy reply.

With a sideway glance, Gibby mumbled under his breath. "Our job isn't too exciting. Seems like any monkey could do our task."

"What if something goes wrong?" replied Carla Jo.

"Like what?"

"Well, what if the computer goes down? Or what if we lose visuals from the UAV cameras? Maybe the satellite doesn't synch up? I mean potentially, we could be asked to restart the programs and perform the uploads blind," expounded Carla Jo while shrugging her shoulders.

Gibby turned away and said, "Okay, now you're stressing me out."

Carla Jo smiled and turned toward the door. Kyle and Lt. Elliott walked inside the simulator dome area. They were decked out in full flight gear, even down to their boots and pressurized suits. With a quick nod, they passed Gibby and Carla Jo and proceeded into their assigned simulator cockpits. Not having to worry about an active ejection bar, they slung themselves over the edge and their bodies disappeared inside cockpits.

"Gibby and CJ, this is Lt. Elliott. For this mission, my call sign is Moon Doggie," said with a smile.

"Copy that Moon Doggie. I hear you loud and clear. This is Gibby. Out."

"This is CJ. Copy that Moon Doggie. Loud and clear," she replied in a calm steady voice.

Several simulator technicians peered out a set of windows up from the bird's nest control room looking down. Each technician gave a thumbs up.

"Breaker, breaker. This is the side kick Kyle. My call sign will be GI Joe," said Kyle with a smirk.

"Copy that GI Joe. I hear you loud and clear. CJ out."

"Copy that. Gibby out."

"Okay, people. Let's keep cool, calm and collected. Before we take off, we're gonna run a simulation with CJ and Gibby manning the computer consoles. We've been running these situational simulations hundreds of times. We want you to get the feel, and timing of everything," explained Moon Dog.

"Roger that," replied Gibby.

"Copy that," said Carla Jo as she adjusted her headset.

"We're gonna start the simulation mid-flight after we've already matched the missile's speed running side-by-side. You guys only have 45 seconds to finish your uploads," explained Kyle.

"Gibby and I will focus on initiating the missile redirection, while GI Joe and CJ will focus on deactivating the nuclear detonation," explained Moon Dog as he glanced up at the simulator techs and gave them a thumbs up signal. Within seconds, the oversized wall monitors blinked on but was frozen in a still motion like a picture. Moon Dog and Kyle were used to the images. Gibby and

Carla Jo were getting a baptism by fire. The huge wall to ceiling images gave a realistic affect tricking their mind to believe they were truly flying. While controlling the UAV SR-72, Moon Doggie outlined the objective to Gibby and CJ.

"As we navigate up next to the missile, look to the upper right corner of the monitor. Those numbers are stabilization percentages. It's currently showing 82 percent."

"Roger that," replied Gibby followed by CJ's "Copy that, 82 percent."

"Once we snuggle up tight, I'll be on the left side and GI Joe will be on the right. We'll lock on the speed and trajectory. The missile is designed to move in a straight line upon re-entry. So, there isn't any fear of it changing course. The goal is 100 percent stabilization, but our training has proved that 95 percent is good enough. Anything less, and the data won't properly transmit from the UAV to the missile. We're guessing that the software coding gets lost in the translation. It won't work, we've tried," explained Moon Dog.

Moon Dog craned his neck and partially raised out of his seat to check on Kyle. "You ready GI Joe?"

"Copy that Moon Doggie!" replied Kyle. Kyle glanced up and watched Moon Dog slump back into his seat and disappear inside the jet black UAV simulator cockpit.

"On my mark, start the simulation. Three, two, one, mark," ordered Moon Dog.

"Roger that Moon Doggie," replied Kyle as the image on the huge floor to ceiling monitor began moving. It gave everyone watching a sense of flying at supersonic speed.

"Gibby and CJ, when we get within 50 feet, watch the stabilization percentage. If you get a reading of 95 percent or better, start you upload."

"How long will it take to upload?" asked CJ.

"Yours is quick. Five seconds," answered GI Joe.

"And ours?" asked Gibby.

"Up to 30 seconds," replied Moon Doggie.

"What's the difference?" asked CJ.

"Yours is deactivating the nuke. Ours transfers the missile's guidance to my SR-72 UAV and takes a lot more data and time," explained Moon Doggie.

"I'm inside 50 feet," announced GI Joe. "I'm activating the synchronization program."

"Copy that," replied CJ. "The stabilization percent is only 40 percent."

"Steady," added Moon Doggie. "I'm holding back until you're done."

"Copy that," said GI Joe in a calm controlled voice still chomping down pulverizing his gum."

"I'm locked!" announced GI Joe.

"Confirmed," said CJ as she watched the stabilization percentage jump up to 88 percent. "Waiting to initiate upload," continued CJ as she called out the percentage points. "Now it's 91 percent."

Gibby stared at the wall monitor. Hearing the verbal exchanges and watching the simulation challenged his mind to remember that this wasn't real. But the complex human mind was a system designed to solve problems and adapt. The human brain is amazing. It allows the body to concentrate with a laser focus without any conscious effort to keep its other involuntary systems working; digestive, circulative and central nervous systems running on autopilot. Given our complex nature, it's as if the brain needs to be challenged. So much so that if it isn't, humans create puzzles and conflicts to force their brains to solve problems as a form of cerebral entertainment; chess, checkers, board games, and cards. Even in isolation, when there are no others to compete with, humans will challenge their own mental sharpness through crossword, Sudoku and other self-challenging puzzles.

"Stabilization percentage is increasing," continued CJ. "...93...94..."

"Get ready CJ," said Moon Doggie.

"95! Initiating upload," said CJ as she depressed the enter key. An icon appeared on her monitor screen and began confirming the percentage upload. As the program reached 43 percent, the ICON vanished and replaced with a prompt message "UPLOAD UNSUCCESSFUL."

CJ glanced at the stabilization percentage. "It stopped uploading," announced CJ.

"We hit some turbulence reducing the stabilization between the missile and the UAV," explained GI Joe. Kyle adjusted his controls and then switched to automated stabilization program again. "CJ, get ready to try again."

The stabilization numbers reappeared in the upper right corner. "We're back online...now 88," said CJ.

With a deep sigh, Gibby looked up absorbing the entire image blasting on the oversized monitor. He glanced from the technicians staring down from their glass window, then back to the two black SR-72 cockpit simulators. Hearing CJ continuing her count down, Gibby returned his attention to the oversized wall monitor.

"Almost there...91...93....94..."

"This time let it get to 96 before you start the upload," said Moon Doggie.

"Copy that," replied CJ. After a deep exhale, she continued calling out the stabilization percentages, "...95...96! Initiating upload."

Everyone watched as the upload icon reappeared. This time, without stopping, the upload continued uninterrupted with a sequential escalation percentage before vanishing and displaying "UPLOAD COMPLETE." It took less than five seconds.

"Upload complete," announced CJ in a raised excited voice.

"Good job, CJ. Gibby, we're next," said Moon Doggie.

"Veering right and will follow from a distance," said GI Joe. With a slight movement of his wrist, Kyle maneuvered the SR-72 away from the missile. Without any hesitation, Lt. Elliott maneuvered his SR-72 closer. Having to make two attempts on the prior upload, ate into the available time for his part of the mission.

Moon Dog maneuvered his SR-72 UAV even closer. Knowing this was only a simulation, he wasn't worried about crashing. Without any reluctance, he slid the jet within 40 feet before activating the automatic stabilization system.

"Initiating stabilization. Get ready Gibby."

"Copy that," replied Gibby somewhat shocked at how quick his turn came up. Without delay, the stabilization percentage started at 54 percent. Glancing at the view being projected on the oversized wall monitor, he noticed the area under the SR-72 UAV showed buildings and roads as opposed to continuous mountain landscapes.

"The area below? We must be approaching the city boundary," guessed Gibby.

Moon Doggie glanced at his instruments. "We are just inside 200 miles from Moscow. I show 88 stabilization percentage," responded Moon Doggie. "Get ready, Gibby. Initiate the upload at 96."

"...93...94...95...initiate upload!"

"Initializing now," replied Gibby.

The same icon appeared. This time, the upload percentage ticked by much slower. Everyone watched the upload percentage count change on the oversized wall monitor. Under the SR-72 and missile, more buildings and roads began appearing as opposed to natural landscape.

"Gibby, once the upload is complete, the missile will be under your control. Use the stick and I'll bark out my movements. We won't have eyes from the missile. We'll switch over to the camera on my SR-72 UAV as well as from the satellite above. You'll have to fly using these visual cues and your instruments," explained Moon Doggie.

"It sure would have been nice to have been part of the prior simulation runs," replied Gibby.

"We would have. It was part of the plan when we got to this phase in L.I.S.A. It happened so fast. It caught us by surprise. We thought it would be years before something like this was even possible," said Moon Doggie.

"Understood," said Gibby as the UPLOAD continued.

"You're almost there," said CJ. Her part of the mission took under five seconds to upload. Gibby's would be around 30 seconds. Watching the upload percentages, seemed to take forever. The landscape below the SR-72 continued to look more metropolitan than semi-rural. As everyone continued to wait, on the horizon, two jets of unknown origin appeared.

"I have a visual on two bogies to our eleven o'clock," said Moon Doggie. He'd been training for months and expected this type of scenario variation. However, Gibby was so focused on the software uploading knowing he would need to maneuver the missile later. He wasn't expecting this. Knowing the various scenarios, Kyle and Moon Dog purposely withheld this information. They wanted it to feel more real.

Gibby's prior flight school training, although taking place decades earlier, his hundreds of hours in his A4 phantom, including night air-craft carrier landings, enabled him to take the extra distraction in stride. Unfazed, Gibby continued waiting for the UPLOAD to complete. The simulator technicians were prepared for this variable. Watching Gibby's composure, raised his stock. Without missing a beat, Gibby started calling out the upload percentages.

"We're at 94,..97,...UPLOAD COMPLETE," said Gibby in a steady controlled voice. Moving the controller stick, he watched the missile begin to move off its previous straight approach. "I'm in control of the missile," announced Gibby. "Switching to the satellite and SR-72 split screen view."

Just as Gibby began to maneuver the missile away from Moscow, the screen went dark.

"What happened?" asked Gibby still holding the stick and staring at the blank oversized wall monitor. He glanced over at Carla Jo, and they exchanged puzzled looks. After a brief pause, Kyle and Moon Dog raised up out of their SR-72 simulator cockpits and laughed.

"The missile was shot down by the bogies," explained Moon Doggie while Kyle was rocking back and forth in uncontrollable laughter.

"Not funny," said Gibby as he glanced away.

"Kind of," added Carla Jo as she suppressed a snicker. With pursed lips, Gibby avoided eye contact and replied, "Well, okay...kind of."

"Congratulations you two," replied Moon Doggie, "the simulator mission is complete. Let's hope it doesn't come to this."

One of the simulator technicians slid open the observation window. "It's time people. Director Valdez just called. She wants the real SR-72 UAVs airborne. Training time is over," announced X.O. Newland.

"Where is she?" asked Carla Jo.

"What's happening?" asked Kyle.

The simulator techs exchanged concerned looks. "She's at Kadena AFB. The ICBM is in pre-launch. General Blair is trying to abort the launch," explained the X.O.

The oversized wall monitor came back on. This time, the view came from cameras attached to the SR-72 UAVs facing toward a large set of hanger doors. The doors were sliding open. As it retracted, the view opened onto the setting sun and looked like a sliver of orange on the horizon. Soon, it would be dark.

"I'm switching to night vision camera view," announced one of the simulator techs.

"We have rotating refueling tankers throughout the region, enough to keep both birds airborne for 48 hours straight, explained the other simulator tech.

As Moon Dog and Kyle maneuvered the UAVs out of the hanger, Gibby glanced over to Carla Jo. "So much for dinner," said Gibby.

"It's gonna be a long night," Carla Jo replied.

Launch Officer Owens held a pair of night-vision binoculars, standard issue for anyone in his position. He couldn't see General Blair. Before sun set, he saw a woman and Technician Buehler standing at the bottom of the huge Douglas fir staring up. Since the sun set, Owens was still trying to locate the General in the tree. Owens was about to panic, when he saw a strong light appear in the top portion of the tree.

"Okay, I see him now," announced Owens as the General began transmitting Morse code. "Write this down," ordered Owens.

The soldier held the paper pad and readied his pen and waited. Without delay, General Blair started tapping out Morse code using a flashlight. Owens began translating.

"A, B, O, R, T," said Launch Officer Owens as he translated the coded light message.

"Again, he's saying, A, B, O, R, T," repeated Owens. But he needed the General's code. Without delay, Owens replied.

General Blair saw the blinking light Morse code reply and was grateful to know that Owens was receiving the message. He thought, "This will work!" Owens repeated the message allowing the General time to decode it again. Dicky realized Owens needed his authentication code. He froze. "My code?" For a split second, he had a momentary loss of memory.

During that moment of lost concentration, his right boot hook slid away from the bark siding and detached. He began to fall away from the tree. Dicky grabbed out reaching onto one of the branches and lost grip of the flashlight. The oversized flashlight fell. A light beam bounced about as it tumbled down the tree. Owens was watching through his binoculars. His heart stopped as he saw the light descending toward the ground. "No!" yelled Owens.

"What happened?" asked the soldier.

"The General! He dropped the light." After a deep breath, Owens raised the night-vision binoculars and tried to reacquire the General.

"I can see him climbing down," reported Owens. He noticed a light glow coming from a group of branches just beneath the General. It must have landed there. Owens focused on that illuminated section. Fate kept the oversized flashlight balanced on the evergreen foliage. Otherwise, it would have fallen down to the ground.

*   *   *   *   *

Nena and Technician Buehler waited at the base of the tree. Several other soldiers noticed them looking up. Out of curiosity, a small crowd formed below.

"I think he dropped the flashlight," said Nena without looking away. With her head still aimed up toward the top of the tree, she heard an unfamiliar voice standing next to her. "Is he okay?"

Nena glanced down and discovered at least a half dozen bystanders all soldiers, gathered around staring up into the tree. "Buehler," said Nena.

Buehler looked down and noticed the crowd. Turning to Nena with raised eyebrows as if asking "should I clear the crowd?" She nodded.

"Soldiers, we need everyone to clear the area. Please move on." Noticing that the soldier was taking orders from a woman, everyone disbursed. The rumor mill was running rampant. The power outage and the arrival of a VIP welcomed on the tarmac by the General hadn't gone unnoticed. For an apparent civilian to be ordering around a Lieutenant, they knew something was up. Without delay, they vanished into the night.

Nena and Buehler returned their attention to the top of the Douglas fir. Buehler checked his wristwatch. With a deep sigh, he glanced back toward the missile silo. There were only four minutes left.

12

Van Aelst was placed in one of the secure Agency conference rooms. Director Valdez's four person security detail found themselves without having anyone to protect. Knowing Director Valdez wanted to keep Van Aelst isolated, they focused on protecting him. They kept him under constant surveillance and rotated positions, everyone swapping detail inside the conference room every two hours.

Normally, Van Aelst would have felt trapped. But with so much happening, his mind was spinning through all the possibilities. From what he could gather, it seemed clear that the Chinese had kicked a hornet's nest. Van Aelst hoped the Chinese knew what they were doing. The Americans were historically inflexible and paranoid when it came to their nuclear arsenal. The tap against the conference door startled both Van Aelst and the bodyguard inside.

"Excuse me," explained a female secretary as she opened the door and held out a SAT phone. "Director Valdez is on the line for you Herr Van Aelst."

His bright blue eyes fixated on the phone. He grabbed it out of her hand and jammed it against his head and started talking.

"Nena, were you able to meet with the General? Is everything okay?" asked Van Aelst in a set of rapid fire questions.

"Yes. But we have a situation." From the tone of her voice, he could tell it was something serious.

"What is it, Nena?"

"It looks like someone, most likely the Chinese hacked into one of the missiles." She paused, knowing what Van Aelst would do if he had all the information. But for some reason, with all his global connections, it seemed like the right move. Maybe he could pull some strings. Just in case the missile launched, the U.S. needed Russia to know that it wasn't them. "...and they started the initialization sequence. It's preparing to launch."

"Can't you stop it?"

"We can, but an EMP was detonated which disabled every form of communication, their phones, computers and access to satellites. Even those not damaged by the burst, because the networks were fried, they offer no help. My SAT phone is one of the only connections on the island."

"How much time is left?"

"Only a few more minutes. But just because the pre-launch phase is initiated doesn't necessarily mean they will go through with the launch."

"Has the General aborted the launch? Has he provided his code?"

"*How does he know so much about their process?*" wondered Nena. "He is trying. Without communication lines, he is trying to manually send the information to the silo complex. They need his codes to terminate the launch. The Chinese, or whoever hacked inside, may still choose to launch. We just don't know."

"Manually?"

"Morse Code," Nena replied.

"Oh my."

After a brief pause, Nena continued. "Cornelius, we have to plan on the worst case scenario. There's no time. During my flight over here, the National Agency Director

Allwardt was authorized by the President to bring you in. We desperately need your help."

"Yes, of course. What do you need?"

"Contact Russia. The secretary that handed you the SAT phone has the direct numbers. But you know best. You have to decide how best to convince the Russians that we're not planning any attack. You must give them fair warning before it launches. I pray to God it doesn't come to that. If it does...Cornelius, the Russians have to know it wasn't us."

"I will. I still have contacts there. What city is being targeting?"

"Moscow. But Cornelius, we have special supersonic high speed jets, SR-72's that will take them down. Russia cannot try to destroy the missile in flight. We've been planning for this possibility. Our concern is that no conventional missile defense will be able to completely destroy it. If it's only damaged and potentially even shot down, our jets won't be able to disarm the missile and the ICBM will detonate anyway."

"Understood."

"Something else," Nena paused, "...we have two separate training missions; a group of B-52's in the Atlantic and B-2 Stealth's in the Pacific. Both have been compromised. The Chinese somehow coerced some bomb ordinance technicians forcing them to load special ordinance."

"Both groups are carrying nuclear bombs?" asked Van Aelst in a shocked manner.

"They are. They pose no threat of danger. We have them hovering in circles with refueling tankers keeping them there. If the Chinese remote detonate either group, they will explode over the ocean."

"This complicates things, Nena."

"I know." After a brief pause, she continued. "Do your best. That's all we can ask for. Make your calls as soon as I hang up. POTUS will call the Kremlin only after we've confirmed that the missile has launched."

"I will," answered Van Aelst.

"Good luck," said Nena and ended the call.

Cornelius stared at the boxy oversized SAT phone. Wasting no time, he started dialing. He knew the numbers by heart and knew how to work the SAT phone. It was the primary mode of his communication from his subterranean spot under his abandoned Eastern Berlin hideout.

*   *   *   *   *

Gibby and Carla Jo exchanged knowing glances. Until that moment, they had only heard rumors. Seeing firsthand the speed and versatility of the SR-72 Hypersonic UAVs was mind boggling. It had a top speed of 13,000 mph. They could literally fly around the world, traveling over 25,000 nautical miles, in less than two hours.

Waiting for orders, the UAV SR-72 drones flew in the stratosphere circling just outside of Russia. If the missile launched, it would take seconds for the Agency to reverse calculate the trajectory and provide accurate GPS coordinates and time of impact numbers. Having that information, the UAVs could swoop down as the missile re-entered and decelerated preparing to arm its nuclear weapon.

"Anything?" asked Gibby as he looked up at the simulator techs with X.O. Newland above. He could see them talking through the window. Newland heard Gibby through the shared communications. "Nothing yet, Gibby," replied the X.O.

There were four images being projected on the oversized floor to ceiling wall monitor; one from each UAV and another view from two satellites above tracking the UAVs independently. The images appeared dull with a mint green glow using night vision technology. Everyone continued watching the live images on the oversized wall monitor and waited.

*　　*　　*　　*　　*

Dicky struggled through the Douglas fir's thick evergreen branches and continued reaching toward the illuminated area just below. His eyes bulged with concern as he leaned down for the flashlight. He could only hope it didn't fall away before he grabbed it. With a determined focus, he concentrated trying not to disturb the supporting branches. As his arm stretched out, he felt the cool metallic casing. The sensation sent a surge of adrenalin as his fingers encircled the flashlight. Securing it with a tight grip, he finally relaxed.

Wasting no time, Dicky dug his hooks into the tree bark. Certain they had a solid hold to the tree, Dicky started transmitting his code. He repeated the numbers and hoped no one would later question him for using his birthday in reverse order.

On the ground, waiting near the missile silo complex, Launch Officer Owens had a huge grin as he saw the General recover the flashlight and start to transmit his authorization code. Owens called out each digit and the soldier wrote them down. Wanting to make certain he transcribed the numbers correctly Owens repeated the numbers back to the General. Within seconds, Owens received a reply "YES."

"Okay!" yelled Owens. "We have it! Let's go!" he screamed as he grabbed the notes from the soldier and raced back inside the silo complex sprinting full-speed. Without stopping, still gripping the paper pad, Owens ran down the stairwell and raced down toward the launch control center below. The other soldiers followed. The pounding of their boots echoed throughout the complex and sounded like drums beating. When they reached the bottom, they gasped for air and pushed on.

Owens ran straight to the console and took a deep breath to calm his nerves before entering the General's code. This was the only way the launch could be aborted. Without realizing, Owens began calling out the numbers to himself as he entered each number.

"9, 5, 9, 1, 0..."

The other soldier was catching his breath and watched. Owens continued entering the numbers. Taking one of his hands off his hip, the soldier glanced at his wristwatch. There were only a few seconds left. He glanced back up at Owens who was still punching in the code.

"...2, 1, 1!" and pressed enter.

Launch Officer Owens, unaware that he was holding his breath as he glanced about wondering if it worked. The missile silo remained quiet. The other soldier and Lt. Owens exchanged questioning looks.

*　　*　　*　　*　　*

Technician Buehler waited as the General dropped down from the tree. Helping him balance, Nena waited until Dicky was level back on the ground with his wits about him.

"Did you do it?" she asked. "Did they get your number?"

Nodding, Dicky inhaled catching his breath. "Yes. He even confirmed it back."

Their eyes darted about trying to maintain eye contact through the dark. The twinkling reflection off the ornaments decorating the tree were the only source of light. With nothing left to do, they turned and faced the single building that was somewhere on the horizon. It was now too dark to make it out.

*   *   *   *   *

Colonel Fangqi sat on the elevated platform lost in thought. Hearing the door open again caught his attention.

"Colonel, we're still trying to access the inflight bomb. Their firewall is too difficult to overcome," apologized the senior computer technician.

The Colonel looked up. With a deep sigh, he replied, "Contact me on the phone if you get it. I'm going to head home for a quick dinner."

"Yes, sir," replied the senior computer technician taking his time to close the door without a sound.

Colonel Fangqi felt exhausted. The thrill of the chase. The high sense of excitement at achieving the impossible. Then, to have it all come crashing down when General Lee lied, pretending to keep his promise. When in reality, Fangqi was being sent to the northern most outskirts bordering Russia rather than back to Beijing. This new assignment was even worse than his current one. The most disrespectful thing was how General Lee lied. If Fangqi hadn't had access to the General's computer, he wouldn't have known until his flight landed somewhere else.

Fangqi stretched his arms and yawned. An electronic tone emitted from the computer. He glanced down and the mirror program that accessed the General's email confirmed that the General just received a new email. Without much thought, Fangqi opened the message and began reading. To his shock, reading the words caused him to hyperventilate. His eyes dilated and a furious rage began bubbling up throughout his being, like a volcano ready to explode. The treachery and distain the General showed him was one thing. But this news was something else altogether different. More sinister and evil than he could have imagined.

The memo was from the Politburo's senior cabinet member congratulating General Lee for his dedication and success at infiltrating the Imperialist American's nuclear arsenal. For this achievement, he was being promoted to a three-star General and transferred to Beijing. It wasn't possible. The General was receiving accolades for his efforts, being promoted to the location he'd promised to Fangqi. There wasn't even a mention about him and his efforts toward this great Chinese victory. The General was receiving all the glory while Fangqi was being shuttled off hidden away while the General took all the credit.

As the hot tears of betrayal cascaded down his cheeks, Colonel Fangqi stood shamed, humiliated and disrespected. With tight pursed lips a scowl of anguish appeared on his face. Without thinking, he grabbed the computer mouse. In a fit of rage, he maneuvered the cursor over the icon and hit enter. Seeing the LAUNCH icon disappear, he watched the screen return to the prior launch code. The number sequence that took so much effort to obtain. When the code started blinking faster and faster, it registered what he'd just done.

The Colonel's pulse seemed to stop choking as he lost his breath. A sense of panic washed over his entire body. His temperature plummeted as his conscious mind went into overdrive trying to resolve what, in his possessed fury, just did it. He didn't know what to do. The only thing that came to mind was to run. Fangqi glanced about. Seeing no one else present, he dashed for the front door while releasing an uncontrolled scream that reverberated up and down the otherwise empty make-shift computer lab. Still yelling, the sound continued echoing as he pushed through the doors and ran through the empty university halls.

"Nnnnoooooooo!!!!"

The sudden sounds startled the parrot out of his nap. He snapped to and looked about from his perch on the overhead power line. When the yelling stopped, he heard the pounding of boots reporting off the concrete walkway as Fangqi ran toward his small red car, the only car still parked on the street. As the vehicle's headlights illuminated the empty street, the parrot fluttered his wings rising up and flew off following the car. As the parrot caught a favorable tail wind, he squawked out in a sing-song voice, "Bhaaaa…. Fangqi…."

The night breeze helped. African parrots are naturally good flyers. But the extra breeze made it easy for him to keep up as Fangqi jerked the small car along a bumping country road pushing the vehicle as fast as it would go.

*   *   *   *   *

Launch Officer Owens and the other soldier exchanged hopeful expressions. Both their arms were stretched out as if to keep their balance on a surfboard. The desk duty soldier stepped out from the counter and stood on the top step and looked down from above.

"Did you guys do it? Did you stop the launch?"

"I'm not certain," replied Owens as the soldiers' bodies remained rigid and their eyes darting about to sense anything. Then, it happened. The Steam and gases that were leaking out stopped. For a millisecond, the sudden change and absence of hissing steam escaping above ground through the open hatch, enhanced their auditory perception. From chaos and mayhem, to silence.

Launch Office Owens, because of his training knew the significance of what was happening. All his senses seemed to fracture going haywire anticipating what was about to happen. He'd wanted to hear the outer-door slamming shut. But what he heard was something else. His worst nightmare.

*   *   *   *   *

General Blair tilted his head. His eyes seemed to wander trying to heighten his sixth sense and decipher everything that was happening. Without warning, the constant venting of steam and gas and its high pitched hissing sound stopped. Buehler, Nena and Dicky exchanged hopeful expressions. Just as smiles began forming on their faces, preparing to celebrate a great victory, against all odds, their hopes were dashed. The beginnings of what was supposed to evolve into elation, evaporated into despair.

It sounded like hundreds of jet-fighters passing overhead at full throttle. The ground shook followed by an overwhelming roar. The silo complex was designed to distribute the jet wash and accelerant discharge away from the launch site and protect its inhabitants. None of the men inside were injured. Helpless, they ran outside and watched the rocket, "Old Bessie" scream off into the night sky. Owens' attempt to slow the missile by manually locking down the rocket to the stabilizing arms had no effect. They were pulverized on take-off.

Standing under the Douglas fir, Nena, Buehler and the General could only watch with their hands covering their ears as the missile crept upward into the sky almost pausing for a microsecond before catapulting upward emitting exhaust plumes creating a smoke trail into the night sky. The area around the missile silo complex looked like a bright spotlight shining down like an artificial sun. As the rocket climbed, the light it projected on the ground began to disappear.

Every resident on the island saw and heard the missile launch. Those outside stopped and looked up while those inside came running outside to see what was happening. Regardless, they all ended up standing about with their heads pointed upward and watched the missile as it jetted off into the night. The rocket punched through the thicker ground air and ascended toward the different layers that surrounded the earth screaming toward its final destination- outer space.

The senior North Korean agent titled up his cell phone and recorded everything. As he stared at the image on his cell phone, he watched the missile rise up and could hear the roar subsiding. Once the rocket was out of sight, he turned his attention back to disassembling the EMP device. He wanted all the evidence destroyed before they left.

On the other side of the island, standing outside the submarine USS Michelle J Howard SSN-805, Jeanne's head jerked up to the sky and watched a rocket take off from the island and disappear into the night sky. The roar of its engines vibrated the rocks along the sea cliff, along the boulders stacked on the break. The abrupt silence left her wondering if it was all real. The only evidence of its existence was the smoke trail it left in the night sky. The temporary glow dissipated until the small orange dot disappeared.

"Unbelievable," said Buehler.

General Blair was shocked into silence and stood there shaking his head in disbelief. In a soft whisper, he added "I thought we stopped it."

Nena was already dialing her SAT phone.

"X.O. Newland," said Jim as he answered the call.

"It's happened. We couldn't stop it. The ICBM just launched. God help us. Run the trajectory coordinates so we can pinpoint the re-entry and direct the SR-72 UAV there. They have about thirty minutes before the missile re-enters the atmosphere to decelerate and arm. It's all up to you guys now, Jim."

"Yes, ma'am. You can count on us. We'll get it stopped before it gets to Moscow. I'll get back to you in a few minutes, Nena."

"Thanks, Jim."

X.O. Newland ended the call and switched the simulator dome's PA on and linked it to the shared communications line making sure everyone heard. "I just got off the phone with Director Valdez. It's for real. This is no longer an exercise in theoretical possibilities. Joe Erbes, you there?"

"Yes, Jim. I'm listening," replied Erbes.

"We need the exact GPS locations where that flight path takes the inbound ICBM re-entry. We need the SR-72 UAVs waiting when it arrives," ordered Newland.

"We're way ahead of you. We've been watching Kadena on our satellite over here in L.I.S.A. and verified the launch. I'll send you the coordinates now," replied Erbes.

"How fast will it be going when it reduces its speed and prepares to arm the bomb?" asked Newland.

"Around 1,980 mph. Once armed, it is designed to remain perfectly straight at a constant rate. You'll have between 60 to 90 seconds to disable the missile. It depends on the weather and cloud presence. The moisture in the air will reduce the speed. If the pathway contains a lot of moisture in the air, it will incrementally and cumulatively delay its arrival a few seconds for each segment of its journey through the multiple layers that surround the globe."

"Roger that," said Newland. "So, we have between a minute to a minute and a half to get our jobs done, people."

"We just received the coordinates," said Carla Jo.

"GPS location entered. We're heading there straight away maximum speed," said Moon Doggie.

"Roger that," said Gibby.

"Copy that," added GI Joe.

The images displayed on the oversized wall monitor confirmed the directional changes as the SR-72 UAVs sped off to intercept the ICBM.

"I estimate arrival time in 10 minutes, 33 seconds," announced Gibby as he concluded his mathematical calculations.

"Copy that, ETA ten minutes, and 25 seconds...mark," said X.O. Newland accounting for the time from when Gibby made his announcement.

With a deep exhale, X.O. Newland stared down into the simulator dome and watched everyone below busy focused on their jobs. Kyle seemed to be chomping the same piece of gum and looked the part of GI Joe with his oversized pilot helmet and clear visor covering the front of his face. This plan had to work. There was no plan B.

13

The Captain inside the Kremlin's security detail stared at the front door. His eyes shifted back and forth as he cradled the telephone receiver tight against his ear. Through gritted teeth, he replied, "Comrade, such a surprise, and calling on a landline. Is that wise?" said Yuri as he continued searching the area to make sure no one was around.

"There is no time for the cloak and daggers now, my old friend. I need you to get this information to the Russian President. We have no time to waste. There's been a tragic event. A U.S. nuclear missile complex has been infiltrated, presumably by the Chinese."

With a smirk, Yuri replied in an incredulous tone, "Cornelius, if this really is him, please stop playing these games. How do your American imperialist friends say, stop 'yanking my leg'," followed by an awkward forced laugh.

"It's true, Yuri. An ICBM just launched from their Japanese base on Okinawa. It's headed for Moscow."

"Van Aelst, please don't involve me with such fantastic claims. Are you looking to get me transferred to Siberia?" retorted Yuri, but his tone seemed to be shifting.

"The Chinese hacked inside. I'm presuming they were just experimenting, trying to see if it were possible-to make a point. When some overly enthusiastic computer technician, trying to make a name for himself and impress his superiors, pushed the wrong button. Whatever the reason, the Americans are trying to intercept the missile and bring it down safely without it detonating. They've confirmed the existence of their secret hypersonic jets that are waiting to strategically intercept the bomb as it re-enters the atmosphere. Because the rocket is one of theirs, they know all of its workings and characteristics. They will attempt to prevent the bomb from arming, and if there is enough time, redirect it away from Russian soil before it lands," urged Van Aelst in a rushed voice.

After a brief pause, Yuri spoke, "You're serious? One hundred percent truthful? Cornelius, you must understand, if this information is not accurate, there will be ramifications for you and me. You understand, yes?"

"I do my old friend. The South Korean Agency Director Valdez brought me into their meeting. I was there during the briefing and heard it all. Well, enough? She called me from Okinawa on a SAT phone. An EMP was detonated disabling the entire island. Their normal communications are all destroyed."

"The Agency Director that dropped the North Korean invasion tunnel?" asked Yuri.

"Yes, Yuri. She knows of my connections and urged me to make the call, to do everything in my power making sure the Russians understand. The most important point Yuri is you can't attempt to shoot it down or disable it. If you do, it could prevent the Americans from being able to abort the detonation. Merely knocking it out of the sky does not guarantee that the bomb will still not detonate."

"Those crazy Americans finally did it! It's come to this. After all those bad times. All those Cold War years, and now, when we finally have a good respectable, predictable relationship, we are forced into this conflict," said Yuri.

"Yes comrade. But look who everyone turns to – us old relics. During their time of need, Yuri, they all still come to us. They still need us. They've always needed us," replied Van Aelst.

With a deep sigh, Yuri stood. "Okay my friend, I'm laying my thick fat neck on the chopping block."

"He's your brother, Yuri. He'll believe you. Also, let him know the American President will be calling shortly. You need to make sure your brother gets to the Russian President first."

"Of course. You'd better be right Cornelius. Otherwise... your code name will be changed to the Dead Wolf," joked Yuri with a chuckle before he hung up the phone.

Van Aelst stared at the phone. After a few moments, he started calling another number he had memorized a long time ago. It was to Kazakhstan.

*　　*　　*　　*　　*

Colonel Fangqi drove straight to his country cottage. He found a side road that hadn't been used for decades. He glanced about each time he went there making sure no one was around as he pulled down that path. He pulled his car around the house making sure it was obscured by the cottage structure. After running inside, he pushed open the back windows and appreciated the evening breeze as it cooled the interior. With a quick turn of his head, he looked out the open window. Something caught his attention. *"Probably a bird,"* thought Fangqi as he watched what appeared to be an animal outside on a tree branch.

Fangqi turned his attention to his computer and began booting it up. Then something else caught his attention. He thought he heard someone calling his name. With a scrunched expression, he shook his head in disbelief chastising himself. The stress of the situation was getting to him. He was certain that no one was there.

While Fangqi waited for the computer to restart, he glanced at the wall clock. It seemed like an eternity. When in fact, only eight minutes had passed since he'd pushed the button. On his drive over, he convinced himself that just because he pushed some button didn't necessarily mean it worked. *"That would be too simple. A weapon of mass destruction, especially one designed and maintained by the Americans, certainly would be more full-proof than that, right?"* he told himself.

Fangqi found himself rationalizing away what he'd done. If he really wanted to know, he could call any one of his senior technicians. They'd been allocated five satellites for this mission. They could confirm the launch without others knowing. Fangqi had another idea.

There was the SAT phone used by the North Koreans. The senior agent. They'd used it to speak earlier making certain the EMP attack was a success. Fangqi stared at the SAT phone sitting next to the computer. He'd set it there when he came inside. He recalled grabbing it as he ran out of the make-shift computer lab. Until that moment, he didn't remember even doing it. He could barely remember driving to the cottage. The sound of the computer completing its set up caught his attention. The musical tones brought him back to the present, and out from his confused and rambling thoughts.

Fangqi again, for the tenth time since his arrival, stared at the wall clock. It was now ten minutes. A quiet whispering voice sounded in his mind, asking, *"Did the missile launch?"* His mind was stuck on a treadmill. As he closed his eyes and imagined his life if he hadn't pushed the button. If he hadn't launched the missile. He could forget everything. For a split-second, he found himself thinking his transfer to the Northern Province near Russia wasn't so bad after all. It was better than his current reality. The inevitable reality if it had actually worked. If he'd actually launched the ICBM.

Fangqi stared back at the clock again. This time, he stood up and walked toward the SAT phone.

*   *   *   *   *

The senior North Korean agent was stunned. He was told the mission only entailed infiltrating the American missile control. The Chinese were only supposed to prove they could manipulate the rockets. To prove that the Imperialists weren't invincible. That even with all their technology, they weren't infallible. His Chinese handler said they only wanted to teach the Americans a lesson in respect.

Seeing the missile launch across the otherwise black sky, his team froze in their tracks and watched in terror from their cheap hotel room. The missile's force caused their room to vibrate as the awesome roar echoed out over the island filling the sky with a streak of bright orange and blue flames as the rocket pass overhead. The roar become louder and louder. He didn't even remember stepping out onto the small balcony to watch the missile disappear into the stars. Without haste, using the SAT phone he called his handler in Pyongyang. Hearing the news, his handler ordered him and his team to leave Okinawa immediately.

There was no time or need to pack or attempt to dispose of the evidence. The handler correctly assumed the Americans and other common security cameras would be discovered and their tapes reviewed. In no time, they would have photographic proof of their presence, actions as well as their identities. The handler gave explicit instructions that no one could be captured alive. He knew that this was always a chance in such covert missions. If detained, they were ordered to swallow their cyanide capsule. Defection and cooperation would result in the death of their loved ones back in North Korea. Unlike other clandestine organizations, having families was a good thing for the DPRK. It allowed the North Koreans a guaranteed means to increase the likelihood of cooperation. While the western agencies, viewed families as a liability. The North Koreans felt they created a way to blackmail an agent into cooperating.

As the North Korean team left the hotel, the SAT phone rang. The senior agent stared at the incoming call. It was Colonel Fangqi. He didn't wait. He turned and walked for the door. Holding the boxy SAT phone, he depressed the button with his thumb and rejected the call. His handler ordered him not to speak to the Colonel.

With the team loaded in the two cars, they drove toward the dock. A Chinese owned fishing boat was waiting. The agents stared out the windows as they passed through the vacant streets following all the laws and driving on the correct side of the road. Everyone on Okinawa witnessed the missile launch. The island inhabitants were hunkered down inside their homes, wondering amongst themselves what this all meant. The streets were empty as the North Koreans continued their way to the docks.

*   *   *   *   *

Old Bessie continued its flight into the sky. It passed through the troposphere, stratosphere, and then the mesosphere. It was just exiting the thermosphere some 372 miles above the earth into the exosphere. The area above this gradually fades into interplanetary space. Like the NASA rockets, this ICBM dropped its fuselage as the rocket burned through each stage. By now, there were already several multiple separations that took place all at pre-determined altitudes. At the final stage, the outer shroud casing was jettisoned, and a post boost maneuver carried the missile to a pre-determined area in space.

As it turned to begin its descent and re-entry back through the different layers, a generator fired placing the rocket into a gas spin to stabilize the projectile toward its target. Like the rotating inner grooves on the inside barrel of a rife keeping the projectile on a straight course. Only 13 minutes remained before the ICBM re-entered the troposphere and began to slow. Once the missile was level only the atmospheric turbulence would prevent a smooth ride. During this last phase, the nuclear component was armed. With the recent refitting back in Kadena, Old Bessie was running like clockwork, just as it was designed.

*   *   *   *   *

The front doors to the missile silo complex burst open. General Blair's hair was pushed up and back, wind-whipped from riding along with Buehler on his motorcycle without a helmet. With a frustrated expression, he approached the Launch Officer Owens.

"What happened, Brian?" asked Dicky.

"I don't know General. I entered your code. I thought we keyed the numbers in time. For a second, the launch seemed to stop," explained Owens. "I'm guessing whoever hacked into the system, may have also locked us out. We'll never know."

Buehler came through the doors. With his hands on his hips, he scanned the room. Everyone seemed dazed not knowing what to do.

"Buehler," asked the General.

"Yes sir, General."

"Where's Nena...I mean Director Valdez?"

"Her pilot commandeered a helicopter and is taking her to the dock. She has a meeting set up on the USS Michelle J Howard," replied Buehler.

"Why?" asked the General.

"The submarines thick outer metal casing protected its communication system from the EMP attack. She's going to brief the National Agency Director and POTUS using the sub's communication room."

With a deep sigh, everyone exchanged blank stares of concern. Without speaking, everyone knew what the others were thinking, "What are the Russians going to do?"

*　　*　　*　　*　　*

"This way Director Valdez," said the Submarine Captain as he helped her down the main mast ladder. "Everything is set up in the Comm's area. POTUS and your National Agency Director Allwardt are waiting for you to arrive."

Nena made her way through the submarine ducking through the narrow doorways. Several sailors backed up to the wall to give her room to pass. This was her first time inside a submarine. The confined quarters took some getting used to.

"Ma'am, this way," directed the Captain.

After leading her through another set of openings, the area opened into a large Command Control Center. There were several sailors tending to the area with the boat's X.O. looking through the periscope. All conversation ceased as Nena appeared.

"Ma'am let's proceed to my room. It's as private as it gets inside a submarine," the Captain explained. Nena followed the Captain through the mess area, then past several 6-man and 9-man bunks, before going by the engine room and one of the enlisted heads; an all-purpose shower and toilet combination. Finally, they reached the Captain's quarters. As she entered, she saw two large flat screen television screens doubling as monitors. She saw POTUS on one screen and NATD Allwardt on the other.

"Mr. President, Director Allwardt, I've brought Director Valdez," said the Captain as he raised his hand in her direction. The Captain was preparing to exit, when POTUS spoke.

"Captain, could you stay please. We're hoping things work out. But, in case it doesn't you may be the first ones we call into play. It's best you hear everything."

"Of course, Mr. President," said the Captain as he closed the door and took a seat.

"Nena," said National Agency Director Allwardt. "Where are we with regard to your team?"

"We have two SR-72 UAVs that have moved into position just outside of Moscow. We've triangulated the missile's re-entry location and are waiting in that location as we speak. Our primary goal is to deactivate the bomb so that the nuclear reaction won't take place. From what our people say, this may not be as difficult as one would assume," she explained.

"How so?" asked POTUS.

"Until recently, no one had jets that could fly fast enough to arrive and position at the exact re-entry position. Also, the advanced computer software systems inside the modern ICBM accounts for remote launches. Since the missile is ours, we know all the inner workings of this rocket. Our new powerful satellites give us everything we need to pull this stunt off. In years past, it just wasn't possible," Nena explained

"If the missile was from another country, even with all the advantages Nena outlined, not having the launch code and deep understanding of the inner workings, this wouldn't be an option," added Allwardt.

With a deep sigh, POTUS said, "I hope so. Still, I have contacted our European base commanders closest to Moscow. They could still arrive there in time to destroy the missile."

"It's too risky, sir," explained Nena. "If we only disable the missile, or even bring it out of the air, we have no guarantee that the nuclear device still won't detonate.

We may save Moscow from a direct hit, but the bomb could still cause catastrophic damage to other parts of Russia. Theoretically, the post explosion side-effects will still rain radiation throughout most of Moscow. It wouldn't be as dramatic given the impact location, but the toll on life will still be devastating. If we try this approach unless we completely destroy it, virtually vaporize the entire inbound missile, we run the risk that the nuke will still detonate," she elaborated.

"It's a hell of a position were in," said POTUS as he pursed his lips and rubbed his temples. "I just got off the phone with the Kremlin. They were given the heads up prior to my call, presumably Van Aelst. I'm hoping that they cooperate. For now, the Russian President, said they wouldn't delay launching their defensive missiles giving our SR-72's time to at least disarm the missile. But I'm skeptical they'll let it get anywhere near the Kremlin or Moscow." After a pause, POTUS added, "I'm not certain I would either if it were heading to Washington. I'd rather take my luck dealing with the fallout as opposed to a potential direct hit."

Nena checked her wristwatch. Everything happened so fast. She stared at the two television monitors and spoke. "Gentlemen, in ten minutes, the missile will enter the atmosphere at its lowest altitude and slowest speed, around 1,900 mph. I wish we had more alternatives, but we don't. Thanks to L.I.S.A. project, we had an early warning heads up that gives us a strong chance of still getting out of this mess."

Nena dialed her SAT phone. X.O. Newland picked up on the first ring. "Yes, Director."

"Jim, we have Director Allwardt, the submarine's Captain, and the President of the United States on the line. Where are we, Jim?" asked Nena.

X.O. Newland was taken aback. Without missing a beat, he proceeded as if this call was a normal everyday occurrence. "Ma'am, our SR-72 UAVs are in position. We've been tracking the missile through the L.I.S.A. team. Have the Russians been notified?"

"Yes, they have," replied POTUS.

Hearing his voice, Newland flinched realizing he was speaking directly to POTUS. "Will they cooperate Mr. President?"

"I'm certain, like us, they've been caught off guard. I'm confident they will give us the first few moments after the missile re-entry. However, if we can't redirect the missile in short order, I'd have to guess that they'll attempt to knock it out of the sky and roll the dice with the fallout later," said the President.

Just then, there was a knock on the Captain's door. "Yes," said the Captain looking over his shoulder.

"We have another connection coming through from South Korea Agency located in Camp Bonifas. We're patching it through to your desktop computer, sir," said the sailor. The sailor entered the room. After seeing the President's face on one screen, he became self-conscious. He approached the Captain's computer, brought up the connection giving everyone in the room access to the oversized floor to ceiling wall monitor view so they could see in real time what everyone back in the domed SR-72 simulator complex was seeing and hearing.

Everyone on the teleconference seemed mesmerized by the mission and listened in on Moon Dog, Kyle, Gibby and Carla Jo. The camera view from POTUS's camera changed views and panned out. With this new point of view, everyone discovered that POTUS was accompanied by the six members of the Joint Chiefs of Staff, his National Security Advisor and the heads of the DOD.

A side monitor wasn't visible by the group watching the oversized wall monitor feed from the teleconference. But this monitor was displayed for the benefit of the L.I.S.A. project. They needed to know who was watching. Carla Jo was the first one to notice and glanced over at Gibby mouthing "we have company," as she tilted her head toward the side monitor. X.O. Newland noticed Kyle stop chewing his gum and stare at the side monitor.

"Director Valdez," announced Newland over the loud PA system. His voice echoed throughout the domed simulator room. He wanted to make sure everyone knew that the VIP's were in the room watching their every move. "We're set. The satellites have confirmed the trajectory and the L.I.S.A. team has dialed in our coordinates. Based on our calculations, the UAVs will circle waiting for the missile to reach its floor elevation and establish a constant speed. We're guessing that to be around 1,980 mph." As if there wasn't enough pressure, having the President and these countless others watching, seemed to notch the stress level up to another level.

"Inbound bogie is two minutes out, prepare to rendezvous at the vector coordinates," announced Joe Erbes from the L.I.S.A. area.

"Copy that. Two minutes," repeated the X.O. Moon Dog, Kyle, Carla Jo and Gibby scanned their instruments and oversized wall monitor as they maneuvered the UAVs into position.

"Mr. President, we have the Kremlin on the line," came some unknown voice that echoed unfiltered allowing everyone to hear.

"Pass it through," said POTUS.

"Hello?" came the voice of the Russian President spoken with a thick accent.

"Yes, Mr. President. You are on speaker with my entire team. We're listening in on the mission live. The missile is about to re-enter and level out," POTUS explained.

"That's why I called. We've been tracking the missile as well and came to the same conclusion. Mr. President, are you sure you don't want us to release our surface-to-air defenses?" Asked the Russian President. His voice reflected his concern and was trying his best to suppress his agitation and uncertainty in such a decision.

"Mr. President," interjected Nena. "The guidance and arming mechanisms are known variables. Because it's one of ours, we understand how it functions, and therefore, are confident about how to disarm it."

"Yet, it was launched by someone else, nonetheless," replied the Russian President, suggesting the Americans aren't in control. In the background, several Russian voices were interjecting something. A Russian translator was part of the Joint Chiefs entourage anticipating the possibility that the Russians would call at the last second. The interpreter muted the call and confirmed that one of the Russian generals is reminding the Russian President about the two groups of bombers, each group carrying nuclear weapons, before unmuting the call.

"The missile arrives in 90 seconds," announced Newland over the PA.

Director Valdez spoke up again, "We urge you, Mr. President, please allow us enough time to deactivate the bomb before you authorize any shots. If the missile is only damaged prior to impact, we may not be able to disarm it, let alone redirect it," urged Nena.

After a brief pause, the Russian President finally replied. "I wish it were so simple. Unfortunately, we are the ones that will suffer the consequences of any failure. Our forces have been instructed to delay retaliation allowing the missile time to reach its pre-detonation altitude. Our scientists are estimating you have 70 seconds from that point before detonation. We will give you 60 seconds from this re-entry to work your magic. After that time has expired, our missiles will fire. If what you're saying is correct, you should have at least disarmed the missile."

The Russian President's words were heard by everyone. It wasn't ideal, but certainly understandable. They were giving the Americans as much time as they could without jeopardizing their ability to strike it down before it entered Moscow air space.

With stern tight lips, POTUS nodded, "Thank you, Mr. President."

For a solemn moment, it was as if the world stood still. No one spoke from any of the sites patched in from across the globe; South Korea's Agency site inside Camp Bonifas's domed simulator building, from the L.I.S.A.

project, from inside the Captain's room aboard the USS Michelle J Howard submarine, deep inside a bunker conference room somewhere near Washington D.C., nor from the Kremlin. It was as if no one noticed the silence, everyone lost in thought. It was X.O. Newland's voice that broke the silence. "Fifty seconds until re-entry."

Gibby and Carla Jo exchanged a quick glance, while Moon Dog and Kyle continued their circular routes waiting for the missile to arrive. The SR-72 UAVs passed each other as they made their final loop. The night sky was filled with stars, and the images displaying on the oversized floor to ceiling wall monitor appeared a dull mint green color as they relied on night vision technology.

"Mr. President," said the Russian President. "This has to work." The Russian president's expression and tone said it all. If the bomb exploded in Russia, there would be consequences. POTUS and everyone present understood its meaning. If the nuclear bomb detonated, things could spiral out of control.

"I understand," replied POTUS.

14

The missile was making its way back through the different layers around the earth. This time, in reverse order; the exosphere, thermosphere, mesosphere, stratosphere and troposphere. The missile, having jettisoned the multiple fuel stages, revealed an ICBM that was much smaller and represented only the top ten percent positioned at the top section where the deployment and re-entry systems were located. The missile continued altering its decent angle in preparation for the final phase of its journey where it would run parallel to the earth's surface.

People all over the region would later report seeing what looked like a falling star or meteorite glowing, emitting a bright light as it skipped across the sky making its re-entry. The EMP attack knocked out all communications preventing any news being reported to the outside world. Only the U.S. military was partially back on-line with limited communications. With the Internet and its social media popularity being a global phenomenon, the EMP attack played to their advantage by not having to also worry about the media interfering and riling everyone up. Given the remote re-entry over a sparse area of mostly desert terrain, they didn't have to contend with heavy commercial airline traffic. For those very few planes flying about, the U.S. military casually intervened and redirected them through AWAC (Airborne Warning and Control Systems) radioing those pilots away from potential danger. They had no clue that an inbound ICBM would have flown past them had their course not been altered. With all the civilian and commercial satellite uplinks, cell phone towers and computer uplinks on Okinawa fried, only a limited number of U.S. and Russian personnel, and a small group of North Korean agents hiding in the belly of a Chinese fishing boat had any idea what was happening. So, they thought.

*   *   *   *   *

Van Aelst paced inside the conference room. One of Nena's security detail just relieved the prior guard. Van Aelst glanced up at a new face inside his small temporary shelter. He knew they were there for his protection. If they hadn't allowed him to keep the SAT phone and given him unfettered access to the delicious food available through the Director's kitchen staff, he may have felt otherwise.

Van Aelst checked the wall mounted clock. He knew everything was about to happen. With a deep sigh, he glanced at the SAT phone and hoped that his second call was the right thing to do. With a sideways glance at the guard, Van Aelst began second guessing the wisdom of placing that call to Kazakhstan. What's done is done. There was no looking back now.

He imagined he could hear everything that was going on beyond those doors. It's a good thing he didn't know all the action was happening a few hundred yards walk to the nearby domed simulator complex. Otherwise, he may not have been so cooperative. All those decades of experience working with the KGB and Stasi, taught him patience. Those years behind the Eastern Bloc iron curtain taught him a simple axiom- nails that stood up higher than the rest received a flat head when the sledgehammer came down putting it back into its rightful place. He was lucky to survive those years as a covert agent lurking in the shadows known by others as the "Lone Wolf". His most important attribute was patience. Others were lured in by their insatiable curiosity. It was the biggest reason spies were taken down. Van Aelst settled back down in his chair and stared at the boxy SAT phone and continued to wait.

*   *   *   *   *

"Here we go people," announced X.O. Newland. "I'll count you down. Kyle and Moon Dog, you need to time your circular path back to the spot you've been assigned to just as the missile enters the area."

"Erbes, what is the missile's current speed?" barked Moon Dog as he maneuvered the UAV.

"2,500 mph," replied Erbes as he tracked the missile on several satellites.

"UAVs, match that speed," ordered the X.O.

"Copy that, 2,500," replied Moon Dog and then Kyle as they matched the UAVs re-entry speed.

"On my mark," said the X.O. "Here we go...ten..."

From that point, everything slowed down. The plans and players were set. There was nothing else to discuss or strategize. The input provided by all participants was now left in the hands of these four; Kyle, Moon Dog, Carla Jo and Gibby. Everything came down to this group of four, to utilize all of the resources at their disposal and tasked with doing their jobs. This was it.

"...nine...eight...seven..." echoed throughout the domed simulator building as the X.O. continued to count down the seconds.

The oversized floor to ceiling wall monitor showed the view from each UAV SR-72 as well as the synchronized satellites above. Both UAVs were completing their circular turns. It looked similar to airshows where the Thunderbirds or Blue Angles come together in a midair, side-by-side formation. Unlike the airshows, the UAVs didn't need to form up that close to each other and could remain a safe distance apart.

"Here it comes," announced Joe Erbes from the L.I.S.A complex a building away.

"…six…five…four…"

Gibby and Carla Jo exchanged one last glanced. Their eyes bulging, pulses elevated and quickened breaths.

"…three…two…one…MARK!" announced X.O. Newland.

Right on cue, the ICBM reappeared out of nowhere. The UAVs converged and kept the missile between them and matched its speed as the missile leveled and continued reducing speed. The missile was glowing a bright orange from the friction passing through the various levels of space. The simulator hadn't prepared them for the steam cloud that formed around the missile as the winter air, full of moisture, burned from the missile's heat. Moon Dog was the first to adjust.

"The missile is creating off gas clouding my vision. Pulling up to get in front of the steam. Moving up from our simulator positions," announced Moon Dog as he maneuvered the UAV up. "Matching speed and continue to decelerate," he added.

"Copy that," replied Gibby.

Kyle followed suit and pushed up to get in front of the misty steam cloud created by the missile's temperature.

"Moving up as well," announced GI Joe. "Get ready, CJ!"

"Copy that," replied Carla Jo.

"There's a lot of vibration here," said Moon Dog.

"Copy that," replied GI Joe. "It's pretty bumpy."

"I'm gonna get a little closer," explained Moon Dog wanting to make sure the upload had only a short distance to travel. As Moon Dog inched closer, he slid into a pocket next to the missile that was much more stable. It was like ducks or geese flying in a v-formation and using each other's body to draft through the airspace. "There you go. Much better in here."

"Roger that, I'm moving closer," said GI Joe. "Ready to initiate. Stabilization is set."

"We have a problem," announced Erbes from the L.I.S.A. building. "There is a large number of inbound bogies that just appeared out of nowhere on our satellite feed."

Hearing the news, everyone turned toward the image transmitting the Russians.

"How many inbound bogies?" asked POTUS with a disappointing scowl glancing toward the Russian President.

"Thousands," replied Erbes.

"It's not us!" shouted the Russian President.

"The bogies are moving too slow to be surface to air missiles," interjected Erbes.

Kyle and Carla Jo tried blocking out the extra conversations. None of that mattered. Kyle had to keep the SR-72 UAV steady and Carla Jo had to make sure the entire program uploaded.

Everyone looked up to the oversized floor to ceiling wall monitor. The first percentage stabilization numbers came in very high. "We're at 88 percent...92 percent," reported Carla Jo as she continued to wait until it hit 96. "...95...97 percent! Starting my upload!" reported Carla Jo. Without realizing it, she was whispering words of encouragement that echoed inside the domed simulator room. "*Come on baby, you can do it.*"

Even though her part of the mission was going to take only five seconds, those seconds seemed to drag along. The time was counted off to the thousandth of a second and was super-imposed over the upper section of the over-sized wall monitor. At the end of the upload, something happened.

"Almost there," announced Carla Jo as she watched the upload ICON march past 75 percent.

"Copy that," replied GI Joe.

"…80…90…95…"

Just then, a wall of small objects began slamming into the missile and SR-72 UAV.

"I'm hit!" reported GI Joe as he tried to keep the UAV steady. "I'm getting pelted."

"What are those things?" asked the XO.

"I have no clue. But we're okay. No damage."

The SR-72 UAV seemed to wobble. The stabilization percentage immediately decreased from 98 percent to 70. "Did it all upload?" asked the X.O.

"I'm not sure," replied Carla Jo. "The upload ICON froze at 99 percent. It didn't confirm upload complete."

In the excitement of the moment, Gibby started his upload while the first one was uploading. The plan was to wait until the first one was complete. But hearing the Russian President mention their intention to launch, Gibby thought he could save some time by starting a little early. When he saw the upload percentage reach 90 percent, he figured there would be no harm, and everything would be fine.

"Should we have Gibby run the deactivation program again, just to make sure it's deactivated?" suggested the X.O.

"Too late," said Gibby. "Program two is uploading now. I'm afraid to stop and restart it. If it takes too long to reboot, we could run out of time."

Just then, as Kyle was preparing to peel away from the missile, another group of bogies slammed into the SR-72 UAV. This time, some debris found its way into the jet intake. With a sudden jolt, Kyle's engine froze as the debris jammed the fans. The engine exploded and burst into flames. The high speed bank combined with the multiple inbound strikes were too much. The SR-72 UAV's fuselage lost its integrity and tumbled in an uncontrolled roll and broke into pieces. The night vision images were temporarily lost as the exploding UAV fell away and out of view. That UAV's image on the oversized wall monitor went to static.

"We're still good," announced Moon Dog. "We held at 96 plus percent and stable the entire time. It looks like GI Joe's UAV shielded the missile and us from the inbound objects."

"What are those things?" asked Carla Jo as she stood up no longer needing to control the program upload.

"They're geese," explained Erbes speaking from the adjacent L.I.S.A. project building. "We calibrated one of the satellites. There are a lot of high flying V-formations. The geese are migrating south for the winter."

With a deep sigh, everyone redirected their attention watching the last upload and its stabilization percentages as Gibby called out the numbers. "45 percent..."

"How much time until impact?" asked Nena through the shared communication line.

"No more than 45 seconds," said X.O. Newland.

"Do we have time to rerun the first program?" asked POTUS.

The room went silent.

*   *   *   *   *

The parrot was perched on the tree branch outside Fangqi's open window. The parrot followed him here and was getting hungry. This was the longest he'd been away on his own. The sun already set. To the parrot's surprise, more night-time flying animals began appearing; bats, owls and the worrisome hawks and eagles. The parrot decided it was time to leave. He checked his surroundings and started back home. His miniature vest was secure and the micro-camera with GPS tracking had been recording the entire time. It had an extended battery that provided 48 hours of continuous recording. If the vest somehow came off, it would emit a beacon so it could be located and safely retrieved.

As the parrot flew across the meadow, he heard a distinct noise. It was a screech owl's call that pierced through the darkness as it grabbed an unsuspecting rabbit that was busy eating the meadow grass. Although the parrot hadn't lived in the wild, his instincts told him to stay attentive and look out for other birds of prey that hunted at night.

Peering down from above, a sparrow-hawk soared above looking for his next meal. Out of the corner of his eye, something caught his attention. The hawk changed its course and began descending in that direction.

*   *   *   *   *

Kyle glanced about as he climbed out of the SR-72 UAV simulator cockpit and removed his headset. Seeing everyone focusing their attention on the oversized wall monitor, Kyle walked near Carla Jo's desk and sat in the vacant chair. The images on the wall monitor showed Moon Dog's UAV still flying next to the missile. Carla Jo nodded and patted Kyle's hand before returning her attention to the big screen.

"65 percent," reported Gibby.

"Stabilization remains solid at 96 percent," added Moon Doggie.

"70 percent..." said Gibby as he continued counting down.

Carla Jo noticed her desk phone light appear. With all the noise echoing around the domed simulator room, she would have missed the call. Wondering who was calling, she looked up and saw X.O. Newland signaling with his free-hand for her to pick up the call.

"Hey, Jim. What's up?" asked Carla Jo.

"Do you think your upload was complete?" asked the X.O. "The upload icon stopped at 99 percent. It never displayed complete. It just closed."

"I was wondering that as well," replied Carla Jo. "During the simulation, the icon showed upload complete."

With a deep sigh, X.O. Newland said, "I guess we just don't know. We'll have Gibby try and boot up your program again."

"If we have enough time," she added with a doubtful shrug of her shoulders.

"Yeah, if there's enough time," repeated Jim in a concerned tone. "Okay, that's all," said Jim as he hung up the phone.

While Gibby's voice echoed over the loudspeakers continuing his count-down, Carla Jo glanced back up at the window tower above the UAV cockpit area as she returned the telephone receiver back into place.

"...85 percent..."

The area below the SR-72 UAV and missile was no longer passing over constant desert sand, but more rolling hills even a random building or road. For the first time of the night, small dots of lights began appearing below and interrupted the clear night vision optics. The oversized wall monitor looked more like a gigantic video game than real life.

'We're crossing Kazakhstan. Impact and detonation in 20 seconds," announced Erbes from the L.I.S.A. building.

Because most of the program was already uploaded, the percentage complete numbers seemed to quicken. Gibby began to call out the percentage numbers quicker, "...90 percent..." while he unconsciously rocked in his chair, as if he were riding in a golf cart whose battery was running out of juice and needed some extra assistance to keep going. "...92 percent..."

Kyle turned to Carla Jo. "We're not gonna have enough time to boot up the other program again."

Carla Jo stared into Kyle's eyes with a blank stare and covered her mouth with her hand. He was right. Nena had muted the call to prevent POTUS's and the others' remarks from booming into the domed simulator room and distracting her team. As the seconds ticked away, the others watched knowing it was out of their hands. They could no longer alter the circumstances. Without realizing this, the General's and POTUS were shouting words of encouragement.

"Go,..go!!"

"Come on! Hurry up!"

"How much longer?"

"...95...97...99 percent," continued Gibby.

"Ten seconds to impact," announced Erbes.

"Upload complete!" yelled Gibby. "I'm transferring the missile's control to my stick," he announced as he grabbed the stick and gave it a hard right trying to bank the missile away from Moscow. Traveling at almost 2,000 mph, the missile was traveling almost six miles in 10 seconds. In 20 seconds, he could divert the missile 16 miles in the opposite direction which would have a huge positive impact with potential fall-out should it still detonate. Gibby started uploading the first program. It would only take five seconds. There was still time. "Get in tight Moon Dog!" urged Gibby as he continued banking the missile. "We need the stabilization high enough to try the upload again."

Kyle was right. There wasn't enough time to reboot the first program. Everyone watching was leaning forward in their chairs, while their hearts raced mesmerized by the live images projected on the oversized wall monitor. As Gibby continued to steer the missile away from Moscow, Erbes' voice began counting down to impact.

"10...9...8..."

Moon Dog raced up along the missile and started the stabilization program. It went from 70 to 90 percent in less than a second. Gibby kept watching the percentage numbers vowing to wait until it was 96. This was going to be their last chance to get it right. The percentage numbers continued climbing to 95.

"...7...6..."

Gibby was about to attempt to upload the first program for a second time when it happened.

"Multiple inbound bogies, all from ground launches. Definitely surface to air missiles, velocity too fast for biologicals," reported Erbes over the PA speakers.

Everyone turned to the Russian President. Sensing the attention, he said, "It's not us."

These weapons were much faster than the ICBM and UAV and approached them as if they were standing still traveling almost 4,000 mph. The downward view from the last remaining SR-72 UAV and satellite showed multiple smoke trails leading up from the surface. Gibby tried to read the stabilization percentage, but it didn't matter. The surface to air missiles slammed into the missile and UAV simultaneously causing the entire oversized wall-monitor to go fuzzy with static. For a brief moment, the room went still. No one from any of the locations spoke. It was deathly quiet. Not a sound.

Erbes' voice cut through the hollow tomb-like domed simulator building, "I'm magnifying the satellite image and see mobile rocket launchers below." His prior count-down was based on the last second promised by Russia. "This is it people. Now counting down to the last possible moment of detonation. Time to detonation is 10...9..."

"Did it work," asked POTUS.

"We'll have to wait and see," said Nena.

"God help us," said the Submarine Captain.

"We'll all know soon enough," said Moon Dog as he climbed out of the SR-72 UAV simulator cockpit and crossed his arms before standing in front of the oversized wall-monitor now showing the close-up night images of the mobile rocket launches below. No one spoke. The only words were Erbes' voice counting down for the final time, "...5...4...3...2...1..."

15

Van Aelst stared up at the wall clock. He had no clue what was happening or how much time was left. Just then, his SAT phone rang. The unexpected sound combined with the vibration on the table startled Van Aelst.

"Yes?" answered Van Aelst.

The guard glanced over too curious to take his eyes away actually craning his neck to catch the entire conversation. The guard was disappointed hearing only one side of the call.

"Perfect. It's time to get out of there. You know what to do," said Van Aelst, this time speaking Russian. Otherwise, they both would have spoken Kazakh. With a deep satisfied sigh, Van Aelst ended the call. He clasped his hands together and placed them on the table and closed his eyes.

*   *   *   *   *

After hearing the countdown to zero, everyone's shoulders seemed hunched up, as if expecting to be hit over the head by something. But nothing happened. Recognizing what may have happened, they began glancing about at the other members in their group, sharing hopeful expressions, wondering if disaster had been avoided. Erbes' voice again echoed over the PA speakers. "We're not detecting any detonation anywhere near the crash for miles around."

The oversized wall-monitor showed magnified images of what looked like the debris from the SR-72 UAV jets. In the night vision, they looked more like dark pieces of material strewn about the otherwise empty deserted mountain range. The other side of that pass was the beginnings of the outer Moscow jurisdictional border.

"Can it still explode?" asked the Russian President.

"I don't think so, but with your permission, Mr. President, we'd like to send our people in to recover what remains of the missile and our UAVs. I'd hate for some civilians to happen along and find it," offered POTUS.

"That won't be necessary, Mr. President. We'll take it from here. Besides, my hard-liners in the Kremlin will

330

give me this small victory arguing that you Americans have done quite enough for now thank you very much," said the Russian President in a sarcastic but stern tone. He had no intention of missing the opportunity to examine these Top-Secret jets and one of the American nuclear ICBMs. As long as it didn't detonate later, it was a great find.

With a slight nod, POTUS acquiesced realizing the futility of pursing the matter any further. He was grateful how things apparently ended.

"By the way, Mr. President, were those your surface to air missiles?" asked NATD Allwardt.

Without replying, the Russian President smiled and raised his eyebrows. After an awkward silence, POTUS decided it best to terminate the conference call.

"Mr. President, I assure you we did not have anything to do with starting this situation. We believe the Chinese are at fault, probably snooping around where they shouldn't have and accidentally launched our missile," explained POTUS.

"We're hearing similar things over here," replied the Russian President who exchanged a sideways glance to his Kremlin Security Captain. "In fact, I've got a call into China as we speak. I'm grateful it's ended this way, Mr. President, for everyone's concern."

"Likewise," replied POTUS. "Were you guys going to take care of the Chinese loose end, or should we?"

"We can handle it. The missile was heading to Moscow not Washington, yes?" replied the Russian President.

"Understood," said POTUS. "And again, my deepest apologies that this happened."

"Let's get that barn door fixed, yes?" said the Russian President with a smirk taking one last shot using an American euphemism. With one final nod, the Russian President terminated his end of the call.

With the Russians gone, POTUS spoke directly to Nena. "Director Valdez, we need to know what happened. If it really wasn't the Russian's missiles, who were they?"

"I have specialists in the L.I.S.A. building working on it. They will get to the bottom of it. It might be easier at next light," said Nena

"Great job, Nena. I'm not certain whether the uploads worked. It might have been the surface to air missiles. Either way, the ICBM never detonated. I'm very pleased," said POTUS.

"Yes, sir," replied Nena with a relieved smile.

"Keep us posted. As soon as you hear anything, let me know," added NATD Allwardt.

"I will," she said as the call ended. The only locations still connected was between the Captain's quarters on the submarine USS Michelle J. Howard and the South Korean Agency inside Camp Bonifas.

With a deep sigh, she addressed her team. "Well done. It goes without saying things could have gone terrible very fast."

"The Russians had their subs ready with a majority of them steaming toward the eastern seaboard," said Gibby. "We've been tracking them since this whole fiasco started. No need to bring anything up prior. I mean, we'd have done the same thing."

"Losing those SR-72 UAVs will hurt. That's an expensive hit to our little budget," joked Moon Dog.

"Our budget isn't scrutinized, no over-sight committees to worry about," reminded Nena. "And the SR-72s certainly proved their worth today. I'm sure if Congress knew what happened and how much we spent, there wouldn't be any complaints. What's the price tag on one of those anyway?"

"No one knows," answered Gibby. "Another one of Skunk Works pet projects. Too rich for my blood that's for sure. Probably in the multi-billions per copy."

"If it wasn't Russian missiles, whose were they?" asked Carla Jo.

"We were just looking into it," interjected Erbes. "It looks like the old Desert Brigade."

"Never heard of them," said Gibby with most everybody else nodding in agreement.

"It's a group of old-school Cold War cronies that roam the Russian borders. Based on our satellite images, they used mobile rocket launchers. We back tracked the film and saw one of the drivers using a SAT phone before racing the mobile launchers back undercover. They disappeared underground. With the missile incinerated and Russia pretty clear on wanting to recover the debris, I figured we weren't going to look too hard to confirm their recovery. I'm sure they're heading there right now with a recovery team."

"If there are bunch of old geezers with thick glass, we might know somebody who knows," interjected Kyle with a wide grin.

"Right!" added Moon Dog. "And don't forget their crazy hodgepodge of hats."

"And them raising up their arms and extending their middle fingers to the satellite" joked Carla Jo.

Hearing the last part, everyone from the South Korean agency that helped in the Curt Anderson case started laughing. Erbes waited for the noise to subside.

"Now that you mention it," said Erbes. Everyone turned toward his image on the oversized wall-monitor curious as to what he had to say. "We couldn't see their faces because of the night vision optics, but everyone was wearing hats and glasses. And like you said, after the missile and the second UAV was shot down, one of the analysts noticed one group of about ten figures pause. Everyone raised their arm up to the sky. We thought they were shaking their fists. Given the limited vision, I couldn't say if they were actually giving us the bird or not. We actually thought it was a group celebration for downing the missile."

"For real?" asked Kyle with a shocked expression.

"Of course," replied Erbes in a confused serious expression. He wasn't the joking type. Hearing this, they all laughed again even louder.

"Okay, people, remember...that mission is on a need to know basis."

Hearing this reprimand, they regained their composure. More than anything, it was probably just the stress and excitement from what they just went through that caused them to break protocol.

"Sorry, boss," said Moon Dog.

Nena just smiled.

*   *   *   *   *

Colonel Fangqi was almost catatonic. He'd hoped that nothing happened, praying that his decision to launch the nuclear missile was all a dream. But he knew better. He rationalized that the computer program used could have been defective, or the program incomplete. Just because he clicked on the icon didn't necessarily mean anything really happened. Fangqi kept running through different scenarios in his mind, supporting his delusion that nothing had happened; the distance was too great; the coding instructions were flawed; the missile was a dud and never reached its target let alone detonate.

At first, all his wishful thoughts seemed like they were in the realm of possibility. This delusion was reinforced when he realized that since his arrival to the cottage, no one had attempted to call his SAT phone. It was published and used as his principal contact number. As the minutes passed, no calls came through. He picked up the phone, held it in front of his face staring at the display screen and waited. Still nothing. For a brief moment in time, he'd tricked himself into believing his fantasy convincing himself that everything was fine, that nothing had happened, that his prayers were answered.

That all came crashing down as non-stop calls started coming, one after the other. Many from numbers he didn't recognize. He sat there and let the phone ring. Not once did he attempt to answer or disconnect the call. He didn't want anyone to know he was there, still holding the SAT phone. He'd counted 49 missed calls. By the 15th, he knew the truth. He wasn't surprised and expected to see calls from General Lee's office and his private number.

Fangqi knew he could never go back. He had to find some way to avoid detection and slip out of the country. It was the first time since arriving in Xinjiang Province that he was pleased to be assigned so close to the border.

Wasting no time, Fangqi stared out his open window while changing out of his military uniform into regular civilian clothes. As he jammed his arms through a worn jacket he'd found in the closet, he looked out into the dark landscape. He'd never been away from China. He wondered what to expect in Kazakhstan.

*   *   *   *   *

Burt sat on his back patio finishing his third bottle of wine. Feeling more than a little tipsy, he kept Fur Elise blaring at full blast. He didn't care what his neighbors thought. A sense of guilt was setting in. He began chastising himself for sending his pet parrot on such an unimportant mission. It was done more out of intellectual curiosity's sake, expanding the possibility that his parrot could actually help locate somebody. Burt never expected his pet parrot to be gone so long. He wondered if something had happened to him.

As each hour passed, Burt became more distraught. *"What have I done?"* He was gone way too long, the longest he'd ever been out in the world on his own. Leaning on the railing, Burt began hearing a variety of animal cries; owls, hawks, bats and eagles. He took a deep breath trying to calm his nerves and glanced at the wall mounted clock again. Hearing a Chinese Sparrow-hawk screech just over the hill caught his attention.

Burt saw the Sparrow-hawk's silhouette as it floated over the horizon as the moonlight lit the area. Without flapping its wings, the hawk seemed to accelerate as it arched downward into a diving position. Burt tilted his head wondering what it was chasing. To his surprise, he watched the hawk bank and make a beeline heading straight to his back porch.

Burt was so focused on the Sparrow-hawk that he hadn't noticed his pet parrot bobbing and weaving about between the trees making his way back home. It wasn't until Burt saw the hawk's wings unfold and spread wide with its legs and talons outstretched in front of him, did he finally see his pet parrot.

The porch light provided enough illumination to see his parrot flying toward him. Seeking protection, the parrot dove into Burt's chest. Without thinking, Burt cradled the parrot, encircling his arms around the bird while turning away from the oncoming hawk. Burt bent forward and stiffened his back muscles anticipating the impact from the hawk to follow.

Burt's unexpected presence must have startled the hawk. As the Sparrow-hawk saw a man grabbing his prey, the hawk retracted his talons and legs, did a 180 degree mid-air spin and hurried away in the opposite direction. Not feeling the hawk, Burt turned and looked over his shoulder and watched the Sparrow-hawk disappear into the night. To his great pleasure, Burt was hugging his pet parrot and carried him inside and shut the door. Fearing he would take off again never to return, Burt placed him inside his cage and latched the cage door. The mango slices were waiting inside. The parrot was famished and didn't care that the fruit had been out for quite some time.

Burt bent down and stared at his pet parrot watching his best friend eating. It was a reunion he thought might never happen. The parrot seemed unfazed just happy to be home. In between bites, the pet parrot looked up into Burt's face and spoke, "Waaaa...Fangqi," spoken in his sing-song voice.

Burt smiled and started laughing out loud. "Yes, buddy. Colonel Fangqi. Great job!" replied Burt.

Careful not to injure his parrot, Burt opened the cage door and removed the small jacket. After locking the door, he disconnected the tracking monitor and miniature camera. It was at that moment that Burt noticed a single straight edge cut along the back of the parrot's miniature vest. The equipment was not damaged. When he realized that the hawk had almost caught his pet parrot his heart skipped a beat. With a grateful smile, Burt watched his parrot finish the mango unaware of a tear drop sliding down his cheek. He'd almost lost his best friend.

*   *   *   *   *

General Blair sat in his office staring at his Hotshot plaque. He'd reattached the hooks and remounted it back on his wall. It had turned into a very long day. Dicky stared out his window and was grateful to see more lights coming back on around the base. Just then, the SAT phone that Nena left for him to use until everything returned to normal, started ringing. He would keep it as a memento an object he'd cherish to remind him of the day that almost wasn't.

"Hello, this is General Blair," said in his Bostonian accent.

"Dicky, it's Nena."

"Are you back home already?"

"Almost. POTUS and the Joint Chiefs decided to re-route the B-2s and B-52s to Kadena. You'll need to off load their ordinances. Somehow, the Chinese compromised two bomb ordinance techs from two separate bases. You'll need to store the 'special ordinances' for now," explained Nena. "They thought it best not to involve another base. You already know everything. Rumors are soon to be flying off Okinawa, so might as well keep all the speculation circling in one location."

"Like area 51," Dicky said with a chuckle. "Things could have played out horribly. Thank God your team was able to disarm the missile."

After a brief pause, Dicky continued. "Were your guys able to confirm who shot down the missile? Was it the Russians after all?"

"It doesn't look like it General. Our satellites confirm that it was from a large group of mobile rocket launchers. We were able to track them back to several cave openings along the mountain range just outside the far Moscow border. The equipment looked pretty old too, most outdated and used decades prior."

"Good thing they still worked. It got the job done," replied Dicky.

"We're almost back to Camp Bonifas," said Nena. "For what it's worth, Dicky. I thought we'd stopped the launch in time. I have a feeling I may know somebody waiting in one of my conference rooms that has a good idea who those guys were. You take care, Dicky."

"You too, Director Valdez," replied Dicky as they ended the call.

Dicky was setting the SAT phone down on his desk when it rang again. He thought it was Nena again.

"Hello," answered Dicky.

"General Blair, this is National Agency Director Allwardt." Dicky was surprised to hear another voice.

"Yes, Director Allwardt. I was just speaking to one of your superstars, Director Valdez."

"Is she back at Camp Bonifas yet?"

"Almost. She called as they were about to land. What can I do for you?"

By Allwardt's voice, Dicky sensed something was wrong. As he listened to Allwardt, he was taken aback. It had something to do with Nena.

"Obviously, this is beyond Top Secret. Other than POTUS and me, you will be the only other person that knows."

"Understood," replied Dicky.

"If anything turns out to be true, we may need to contact you to intervene. It's an unusual set of circumstances, but protocol dictates that the highest ranking officer in the region must be involved. In all military circumstances, you would be that person for all military branches. However, technically, Nena's classification falls outside the normal military jurisdiction. However, given the Treaty with Japan, certain technical necessities must be followed. For these reasons only, you may have to be part of this process."

Hearing Director Allwardt's words, Dicky knew that this had to be something serious. "How confident are we about the accuracy of the allegations being brought against Nena?"

"It's still too soon to tell. My people don't know everything yet. The Philippine Embassy just notified me. It was the first call I took after our little problem down your neck of the woods was resolved. General, given Director Valdez's access and control over the Asia Region, it may become necessary to pull her from the field on a moment's notice. Unfortunately, depending on how this pans out, politics and perceptions may dominate our decision making."

"That's too bad. I really like her."

"Me too. We all do. Hopefully, it won't come to that," added Allwardt. "Sometimes, life isn't fair. And in light of all the good she's done for us, especially over the last few years, today in particular, it would be very unfortunate."

The conversation lagged as both men contemplated her uncertain future. To avoid the awkwardness, Dicky changed the conversation. "That was pretty exciting today. I'm wondering if anything is showing up on the news yet."

"So far, so good. With Kadena AFB and the Okinawa Island mostly in the dark, we should be able to control the situation with some cover stories."

"Maybe a joint Russian/American Military training exercise," offered the General.

"Something like that," dodged Director Allwardt avoiding further discussion on that topic given the specific steps the Agency were already taking to cover-up everything. "Thanks again General. If necessary, I'll be back in touch with you on Nena," said Director Allwardt before ending the call.

Dicky stared at the SAT phone. For the first time since the EMP attack, he wished for a fleeting moment that he didn't have any contact with the outside world. There always seemed to be something happening.

*   *   *   *   *

Sitting at the bar, Janet nursed her drink. It was busier than normal. The buzz was all about how the Americans dominated the DDD military gaming tournament winning every format. Pictures of the winners were playing on ESPN with each winner holding an oversized novelty check of $250,000, when she noticed the college professor step up to the bar. He appeared to be in an agitated state.

"What can I get you Burt?" asked Susan glancing about concerned for his break in protocol. She could see he was holding something in his hand. Always the professional, with exaggerated eye gestures, she calmed him down enough to revert back to their normal routine. Caught off guard for being so impulsive and out of character, Burt regained his composure and tried to get back on script.

"I'll take a draft today Susan, please," replied Burt. After glancing back, he saw an empty two chair table. "And, I'll take it back at that table," he said as he pointed.

"Perfect," smiled Susan glad to see him under control. "I'll bring it right out, Burt," replied Susan. With a calm unsuspecting demeanor, she glanced about checking to see if anyone was paying too much attention to what was happening. Espionage was still an act punishable by death in China. With a satisfied expression, she met Janet's eyes. Remaining in control, Susan grabbed a chilled mug from the lower refrigerator, tilted the glass and filled it from the spigot leaving a slight head of foam on top. She carried the beer filled mug across the floor toward the table where Burt waited.

Susan set the mug down on the tabletop, while Burt laid a $10 bill next to the perspiring mug. Underneath the bill, was a computer flash-drive. With an exaggerated grin, Burt said, "Keep the change," emptied the mug in one giant swig and practically slammed it down with a thud.

Susan almost laughed out loud as she stared at Burt's foam mustache. She'd never seen him so animated. He was almost giddy with enthusiasm and energy. She knew he had something.

Burt wiped his mouth on his shirt sleeve, stood and walked out the front door never looking back. Unable to contain a slight grin, Susan grabbed the money and found a computer flash-drive, rather than a piece of paper, hidden underneath. In the three years she'd been his handler, she'd never seen him act this way. She was careful taking her time to grab both. She didn't want to drop the flash-drive.

Susan made her way back to the bar and nodded at the cashier. The cashier understood that Susan wanted her to watch the bar. Susan turned and walked into the back office locking the door behind her, then double checking to make sure it was shut tight. After turning on her Agency issued secure desktop-computer, she checked the surveillance cameras while waiting for the computer to boot up. After scanning the security monitors, certain the bar and outside the building was secure, she inserted the flash-drive.

The flash-drive contained two files; a word document and a long continuous MPEG that ran for 6 hours and 22 minutes. She read the document first.

"Found FANGQI. See GPS coordinates below. It's just outside the city limits down a hidden patchy grass covered road. Skip to 4 hours, 34 minutes.

A big thanks to ICARUS! If it weren't for him, we'd never have found FANGQI before he left."

After Susan wrote down the GPS coordinates, she deleted the word document and opened the video clip. As Burt instructed, she fast forwarded the video to the 4 hour 34 minute marker. While watching the clip at normal speed, she wondered, *"Why was Burt congratulating himself?"* And also, *"How did Burt know his CODE name?"* She was certain that she'd never shared that information with him. Burt's prior handler mentioned that he liked birds. Susan arbitrarily chose "ICARUS."

As Susan watched the clip, she realized the video was taken from the air. At the precise video location Burt provided, the camera angle was looking down from above showing an old cottage. Through an open window, she saw Fangqi staring outside. He appeared startled as if searching for someone outside. In the bottom border of the video clip, the GPS location confirmed the coordinates she'd already written down.

Out of curiosity, Susan fast forwarded through the video. She was under the impression that the footage came from some remote drone, like the one she'd given Janet. It wasn't until the end, that she suspected something else. Without warning the camera view became erratic, bobbing up and down, left and right. After some time, the view seemed to stabilize. The view showed a light source coming from a house.

Out of curiosity, she searched and located a volume. After turning up the volume, she was surprised to hear piano music and was certain it was Beethoven. The music was echoing out over the landscape. Toward the end of the clip, the camera view flew down into Burt's waiting arms. And from the reflection off Burt's glasses, she saw that the camera wasn't attached to a drone, but a large parrot.

Susan flinched in surprise. She felt like she was watching a National Geographic documentary or some random Facebook clip on pets. The most touching aspect was to hear the parrot speak. He'd learned the Colonel's name as he blurted out in a sing-song voice, "...Baaa Fangqi... baaa." It wasn't until she heard Burt say, "You did it, Icarus! You did it!" that she realized Icarus was the bird's name. Susan couldn't help but smile and laugh out loud. What a coincidence that she'd randomly selected the same name for Burt's secret code – Icarus.

*   *   *   *   *

General Lee was furious with himself. *"How had it come to this?"* he thought as he walked along an old wooden deck. It continued toward the back side of Beijing's criminal detention building. The back section was enclosed with large cinderblock walls. With his hands tied behind his back, he waited with the rows of other inmates that would suffer the same fate. Once a month, China performed executions by firing squad. There was no fanfare, nor scores of media coverage protesting the wrongful enforcement criticizing this archaic custom. In fact, China still billed each prisoner's family the cost of the bullet.

Lee was pushed along and placed against a concrete wall. All the prisoners, including the General, were lined up and separated every ten feet. Everyone was faced away from the firing squad. No mask or eye coverings were provided. Staring forward, he saw countless indentations on the concrete wall. He glanced around at the others and questioned why he'd asked and was granted permission to wear his uniform. He wanted to feel different, better than the others dressed in shabby prison uniforms. He didn't. As he stared down at his shining freshly polished military boots, he thought back how, in an instant, his life had changed.

Minutes after the ICBM launched, calls were being made throughout China. They knew that Colonel Fangqi was on a special assignment in Xinjiang. He was the only one that would know anything about what was happening at the American base. But Fangqi wasn't answering his SAT phone and no one knew where he was. A special investigative unit was sent to the University and all of his assigned men were being gathered and questioned. Unable to contact the Colonel, General Lee was contacted. Hearing what happened, the General also tried reaching the Colonel. No one knew his whereabouts.

The Chinese President was grateful to hear that the disaster was averted and spoke to both the Russian and American Presidents. He promised he knew nothing about what took place and would root out the conspirators making a swift example of such treachery. It didn't take much investigative work to find out the truth. Colonel Fangqi had told all of his men that his reward would be a promotion and relocation to Beijing. On several occasions, his men had raised toasts wishing him great success on his next position. He was actually well liked by his men. After reviewing the General's emails, and phone logs, it was easy to piece together what happened. They concluded that due to personal differences, Lee went out of his way to hurt Fangqi. The email and call from Fangqi's SAT phone contradicted everything General Lee told the investigators.

Justice is swift in China. The next morning, Lee was apprehended, verbally reprimanded in front of the other Generals and sentenced to death by firing squad. He wasn't allowed to contact any family but was assured they would be notified.

Before the General was taken, he asked his superiors if Colonel Fangqi had been located and was told that was no longer any of his concern. When in fact, from Fangqi's SAT phone, they knew his exact location. The Russians were promised they could take care of Fangqi on their own.

General Lee was lost in his thoughts until he heard a voice booming over the public address speakers. "Prisoners, you are guilty of high crimes against the People's Republic of China and sentenced to death." Without any fanfare, the announcer continued. "Ready, aim..."

General Lee stood alone, staring at a pock-marked cinderblock wall. His legs were shaking uncontrollably. He never imagined things could end this way. The last thing he heard was a thunderous report as hundreds of rifles fired in unison. Then, everything went dark. High above, looking down from hundreds of miles in the sky, an American and Russian satellite recorded the execution. Tapes would be sent to each countries' Presidents confirming his disposal.

*   *   *   *   *

As Director Nena Valdez stepped out of her helicopter, she was surrounded by her four man security detail preparing to enter the back doorway into her Director's office wing when her SAT phone rang. Stopping, she answered the call.

"Director Valdez," answered Nena.

"It's the President, Nena."

"Mr. President."

"Thanks again for all your teams outstanding efforts. Your team has accomplished many amazing things, but this one definitely stands above the others. We're forever in your debt."

"Thank you, Mr. President. I'll be sure to let the team know what you've said."

"Take care, Nena," said POTUS as he ended the call.

With a satisfying smile, Nena stared at the boxy SAT phone. Hearing who she spoke to, her pilot Mr. Davies and four man security team all smiled.

"We have a special job, boss," said Mr. Davies.

"Yes, we do. And it comes with great responsibilities," replied Nena as she followed him surrounded by her guards through the reinforced bunker complex and through the back entrance inside her South Korean Agency located inside Camp Bonifas along the DMZ. As she entered the hallway, she noticed another security detail standing outside one of the conference rooms. Upon her arrival, her team, having the primary task of protecting the Director, had just been replaced by this team. She'd almost forgot about Cornelius. She nodded at the guard. He smiled back and opened the door.

"Welcome back, Director."

"Thank you," smiled Nena. "It's great to be back. How's our guest been?" she said staring inside. Another security guard inside glanced over his shoulder. He'd been standing at attention in front of the door waiting for his rotation to end.

"Hey, Director," the other guard said as Nena walked inside. Cornelius Van Aelst had just finished speaking to someone on his SAT phone. With a tight lipped smile, Van Aelst stared back at Nena. Right away, by the look on his face, she knew something was wrong. Without speaking, she sat next Van Aelst.

"What's wrong?"

*   *   *   *   *

Colonel Fangqi had changed his clothes and packed his duffle bag. He filled two canteens with water. With the batteries removed, he'd placed the SAT phone in his backpack under his change of clothes. He would never use it again but contemplated selling it on the black market. He paused and took a rest on the overstuffed cushion recliner that faced the open window. The adrenaline from all the excitement wore him out.

With the soft evening breeze and drop in temperature, Fangqi had drifted off to sleep. As his eyes opened, he blinked several times to reorient his vision back in focus. Fangqi almost forgot about all the craziness that took place earlier that evening. Seeing his backpack and canteen next to the back door reminded him that it was all real. He was now a fugitive running for his life, destined never to see his homeland China again.

He rose from the recliner and heard a screech echo through the open window. He turned his head and saw a hawk flying away through the night sky. While Fangqi watched the bird fly above the tree line, an unexpected shadow appeared high up in the branches. With a slight tilt of his head, Fangqi wondered why the roof's silhouette appeared against the tree.

Because of the hillside landscape, Fangqi never heard the roar from a pair of Russian MIG-25's flying along the valley floor. The Chinese granted the Russians access to their airspace for this special mission. As the jets swung up along the ridge, they passed close enough to Xinjiang University that the engine roar echoed up and down the now vacant hallways. As the jets cruised along the nap of the earth at 2,000 mph, each jet launched two air-to-ground Kh-25 missiles especially calibrated for this mission. The first missile hit in front of the cottage causing a fireball that created the shadow on the tree. The other three missiles hit the cottage in the center of the roof cutting through the structure toward the center of the building landing within three feet from each other. By the time the MIG-25s passed over the tree, the cottage was already reduced to a smoldering hole in the ground with all neighboring vegetation aflame.

The explosions echoed along the countryside, followed by the jet roar as the MIG's raced across the Chinese border into Kazakhstan. The air traffic in both countries were expecting this flyby. The jets were given a wide berth with unfettered access. Their Air Forces were ordered to stand-down with the promise of being shot and killed by firing squad for anyone interfering.

Later that week, CNN and other international news media sources reported *"improved relations between the Super-Powers, Russia, China and the United States confirmed their joint military training exercises held over Japan and China, going so far as simulating an atomic attack from the U.S. Air Force Base, Kaneda, on the island of Okinawa in Japan."*

*   *   *   *   *

While the Russian MIG-25s flew over the Xinjiang Province, Cornelius Van Aelst was sitting in a conference room inside the South Korean Agency inside Camp Bonifas along the DMZ.

"What's wrong?" asked Nena.

With pursed lips, Van Aelst's deep blue eyes bore into Nena. "I just received a call, Nena. You may be in trouble," explained Van Aelst.

Confused, Nena flinched, scrunching her face and shaking her head. "What do you mean?"

"We don't have much time. We've only known each other a brief time. But in each instance, I've proved my loyalty to not just your country but your team," reminded Van Aelst.

Understanding his concern, she nodded. "Yes, in Berlin. Helping out with Diane. Of course. And now," replied Nena. "Your advance warning probably helped us avoid a disaster with China and Russia. Of course, Cornelius. In our line of business, trust is based on your actions. You've earned mine."

"Are you certain?"

"Yes, without any reservations. What do you know? What happened?"

"It's about your family, back in the Philippines."

"The Philippines?" repeated Nena taken aback. At that moment, her family was the last thing on her mind. "My family?"

"Remember, my duties and responsibilities over these decades took me to places and put me around people. Others have no clue what really happened. But they did happen, Nena," said Van Aelst. "The Stasi, the KGB, and even the old Germany and even Japan. My experiences, my alliances seem to give me access to a lot of important information from both sides of most conflicts. It's all true."

Hearing heels snapping against the concrete floor leading to the conference room, their eyes rolled back toward the sound.

"They're here for you, Nena," said Van Aelst as he looked toward the conference room door. The sound stopped just outside.

"What is it, Cornelius?" Tell me!"

"It's about the gold."

"The gold?" asked Nena in a confused expression. "What gold?"

"They found it on your family's land. In the Philippines," said Van Aelst. By her reaction, he could tell she didn't know anything about the gold.

As the door swung open, Van Aelst leaned toward Nena and whispered in her ear. "It's about Mission Golden Lily. I can help you, Nena. I can help."

Her pilot, Mr. Davies was holding another SAT phone. "It's for you, boss," said Mr. Davies as he passed her the phone. Van Aelst didn't wait to be asked. He stood and started leaving. Before he walked out the door, Nena covered the phone with her hand and reached out touching Van Aelst's shoulder.

"How do you always know everything?"

Without replying, Van Aelst exhaled and flashed a comforting sincere smile. Without replying, he followed Mr. Davies out and shut the door behind him.

Nena stared at the phone. After a deep sigh, she answered the call.

"This is Director Valdez."

"Nena, it's Dicky. We've got a problem."

THE END

Afterword

"Gamers" was inspired by my long-time friend Patrick Gleason. We were both born and raised in Red Bluff, California, and roommates at Sacramento State. One night, I received a text followed by a call. Patrick's son, Riley, thought I could write a book centered around computer game tournaments. After bouncing some ideas around with my sister Suzanne, I developed a story centered on his general idea of computer game tournament while incorporating the South Korean team and other prior cast of characters to complete the novel.

In my books, I use some historical facts and general truths, then create a fictionalized conflict around that idea. In "Gamers," after scouring the Internet, I uncovered some disturbing facts. One story suggests that during the missile Cuban Crises, a secret underground ICBM missile silo on the island of Okinawa, Japan was authorized to launch nuclear bombs. The story about B-52's that mistakenly loaded nuclear bombs and then parked overnight on the tarmac before flying over the continental U.S. also supposedly took place. Rumors abound over the Internet that an SR-72 hypersonic jet capable of flying Mach 20 (13,000 mph) supposedly really exists. However, because the available information is limited, I fictionalized it as an Unmanned Ariel Vehicle (UAV). It is unclear if an on-board pilot is required.

Similarly, although I fictionalized the submarine USS Michelle J Howard SSN-805, her career is fact. Since 1969, the Navy decreed warships would no longer be named after living persons. In my eyes, although Howard is still living, I chose to honor her now in this book. Howard was the first female to achieve two and three Star General Rank. Later, she was promoted to four-star Admiral. Prior to retiring in 2017, she was the second highest ranking officer in the Navy. Finally, the mention of the "Dead Hand" program that automates the release of the entire nuclear arsenal regardless if anyone inside Russia is still alive is also true.

This book hypothesizes that through human intelligence gathering, it's possible to narrow the parameters and system selections, whereby reducing the variables programmed into the computer. In turn, because fewer calculations and permutations are required, the quicker the computer could theoretically unravel a launch code. "Gamers" and this premise is pure conjecture. However, it does raise the question if utilizing this tactic has any merit.

During the creation and selection of the Chinese character's names, Colonel Fangqi and Agent Fennu, I utilized an on-line English to Chinese translator program. Fangqi translates into "give up" and Fennu into "anger". Understanding their English meanings, I tried to develop these characters based on these underlying characteristics and traits. I'm not sure whether such names are actually used in China but thought this was creative.

Finally, part of my book writing process utilizes fans' names. As a way of acknowledging and rewarding my fan base (specifically those that read one of my books and provides a review, or attended a book-signing event), could request their name be used for a character in a future book. When developing key players in the plot for fan based characters, I try to incorporate something unique from these fans' real lives. Although this goal isn't always achieved, these fans still get the benefit of seeing their name in print. At times, this part of my writing process, although rewarding, can be challenging. I try to balance these back-stories, while still being relevant to the main storyline.

Incorporating fans' names into "Gamers" took some extra imagination. I created the acronym L.I.S.A. (Launch Intelligence Sensory Application) to represent Lisa P Blair's name. Also, in Burt Barnow's real life, he actually is a university professor who owns a pet parrot named Icarus. I think Icarus' adventure contributed to the plot and story. I hope the readers also enjoyed their journeys. If not, I beg your apologies and appreciate your patience allowing me to indulge my imagination incorporating Burt's and Icarus' adventure into "Gamers".

Although the final sentences in "Gamers" leads us into another Agency adventure involving Director Valdez titled "Mission Golden Lily", we'll have to wait until 2023 for that story. The next book to be released in 2021 is the first book in a trilogy titled "G3-The Journey". Remaining true to my influences, like in my second book "Michaso", "G3-The Journey" will revisit this other style. Given the COVID pandemic, this next book is timely.

After completing "Gamers", I felt a sense of concern. Over the last few decades, the inherent danger created by the existence of nuclear weapons, no longer seems to be a major concern. Unlike during my childhood, where popular culture and the entertainment industry constantly reminded us about this nuclear dilemma. Back then, we were reminded of the fragile balancing act between the super-powers implying that the world lived in constant fear worrying about an inevitable nuclear confrontation. I was part of that generation subjected to the ridiculous school drill where children climbed underneath flimsy wooden desks seeking protection against a nuclear attack.

During the 1990's, because the Gulf Wars didn't escalate into nuclear exchanges, and as globalized economies became more interdependent, fears over mutually assured destruction evaporated out of consciousness somehow placed on the back-burner no longer relegated as the most pressing issue of our time. Other concerns took the forefront; climate change, social injustices and global pandemics. Today, I no longer feel that sense of nuclear doom that once dominated our media and collective thoughts. However, after writing this book, I'm reminded about the existence of these weapons of mass destruction. Nothing has fundamentally changed. The world is forever vulnerable to potential catastrophes and the real possibility of a nuclear war. Hopefully, someday in our not too distant future, humanity will find a way to put this destructive nuclear genie back in the bottle. Unintentionally, "Gamers" is a reminder that the presence of these weapons may pose the greatest threat to humanity's survival.

"Until we meet again! Sincerely, I thank you for your continued support." - E.A. Padilla

Made in the USA
Las Vegas, NV
03 December 2020

11973292R00218